MYTHBREAKER

An Abaddon Books™ Publication
www.abaddonbooks.com
abaddon@rebellion.co.uk

First published in 2014 by Abaddon Books™, Rebellion Intellectual
Property Limited, Riverside House, Osney Mead, Oxford, OX2 0ES, UK.

10 9 8 7 6 5 4 3 2 1

Editor-in-Chief: Jonathan Oliver
Commissioning Editor: David Moore
Cover: Clint Langley
Design: Pye Parr & Sam Gretton
Marketing and PR: Lydia Gittins
Publishing Manager: Ben Smith
Creative Director and CEO: Jason Kingsley
Chief Technical Officer: Chris Kingsley

ISBN: 978-1-78108-255-3

Printed in the US

GODS & MONSTERS
MYTHBREAKER
STEPHEN BLACKMOORE

ABADDON
BOOKS

CHAPTER ONE

AFTER YEARS OF doing everything from smoking crushed-up Quaaludes in a Skid Row homeless camp to snorting cocaine with Miami "businessmen," Fitz has come to one inescapable conclusion.

Getting high is a huge pain in the ass.

You'd think it wouldn't be that hard. Doesn't matter if it's pot, opium, ecstasy or Viagra; it all works the same way. You take a thing, and put it in your body. It goes up your nose, or down your mouth, in a vein, up your butt. Simple, right? But no.

People, man. Fucking people. Got to make everything complicated. Pipes, domes, vaporizers, spoons, butane torches, screens, papers, irons, ash catchers, straws, grinders, nails, syringes, chillums, hookahs, clips, masks.

Not that that's ever stopped him, of course. Whether he's popping prescription anti-psychotics or doing opium out of a glass pipe, it's all worth it. To keep the voices out of his head.

"Gimme a hit," Marty says. He leans into him on the bed, wraps his leg around Fitz's own. They fucked the sheets off the mattress an hour ago, their clothes scattered across the floor.

Or is it Matty? Marvin? Fitz can't remember. That's fine. He'll be gone by morning, and he'll never see him again. Dark brown hair, thin to the point of ribs showing, eyes a shade of green that makes Fitz think of the ocean. He'll remember those eyes, even if he never remembers his name.

Fitz passes him the pipe, runs the lighter underneath until the dab of opium dissolves into a little dark pool. Marvin sucks down the vapor, holding it in for a moment and then blowing it out through his nostrils.

"Oh, I like that," Matty-Maybe-Marvin says.

Last week there was a girl. Patty? Pamela? He did a lot of coke with her. And the week before was a couple of Mormon missionaries who weren't quite as devout as their nice white shirts and straight black ties would suggest.

"It's good, isn't it?" Fitz takes the pipe from him, packs another dot of opium into it and lights up. He sucks in the vapor and his mind goes still.

If it didn't, there wouldn't be much point. He's not in it for the high. He's in it for the way it shuts his brain up. All the backchatter and noise. Like being in a crowded bar. And the sights. Images that crowd out his own vision, sometimes; make it hard to tell what's real and what isn't.

A mix of anti-psychotics and benzos does the trick most of the time, shuts things up enough where he can function. But sometimes it gets too much. Everything's too loud, too bright, too everything. And that's when he goes out, gets himself a nice little brown ball of pure joy and a twink like Matty here and spends the weekend in a hotel room getting fucked up and sucked off.

"I've never tried it before," Marty says. Dammit, maybe it's Michael? "It's... different. What's the craziest stuff you've ever tried?"

"Toads," Fitz says, his voice hazy like smoke.

"Toads?"

"*Bufo alvarius*," he says. "Colorado river toad. They secrete a toxin on their backs that's like doing acid. It'll really fuck you up."

"So, like, you suck the toad?"

"No. God, no. Eew. They taste nasty," Fitz says, remembering when he'd heard about the toads and tried exactly that. "You squeeze it. And when it starts to secrete the toxin you slap it against a windshield and smear it all over. You get this gross, goopy gel. And then you let it dry in the sun and scrape it off and smoke it."

Marty shudders. "That's disgusting. Seriously?"

Fitz shrugs. "No idea, really. I just smoked the shit."

"But what about the stuff we just did? You got any more? I want another hit."

"Pace yourself. This shit ain't for amateurs. And it costs more than you do."

"Fuck you," Matthew says, less admonishment than suggestion. "I'm plenty expensive."

"My point exactly."

He trails a long fingernail from Fitz's neck to his cock, his fingers wrapping lightly around the shaft. "What'll it take to get another hit?"

"That's a good start."

"How about I smoke *your* toad?"

"Is that what we're calling it now?"

He kisses his way down Fitz's chest and stomach until he's taken him in his mouth. Fitz rides the high of the opium, the feeling of lips around his cock. Drifts away on the sensation.

Then the visions slam into him like a truck through a convenience store window. They punch through the opium haze, sear into his brain.

Panic and howling winds. Angels and demons fucking in mid-air, tearing into each other with swords of fire. A raven-haired woman in green pulls the still-beating heart out of a man's chest and holds it high, before tearing dripping chunks from it with razor teeth. Bulls and bears battle in a pit of money while high above them the sky fills with clouds of numbers in an unending stream of data that watches and waits and passes judgment. The images tear through him, fill him like an empty basin, crack and burst through the sides.

And through it all is the high, keening wail of someone screaming like they're on fire, like their skin is being flayed from their bones, their eyes being put out with nails.

It isn't until the police break down the door that he realizes it's him.

HOSPITALS. FULL OF sick people. The old, the frail, the dying. The constant stink of disease and antiseptic, of rot and bodily fluids seeping out of holes that should never leak. They die in their beds, bleed all over them. Shit in them, too. Beds just like the one Fitz is currently lying in and handcuffed to. He's wearing nothing but a badly fit gown that's cut too high and leaves his ass exposed. His head hurts, and when he reaches up to touch it he feels a bandaged lump on his forehead.

But there is good news, as good news goes. He overheard a cop and a doctor outside his room talking. Fitz isn't being locked up on a 5150, an involuntary psych hold. It's happened a few times and he's narrowly avoided doctors admitting him for a longer stay so they can turn him into a case study. He's not schizophrenic, they say. He's too lucid, they say. He has hallucinations, but not delusions. He's not bipolar, not depressed, not manic. They don't know what he is, though they all agree 'crazier than a shithouse rat' is a pretty good description.

If only that was a listing in the DSM-V.

But of course, there's bad news, too. He's probably going to do some time for the drug charge. He's got a record, and judges don't like records. He got picked up for heroin a while back and avoided an eighteen-month stint in the state penal system by going to rehab. He's probably not going to get that again.

Even with a good lawyer, he's probably going to do a stint in County.

This is a problem. A very big problem.

"Louie Fitzsimmons?" the doctor says as he comes in through the door. He's young, like Doogie Howser young. Asian, with wide, dark eyes. Is this what happens when you get older? You see people in their twenties and they look like they should still be at their mother's tit?

"Far as I know." He's having a hard time remembering everything he saw when he freaked out in the hotel room. Mostly he remembers blood.

The doctor chuckles. "You're doing better than you were. Can you tell me what you were on? The young man you were with didn't say."

"Benadryl. Maybe some Advil. You know. I had a headache. And I got allergies. Must have had a bad reaction."

"Right," the doctor says. "And this Advil it was, uh, smoked, was it?"

"Don't know what you're talkin' about, doc."

"Uh huh. I hope those allergies clear up, Mister Fitzsimmons. I don't think you're going to be getting any Benadryl for a while."

"How about some Advil?"

"Sorry," the doctor says. "We only do Tylenol here." He closes his chart, heads to the door. Stops when a six-foot-plus wall of muscle steps in his way. He looks up at the giant woman standing there.

"I don't think you're supposed to be in here," the doctor says, his voice suddenly very small.

Samantha Kellerman looms. At six-foot-five, with eyes like carved jade and a shock of bright red hair, Sam can't help but loom. It's built into her DNA. She is not fat, she is big-boned. This only explains her girth because those bones are wrapped in two-hundred-and-twenty pounds of densely packed muscle built doing MMA before she lost a bout in a bad way. She is big-boned surrounded by big-meat.

"Cops said I could," she says, pointing over her shoulder with a thumb.

"Oh," is all the doctor can seem to get out. "Okay, then." He edges past Sam and scuttles away down the hall.

"What's eatin' him?" Sam says. She slings a backpack off her shoulder and onto the hospital bed.

"I think you scared him."

"Don't know why. I'm just a big ol' teddy bear. You doin' all right?"

Fitz holds up his left arm as far as the cuff securing him to the hospital bed will let him. "Been better. How'd you get in here, anyway?"

"Couple of the cops are Blake's customers. They gave me a few minutes."

"He got any prosecutors in his pocket?"

Sam shrugs. It's like watching a mountain shrug. Fitz half expects to see boulders tumble to the floor. "Used to. But these days? Dunno."

"I gotta get out of here, man," Fitz says. "I am not going to do well in prison."

"Jail. The prisons are all full up. And you know you won't do a full stretch. Blake'll take care of you, man. He always does. They gotta get you squared away here and then book you. Then they'll probably move you to County for a few days before they get you in front of a judge."

Any other time that would be a relief. Fitz and Sam have known each other, and worked together, for almost twenty years. Fitz to cook books and hide money, and Sam to break legs and hide bodies. All in the service of Blake Kaplan, a record producer who moved into selling drugs when his boy bands didn't quite get there. Wasn't much of a stretch; he was supplying his kids with enough coke to frost the Alps, so moving into a wider distribution was a natural progression.

No matter what happened, Blake always took care of his boys. Then, as now, whether it's getting someone out of jail, fixing a parking ticket, scoring some Zoloft and Haldol for Fitz to take the edge off, Blake's always come through.

But as soon as Blake figures out a couple of things Fitz has done, that's all going to stop, and Fitz needs to get out of here before it does.

"Yeah," Fitz says.

"Oh, come on. Why so glum? You've done time before."

"I got a suspended sentence and rehab," Fitz says. "I was in for a weekend."

"And that's what this is. Three days max and Blake'll post bail." Sam pulls up a chair. "So what happened? You have another one of those episodes?"

Those episodes. Explaining to Sam that when they hit it's like having his mind turned inside out and poured down the drain is like trying to teach a dog orbital mechanics. Sam's good as murderous thugs go, but anything outside of MMA, craft beer and the best places in Los Angeles to hide a body never seems to fully register with her.

"This one was pretty bad."

"Huh. Well, Blake wanted me to tell you he's got you covered. He has all the updated passwords, right? He'll take over the books while you're out of commission."

"He can't do that," Fitz says a little too quickly, trying to hold his panic down.

"How come?"

"I need to clean a few things up. The numbers are off. I think I transposed some digits. They won't add up."

"I don't know what any of that means," Sam says. "But Blake'll figure it out." She gets up, pats Fitz's hand. It feels like she's slamming a Christmas ham across Fitz's knuckles. "We'll get you taken care of. I know you don't want nobody to help you with these episodes, but if they're getting this bad, you need to see somebody. Like, for real this time. Not that dealer in Koreatown you keep talking to."

"But—"

"I mean it. Like a real doctor. But right now, don't worry about it. Oh, before I go." She unzips the backpack, pulls out a shirt, pants, socks, shoes and a jacket. "They said they brought you in naked. So I hit your place and grabbed you some stuff. I wasn't gonna touch your underwear. Figure if you're going to lock-up you should at least have something to wear besides a hospital gown for the ride over. There's nothing else in there. I had to promise the guys outside I wasn't sneaking anything in and I don't want them gettin' into trouble."

"You're the most honest crook I know."

"Thanks. So take care and don't worry. We got your back."

Fitz waits until Sam disappears through the door before he really starts to lose his shit. Blake's going to look at the books. And when he does he's going to figure out that things aren't adding up. It won't take him long to see it.

After all, it's hard to hide fifteen million dollars.

Not that Fitz hasn't tried. He's been skimming from Blake for almost ten years now. He doesn't want to be an accountant the rest of his life, after all. He'd like to retire sooner rather than later. So he's taken a little bit here, little bit there. Funneled it all into an offshore account in the Caymans and covered his tracks.

But in the last few months he's gotten more aggressive about it, and just a week ago he grabbed nine million out of some of Blake's own offshore accounts and he hasn't figured out how to hide it all yet. When Blake goes looking, he's going to find it.

And the next time Fitz sees Sam, she's not going to be bringing him a change of clothes.

CHAPTER TWO

MEDEINA HATES CELL phones.

Disgusting things. All glass and steel and tiny little screws, an infernal intricacy that defies her divine sight. Where is the manna that fuels them? What are the incantations that fling the voices through the ether? This should be simple for her, she who rules magic in all its forms, gives shape to the Ten Thousand Stars, keeps the laws of war and the hunt. No prey has ever escaped her. No enemy has ever eluded her. She has never encountered a magic she could not master.

Except for this fucking phone.

Thwarted by a mortal machine. Clever little monkeys, mortals, but monkeys nonetheless. If it wasn't for her they wouldn't even have figured out how to make fire with sticks. Ungrateful little bastards. Medeina looks at the disgusting monkeys all around her and breathes deeply of their stink. All running off to things they think are so very important. Appointments, meetings, trysts. So caught up in which monkey is stronger, faster, better, with a longer cock or bigger tits, and they never stop long enough to realize it's all just pointless fuckery.

They are a chancre on the cock of the universe, running pustules of meat and bone, so fragile, so easily popped. She would kill them, but she has things to do. Perhaps later.

She remembers when her world shrank, when the heavens became smaller, more crowded. She knew the other gods of her line—Dievas, who ruled them all, Dalia, who wove fate in her strands of silk, Perkūnas, who made the heavens shake with his thunder—but it wasn't until she encountered the Christian god that her world began to crumble.

Battle and loss. So many dead. Gods are not so easily killed, but they can be shunted aside when their believers are murdered, subjugated or simply led to believe in something else. The power of an old god is a fickle thing, waxing and waning as belief shifts over centuries.

Still, she persevered, survived the loss of belief, the shadows of obscurity that fell upon her and her fellow deities. She fell back, licked her wounds, went on with immortality as best she could with the others from her pantheon. She adjusted, changed, learned pragmatism and the need for new alliances. But the worst was yet to come.

She has a sudden urge to break out of hiding among the monkeys. To show herself to these mortals as the goddess she really is. Right now, they all see her as just a raven-haired, statuesque woman in jeans and a leather jacket, their magicked vision providing her disguise, blending in outside a building full of the sick and dying in Beverly Hills.

If only these people could see her true self, they would believe. They would believe so fucking hard they would shit themselves with reverence.

Or would they even notice?

Things were bad before, when the old gods were shunted aside by the new, but it's truly fucked now. Not just for her, for all of them. Ever since they were kicked from the heavens by that assclown Yahweh. Then He went and shuffled off to who knows where. All the gods are on Earth now. All the heavens locked away from them. Gods in exile, gods without thrones. And so many of them are gods without followers.

What good is a goddess if there is no one to believe in her?

Medeina stares at the device in her hand, a thin brick of black glass, considers willing it into a snake that she can squeeze between her fingers until it is nothing but pulped meat and bone. But the last time she did that, she couldn't change it back. And, distasteful though it might be, she has to make a phone call.

Her finger hovers over the phone. Does she really want to do this? She's learned to work with her pantheon's conquerors, to ally herself with their greater numbers and stronger believers. But it rubs her raw to do it. There's no helping it. She's thrown in with them, and now is not the time to rebel.

She stabs at the phone's screen. Misdials, hangs up, tries again. She presses the device to her ear. It picks up on the third ring.

"You have him?" says Zaphiel on the other end of the line. The Cherub's voice reverberates through Medeina's skull like the buzzing of a thousand bees, each of Zaphiel's four bestial mouths lending its own peculiar tone to the words.

"He is in one of their houses of healing," she says. "In Beverly Hills."

"It's called a hospital," Zaphiel says. "You should learn the lingo. Why is he there?"

"They pulled him in ranting and screaming," she says, seething. "He is locked away inside." *Learn the lingo.* She knows the lingo. She refuses to use it. This age's terms are ridiculous. YOLO?

She pinches the bridge of her nose. Zaphiel's voices give her a headache. She hates angels. Worse than mosquitoes, with their constant buzzing and flapping of wings. Seraphim, Cherubim, Thrones, Dominions, the whole lot of them. Pompous, self-righteous. Almost as bad as their pig-fucked father, may He rot in whatever corner of the universe He's hidden Himself in.

"Who is he?"

"A shadow of a man," Medeina says. "A derelict husk of fetid meat who—"

"Skip the poetry," Zaphiel says. "A name."

Medeina glares at the phone until smoke begins to curl out of its shell. She still isn't entirely sure what Zaphiel wants with this man and she certainly doesn't trust him. But the Cherub has managed to convince his cohorts that he's necessary, and so, like a treacherous soldier who knows a winning side whether she likes it or not, Medeina has gone to hunt him down.

"Louie Fitzsimmons, though he is called 'Fitz,'" she says. Medeina has tracked him, dug into the secrets of his past, pulled the names of his friends from the aether. At least as much as she can. He seems to have a shroud over him, making sight of his movements difficult. It should only have taken her moments to track him down, once she was sent on this task, but it has taken days. It wasn't until earlier tonight that she could see him.

"What am I to do now? Bring you his head? If I knew more of why I am here, I could—"

Of all the things on this mission—the prey, the cellphones, that she must defer to these cockless buzzards—the fact that she doesn't even know *why* this man is important to Zaphiel chafes. She's accepted many things with this alliance, but it is beginning to try her patience.

"No," Zaphiel says, cutting her off. "If they don't already know, the moment you make contact, others will find out about him. We need him compliant. What we need of him he must do for us willingly."

"I can make him compliant," Medeina says. "I will strip the meat from his bones and—"

"Enough," Zaphiel says, his voice punching through the phone and splitting the glass. "Know your place, goddess of the hunt. Or do you forget the last time we fought?"

Medeina remembers it all too well, the thrashing she took at the Cherub's hands, so many of her pantheon slain.

"I know my place, Zaphiel. Do you know yours? Unlike you, my brothers and sisters died fighting to protect us all. They did not turn on me when my father went missing. They did not fight for an empty throne. And if they had, I would not have run like a coward and let it be destroyed. *My* father did not doom us all to this existence."

Zaphiel says nothing for a long time. It's a sore spot with him, what he did when the heavens were closed off, and Medeina never fails to remind him of it. The silence stretches and Medeina thinks the Cherub must have hung up on her, but then his voice comes across the line.

"Leave him," Zaphiel says, as if nothing has just happened. "Keep him from leaving the city, but do not touch him. I will send someone to bring him to us."

"I can bring him."

"You would slaughter him with your incompetence," Zaphiel says, an undercurrent of the lion's roar in his voices, "not protect him from our enemies. I grow weary of your insolence and stupidity, goddess. Do as you're told."

Furiously, Medeina twists reality, turning the cellphone into a snake, writhing and squirming in her grasp. "And I grow weary of this alliance, angel. I will teach you your place. How will you like it when I chase you down and skin you like a rat?"

The snake stills, turns its head toward her. Instead of a hiss, Zaphiel's unearthly voices come from its mouth. "I'm still on the line," he says.

Medeina squeezes the snake into pulp, its head popping between her fingers. The lifeless thing falls to the ground, landing with a wet plop.

This is the last straw. Zaphiel's disrespect will not go unanswered. She can see what the Cherub is trying to do. He'll lock her out of the plan and leave her holding the bag. Well, fuck him. Fuck all of them.

She looks up at the hospital where Louie Fitzsimmons lies in a bed. He is helpless, defenseless.

If Zaphiel wants him, then he's going to have to bow to Medeina to get him back.

"Hey!" Fitz yells, pulling on his handcuffs and shaking the bed. "Somebody! Anybody!" He hits the nurse call button over and over again. They won't come, but he knows who will.

"Jesus, you better be fuckin' dying in here," the cop says, coming into the room with his hand firmly on the butt of his gun. He's lean and young, with buzz-cut hair and a just-out-of-high-school face, but his eyes say he's dealt with more than his fair share of emergency room freakouts and he's not fucking around. Let your guard down on some tweaker you brought in to get some stitches and somebody's liable to get stabbed. Or worse.

"I gotta take a piss, man."

"Oh, for fuck sake."

"No, seriously. I've been here for hours. And I'm freezing my ass off. I don't even know why you haven't carted me off to jail."

"Doctor hasn't cleared you to go, yet."

"Well, when he does I'd like to not piss in the back of your cruiser." He holds up the pants Sam left him. "And you don't want to have to haul me in naked."

The cop makes a face like he just bit a lemon made of ass. One thing they don't tell you when they recruit you: law enforcement is loaded with nudity, and none of it's fun.

"Come on. Sam vouched for me, right?" Fitz hopes this is one of the cops on Blake's payroll. "What am I gonna do to you besides take a leak on your shoes?"

The cop considers it. "Fine." He uncuffs Fitz from the bed, taking care to keep himself between Fitz and his gun. "You try anything and I will shoot you."

"Wow. Community policing at its finest, huh?"

"How much do you remember when you came in here?"

Blood. Fitz remembers blood. The sight of a woman in a green cloak, angels, demons, sights and sounds that he can't process. It's all a blur, all a distorted, screaming dream that even now he can only half remember.

He's never had hallucinations so vivid before. Usually they're vague images in his mind that leave him unsettled at best, shaky and lost at worst. But he's never lost time.

"Waking up. Cuffed to the bed. Hey, you know what happened to the guy I was with?"

"He's fine. He's the one called us. The arresting officer and the paramedics, not so much. You broke one guy's wrist and gave another a concussion. And just so you know, I wouldn't be letting you out of these cuffs if it wasn't for Sam. And also because the guy whose wrist you broke is kind of an asshole."

Great. On top of everything else, he'll probably land an assault charge. But that doesn't make sense. Not only does he never lose time when he's in the middle of one of his episodes, he doesn't get violent, either. And even if he did, that should never have happened on the opium. What the hell happened back there?

"You're a true humanitarian," Fitz says.

The cop shrugs. "He was fucking my girlfriend. Hit the can and I'll be back in three to cuff you back to the bed."

Fitz dresses quickly. He needs to find a way out of the room that won't have him trying to sneak past the cop. But besides the door, the only other way out is a window and they're three stories up. Few options and none of them good.

The window is an awning style, that pushes out from the bottom and hinges at the top. He shoves at it, but it won't open far enough to get himself out. The only way he's going out the window is if somebody throws him through it.

"What are you doing?"

He turns to see the cop standing in the doorway, hand tight on his gun. Fitz wonders if he'd actually shoot him. From the look on his face he'd have to say yes.

"Just getting some air," Fitz says.

"Uh huh. Get your ass back on the bed."

"Sure, no problem." Fitz's mind races, looking for anything that will get him out of there. He could try to run for it, but getting a beatdown from the LAPD isn't his idea of a good time. Jumping out the window is looking more and more appealing.

He starts over to the bed and pauses when he sees the hallway behind the cop darken, the light not so much dimming as draining away, colors siphoning off of everything, the walls turning gray. And as the light leaches out of everything, a shadow coalesces behind the officer like solidifying smoke.

"Hey, there's something—" Fitz starts but is cut off by the cop's surprised gurgle as the head of a bronze spear, its edge serrated with nasty looking barbs, punches through the front of his uniform. The cop clutches at it, wheezing as his shredded lungs refuse to inflate, his ruptured heart stops pumping. Blood runs thick and fast down his chin. And when the saw-like blade is pulled back out, he falls, making a sound like a side of beef hitting a slaughterhouse floor.

A woman in a heavy green cloak and some kind of banded armor steps over the officer's body out of the inky smoke in the hallway. She is enormous, taller than Sam, curvy and heavily muscled, with pale white skin and hair so black it's like falling into the night sky. She grins, showing teeth too white and too sharp, her mouth cutting a wide swath through a face that radiates menace.

"You," the woman says, pointing at Fitz with her spear, spraying blood across the floor as she steps into the room.

"No," Fitz says, panic making him babble. "Not me. Somebody else. Seriously. I don't know what your problem is, big scary spear lady, but it's not with me."

"You are Louie Fitzsimmons. The man they call Fitz. I know. I have tracked you here. Others are coming for you, and I will know why before they get here. And then I will kill you." Her voice is heavy, like trees falling in the forest, with a thick Slavic accent.

Fitz backs up until his butt hits the window sill. "You had me up until the killing me part." Now he *has* to get out of here. The window's probably not going to work. He'd need a running start get through it.

"You will tell me why the Cherub wants you. What power do you possess that makes you so important to him?"

"I have no idea what the hell you're talking about." Cherub? Power? Fitz was crazy, but he was never this crazy. Hallucinations, sure, but not like this. Hallucinations didn't murder police. Weren't there more cops in this hospital? Nurses? Orderlies? *Anybody?*

The woman takes a step closer and her presence fills him, crawling through the nooks and crannies of his mind like smoke. He can feel a buzzing behind his eyes, like radio static slowly rising in volume. Fitz's eye starts to twitch as he looks for some way out.

"St-stop," he says. He pushes out with his arms as if to keep her back. She feels so close, so loud, so *present*, but she's still only on the other side of the room. His arm starts to twitch, the tempo increasing with each step she takes like a Parkinson's patient who forgot his meds. The buzzing is an angry hornet's nest tearing through his head.

"You will tell me," the woman says, her voice a distant sound over all the noise in Fitz's ears. "I am Medeina. I am keeper of—"

Something in Fitz's head pops. He can feel the force of her personality pummeling at him like hail. The pain running through him is excruciating, terrifying. It drives him to the floor, his eyes burning and blood dripping from his nose. The buzzing in his ears thins into a long, high whine and then fades to nothing. Everything is crystal clear. Everything makes perfect sense.

"You are keeper of the forest, ruler of the green spaces, tamer of the wilds," Fitz says. "You are hunter, killer, protector, avenger. Holder of the laws of war and the hunt." The words tumble out of him, images of blood and battle filling his mind. "You are Zvoruna, daughter of Andajus, sister of Perkūnas. The greatest hunter to exist, the whisper in the leaves, the killer in the fog." Medeina's history unspools before him, a great carpet of death, vengeance and rage. She is an angry goddess, a cruel goddess. She is a hunter, yes, but she is a murderer, too.

Fitz shakes himself and the vision fades like a television picture winking out, leaving behind an afterimage of all this intimate and sudden knowledge. This isn't one of his seizures; he doesn't know what it is, but he knows that much. It has the shape of it, the taste of it. But the intensity and the clarity is nothing he's ever experienced before.

What the hell is happening to him?

Medeina stops mid-stride, a scant few steps from Fitz dry-heaving on the floor. "What sorcery is this?" she yells.

"What did you do to me?" Medeina is a goddess. Fitz knows this the way he knows that he has two hands, a face and a dick that shrivels up into a little nubbin when it's cold outside. A little voice in the back of his mind is saying *No, that's not possible, there are no such things as gods,* but he knows that that voice is an asshole and tells him things that everybody knows but are never the truth.

"I did nothing, " the goddess says. "I merely showed myself to you. The rest is your own doing."

And just as Fitz knows that Medeina is a goddess steeped in blood and that she was given the task to protect the forests by her king and father Andajus—that she is a brazen warrior who does not know fear—so too does he know that she is going to kill him.

"If you're going to murder me, at least let me be on my feet when you do it."

The goddess considers it, poses in a wide stance, twirls her spear and sets the end of the shaft on the floor where it cracks the linoleum, and gives Fitz a curt nod.

"Stand before Medeina," she says. "Your final wish is granted. Accept your death with the bravery of a warrior."

CHAPTER THREE

"THANK YOU," FITZ says. He knows that Medeina stands on formality. He doesn't understand how or why, just that he knows. She doesn't brook insult, she doesn't let a slander go unanswered, and she doesn't deny a man his dying wish.

Fitz gathers his feet beneath him, but instead of standing, he springs forward between the goddess's legs, skidding along the cold linoleum floor. Medeina swings her spear, barely missing Fitz's feet. It carves a smoking swath through the floor, the tile bubbling with the heat of the blade's passage.

Fitz lurches to his feet, grabs the gun from the dead officer's holster, careens off the hallway wall outside the room, keeps running. He knows the gun won't do anything to Medeina, but its solid weight makes him feel safer. Of all the stories of her now bouncing through his head like ping pong balls, none of them say that she will die. Or even that she can.

He bolts down the hall, looking for help, realizes it's not coming when he runs into the first corpse.

The doctor has been decapitated, his severed head set neatly on the top of a trashcan. Just past him is another body, a nurse lying against the wall, his dead hands clutching at a massive wound in his chest. And there are two more, paramedics, and then a patient and another nurse and another and another and...

His eyes travel the length of the corridor, lighting on each body in turn. There are at least twenty people here, all hacked to pieces. The room begins to spin, he fights down the urge to vomit.

Did Medeina kill everyone on this floor? In the whole hospital? She couldn't have. Could she? There must still be people in the rooms. He resists the urge to check behind any of the closed doors for fear that he's wrong.

People will have to come up soon enough. And when they do either Medeina will kill them all, or they'll find Fitz alone with a gun in his hand. Or worse, they'll just find Fitz lying here among the corpses, his head shoved up his ass.

There has to be an elevator nearby, stairs, something. Then it hits him; all he has to do is backtrack along the trail of corpses and he'll find his way out.

He starts to pick his way over the bodies, trying not to step in pooling blood. It's impossible. There's too much of it. His foot slides out from under him as he hits a patch. His ass hits hard in one of the orderlies' guts and he panics. He tries to stand, flailing and spreading blood and viscera all over himself in the process. The gun flies from his hand and skitters across the floor.

"I can smell you," Medeina yells from down the hall. "I have your stink committed to memory. No matter where you run, I will find you. Give up and I will make your death quick."

Fitz pulls himself up, slips and slides his way out of the corpses, leaving bloody footprints in his wake. Salvation comes into view as he rounds the corner. The elevator.

He stabs at the button with a finger like he's jackhammering cement, knowing it won't make it move any faster, doing it anyway. He can't look behind himself. He can already hear Medeina's footsteps slowly coming toward him. He knows that if he looks back he'll start screaming and it'll be all over.

How far away is she? Thirty feet? Twenty? Is she right behind him? Her footfalls echo and bounce in on each other until he can't tell where she is.

The elevator dings, the doors part.

And Fitz is faced with an even bigger nightmare than Medeina could ever hope to be.

The FBI.

The agent, manly and chiseled, steps off the elevator, his suit crisp, his brown hair perfectly conservative. This is a fighter in the War on Terror, on Drugs, on Loud Music, on Whatever the Man wants to be at War with. He is tall, muscled, with a manly jaw, a badge that reads Jones—or maybe it's Smith, Fitz is having a hard time telling. The badge blurs and shifts and he can't get a good look at it. Is he FBI? Or does that say CIA?

The agent looks down at Fitz and Fitz can see himself reflected perfectly in his too-polished mirrored sunglasses. Not a blemish on them. Not a fingerprint, not a smudge. Preternaturally reflective. As if they can throw Fitz's own soul right back at him.

And that's when Fitz realizes there is something terribly, terribly wrong with this man.

The agent steps through the elevator, a gun appearing in his hand that Fitz could swear hadn't been there a moment before. He doesn't look at Fitz so much as *through* him. Not seeming to care whether he is there or not. He pushes Fitz gently to the side and as he touches his arm, Fitz begins to shake uncontrollably. Ice shoots through his veins. Images crawl through his mind the way they did when Medeina threw the force of her personality at him.

Where centuries of Medeina's history hit Fitz with the force of a stampeding bull, this man's history is sketchy, young, full of contradictions and lies. He is the G-Man, the Fed, the Gendarme, the Gestapo. He is every jackbooted thug that ever was. He is every faceless goon that ever oppressed a populace. He is every three-letter agency in every language.

His history is short, but filled with so much bloodshed he makes Medeina look like a fucking saint. He is every Black Helicopter, every tinted window, every interrogation cell.

This man is not an agent. He is *the* Agent.

"What bedevilment is this?" Medeina screams from down the hall, her blade slicing through the air in front of her. "Are you the protector the Cherub sent? One of the others that he spoke of? Answer me!"

The Agent cocks his head to the side, looking at her over Fitz's shoulder the way a dog might, trying to understand an unusual command. A faceless dog.

Medeina spins her spear and goes into a fighting stance. "Come to me. I shall taste your blood." Fitz wonders if she's always that pompous, and then the answer floats up from the memories dumped into his mind.

Yes.

The Agent lowers his head like a bull and rushes the goddess, gun out, firing wildly. Bullets punch through Medeina and she cries out in pain, but she doesn't go down.

Fitz doesn't know how this is going to pan out, and he's not stupid enough to stick around to find out. He bolts to the elevator, leaving a centuries-old Lithuanian goddess to duke it out with a conspiracy theory.

BEST CASE, AND he hates himself for thinking this, everyone on the bottom floor is dead and he can run away and not be seen. Worst case, the place is crawling with police and he gets shot the moment the elevator doors open and they see him covered in blood. He needs a plan he can enact no matter what he's faced with. After a moment he has it.

The doors open, Fitz closes his eyes, falls to the floor and starts screaming.

As plans go he's had better. He's also had worse, and he's taking the fact that he hasn't been shot as an encouraging sign. Rough hands grab him, haul him into the hall. It's not taking a lot to act freaked out and hysterical. He's mostly there already.

Someone shakes him, shouts at him, asks him his name. He doesn't stop screaming until somebody slaps him. He stops and pops his eyes open, doing his best to look crazed. Also not a big leap.

The hospital lobby has the look of a disaster film. Police and paramedics, bodies on the floor, desperate attempts to resuscitate the fallen, get them out of the carnage. He's being held down by three SWAT officers in tactical gear. They rapid-fire questions at him like bullets. What's going on upstairs? What did he see? How did it happen?

Did he do it?

He babbles at them about some crazy woman with a spear on the fourth floor. All the bodies. All the blood. It doesn't take much for them to believe that he's just another victim. Just one more hapless schmuck in the middle of some seriously batshit crazy. The fact that he's covered head to toe in gore helps sell it.

It won't last forever. Triage first, questions later. And they are going to be messy questions that he can't answer.

They get him onto a gurney fast, wheel him out to the ambulance bay, pass him off to a paramedic, a heavily muscled man who looks more MMA fighter than medical professional. His hair is cropped in a flat-top, tattoos creep up his neck and into his hair.

"They're not going up there, are they?" Fitz says as the paramedic straps a blood pressure cuff around his bicep and takes a reading. "It's a fucking slaughterhouse up there."

"You don't need to worry about that," the man says. "Got you covered right here." He pops the cap on a syringe and before Fitz can say a word, jabs it into the side of his neck.

"What the fuck, man?" Fitz tries to move, but the paramedic has him pinned.

"Trust me," the paramedic says. "I'm a professional." Fitz struggles but it's no use. The paramedic isn't a big guy, but he feels like he's made out of steel. Fitz's neck burns as his veins fill with whatever shit this crazy bastard just dumped into them.

Fitz's vision blurs, his body feels heavy, his tongue thick. "Wha the fug was tha," is all he can say as the drug hits him.

"Just a sedative, Mister Fitzsimmons. It will make things easier. And then we can get you away from Medeina. She's pretty hot-headed."

Fitz tries to scream for help, but nothing comes out.

*   *   *

FITZ'S EYES SNAP open to see the paramedic standing over him, his head wreathed in a halo from a hanging overhead lamp. Fitz sits up on the folding table he's been laid out on and looks around.

The hospital parking lot is gone. In its place, a wide room with louvered windows all along the sides and a single doorway. Old newspapers and tarp-covered machining equipment sit shoved in the corner, and support columns and lamps hang from the ceiling, breaking the empty space.

"Good. You're awake," the paramedic says. He pulls a chair up to the table and sits in it. He's changed out of his paramedic's uniform and into a pair of jeans and a T-shirt. His tattoos crawl up his neck. Literally. They're moving like snakes. Fitz's eyes must still be adjusting, because for a second it looks as though the glow from the lamp behind the paramedic's head is still there. He blinks and the effect is gone.

"What the fuck did you do to me?" Fitz says.

"You needed some rest. I'm surprised, happily surprised, that you got away from Medeina. Not many do. How are you feeling?"

"Kidnapped." And terrified. "The hell was that all about?"

"Like I said, you needed some rest. Also, you needed to get out of there. Being in jail would have been a very bad choice, don't you think?" Fitz does think, but he's not entirely sure if this is any better. Or much different.

"A cell's a cell," he says. "Helps if I know who the jailer is."

The paramedic sits back in the chair, hands lightly on his legs. "Rightly so," he says. He sticks out his hand to shake. "My name is Zaphiel. Archangel of the Lord. At your service."

"Okay." Any other day, Fitz would have written this guy off as a nutball. But after experiencing Medeina and the Agent, he's not sure what to believe anymore. "An angel?"

"An Archangel," Zaphiel says, correcting him gently. "Chief of the Cherubim." His voice is mild, with a slight harmonic behind it. Fitz looks at the tattoos crawling along his neck and sees that they're not snakes. They're bands of tightly spaced characters. Letters of a type he's never seen.

Fitz looks at the proffered hand like it's a dead rat. He's afraid to touch it. Zaphiel holds it there a moment longer and then lets it drop.

"This must all seem kind of crazy to you," he says.

"Little bit, yeah."

"Understandable. I'm sure you have some questions."

"What's going on?" Fitz says. "Why did you kidnap me? Why did..." He trails off, not wanting to say her name. If he says her name, she might be real. And if she's real, then this guy is real and gods are real and everything Fitz thought he knew about the world is wrong.

"...Medeina try to kill you?" Zaphiel finishes. He shrugs. "No idea. She was just supposed to find you. I suppose it's my fault. She's become increasingly unstable lately. I was hoping that this would be good for her. That maybe she'd find some purpose with this task. I suppose that was too much to hope for."

"People are dead," Fitz says. "A lot of people."

Zaphiel looks down. "I know. And I wish I could have prevented it. But they have moved on now. To a better place."

Fitz presses the palms of his hands hard into his eyes, hoping the stars that burst into his vision will somehow have an answer to all this insanity.

"That's all you have to say? What the hell is going on? What do you people want from me?"

"You're special, Fitz. Can I call you Fitz?" Zaphiel doesn't wait for an answer. "You're important. Not just to me, but to so many. Possibly to the world."

"Important how?" Fitz says.

"You're a Chronicler, Fitz. A prophet. Like Hesiod, Isaiah, Ezekiel, Muhammad. Like a thousand others who history has left nameless. You should be honored. When the gods speak, you hear it."

"I thought there was only one god. Isn't that your thing?"

"I am a servant of the One True God, yes, but think about that phrasing. There's an inherent idea in that. If there is One

29

True God that implies that there are other gods. Lesser gods, to be sure—false gods—but gods nonetheless. And there are. So many of them. Our innermost desires are like an open book to you. Our will channels through you so that we may spread our word across the globe. Humanity has been too long without guidance. You will change that."

There's something wrong here. It takes a second for Fitz to see it. "What do you mean 'our'? You're not a god. And what do you mean, no guidance? Don't your lot have churches and, I dunno, the Pope?" Fitz smells a con here, but he can't place where or what it is. "Does your boss know you're here?"

Zaphiel laughs. "Caught me," he says. "No, my boss doesn't know I'm here. Things have changed. I know it's not something you could understand, but the gods and goddesses, the monsters and heroes of myth, even Archangels like me, we used to stay pretty separate. We all had our domains, all took care of our own."

"I hear a *but* coming."

"It's a big one," Zaphiel says. "Something happened. It's hard to explain, so forgive me for not trying. But we're in a bit of a jam. All of us. And we could really use your help. You see, you've got an ability that no one's seen in a very long time. There have been people who can do it, but for various reasons they, well, they don't last long. But you, you're a talent."

"Since when?" Fitz says, his insides churning. He's getting a feeling he knows, but he wants confirmation. He hopes he's wrong. Hopes that whatever Zaphiel says next it isn't what he thinks it will be.

"Your entire life," Zaphiel says.

His entire life. Through all the foster homes, the involuntary psych holds, the pills and shots and shock treatments. Through the midnight seizures, the desperate attempts to quell the noise, the ruined relationships, the shattered friendships, there has always been one common thread.

The voices.

"This is all your fault," Fitz says, his voice quiet. "You ruined my life. You destroyed everything."

"Fault?" Zaphiel says. "No, Fitz. We've granted you a gift. You should be—"

"Honored," Fitz says. "I got that, yeah. Honored to have my life destroyed before it got started. Honored to be in and out of institutions. Honored to have this screaming in my fucking head my entire life. Because of you."

"No Fitz, I don't think—"

"Who the fuck cares *what* you think?" Fitz screams, leaping off the table and grabbing Zaphiel by the collar. "*You ruined my life.*"

Zaphiel's eyes turn red, pupils shrinking into points. "Ruined?" he says, his voice taking on more of that strange harmonic. "This is an honor, you ungrateful little turd." His neck thickens, tearing the collar of his shirt open. Fitz lets go, falls back against the table and scrambles to get it between him and the transforming Archangel.

"This is a *gift,*" Zaphiel screams. His head bulges on the sides, distending into something twisted and unrecognizable. "Something you fucking mortals just don't understand. You are given the greatest gifts and you piss them away. Rail against the heavens, that you didn't get what you wanted, didn't have it easy."

The bulges along Zaphiel's head crease, holes tearing through the flesh. Fitz watches, horrified, as new faces appear on the sides of Zaphiel's head, which spins like a top to show each one in turn. A lion's face with massive teeth, a razor-beaked eagle, an ox with horns still erupting from its forehead.

Zaphiel roars, each head adding its own sound to the cacophony. "All you thankless worms ever do is bitch and moan about how tough you have it. Well, if it hadn't been for you not knowing your fucking place, this would all still be a paradise."

He kicks the table out of his way and it sails across the room to shatter against a drill press. Two long strides and he's standing over Fitz. He reaches down, picks him up, shakes him.

"You will do what you are fucking told, Chronicler. Do you understand me?"

"Y-yes," Fitz stammers.

"Good." He drops Fitz to the floor, each of his faces twisting to get a good look at him. "Do not try to leave. Or I will tear out your still-beating heart and eat it while you watch."

He turns on his heel and walks out the door, slamming it hard behind him and throwing a bolt to lock it, leaving Fitz shaking on the floor.

CHAPTER FOUR

FITZ IS THROWING up. He's trying not to, but what just happened was horrific and intense. His brain can't process it all and his body has decided that the best way to cope is to empty everything in it as violently and loudly as possible.

After a while his stomach settles down and he lies on the cement floor, his breath coming in shallow, ragged gasps. He's reeling from what Zaphiel has told him. He'd like to believe it isn't true, that he's just sitting in a padded cell somewhere having an extended psychotic break, but everything about it feels too solid, too real. He has a hard time believing that he's completely snapped.

And if it is true, then he's not insane at all. He's just some sort of god radio with the volume knob snapped off, and he's been picking up signals for years from any passing immortal who happens to be screaming on his frequency.

Those fuckers.

Does it work with any god? He didn't get anything off Zaphiel the way he did off Medeina and the Agent. How come? Is it because Zaphiel is an angel, not a god?

And what do the gods want with him? He's some sort of prophet? A Chronicler? The hell does that even mean? They want him to tell their stories and—what? Make people believe in them?

How many gods are there? Well, he knows about Medeina and all of Medeina's Lithuanian pantheon. That's, what, fifteen or so? Plus all the gods he's heard of, like Zeus and Thor and, well, God. Are they all real? If some pissed off Lithuanian hunting goddess and an Archangel can be real, why not?

And then there's the Agent. Is it one of them? He didn't get a sense from it that it was a god, more of... an idea? Not quite fully formed, either. That much came through when he got that infodump in the hospital. But if it isn't a god, then why would he have gotten any sense of it at all?

There are too many questions and not enough answers, and he's not going to get them from the fucking monstrosity that's locked him up in here.

He thinks back to something Medeina said. She mentioned a Cherub. She must have been talking about Zaphiel. He obviously knows her; it stands to reason that she would know him.

Fitz's head pounds the more he thinks about it. If only he could have gotten more from Medeina. How is it he can pick up all of Medeina's history, all of her names, what she does, how she thinks, but he couldn't actually pick up what she's thinking? Aside from what Zaphiel has told him, he has no idea what's going on here.

As holy powers go, this one sucks.

He needs to find someone who can get him answers. He has no idea who that might be, but he knows he's not going to find them sitting in an abandoned warehouse waiting for some psychotic four-faced nightmare to come eat his face off.

He paces past one of the industrial machines and hears something buzz. At first he thinks it's maybe traffic, a truck going by, something like that. Then he hears it again and wonders if he's about to have another seizure. Maybe there's another god coming, one he's tuned into. It might not give him answers, but it will give him more information, and maybe he can start piecing together the truth.

But the pattern of the buzzing is wrong. It's not a continuous buzz, but a burst of two shorts and one long. And it's not in his head.

He stops, straining to hear it. It's like looking for a cricket trapped somewhere inside a house. He can hear it, but can't figure out where it's coming from.

He ducks behind a machine in search of the noise, roots around under a drill press, his hand snagging something small. He pulls it out.

A smartphone. Ringing.

He hits the button, and the screen lights up with a text message from a blocked number.

ARE YOU ALONE?

He tries to exit the messaging app, get to the phone so he can call the police. But it won't let him. The phone buzzes again.

ARE YOU ALONE. Same words, but somehow they feel more insistent.

Yes, he types. *Who R U? I need help. Angel has me trapped.* He'd like to think this was the strangest text he's sent, but there was a time when he'd just smoked a bunch of hash and sent pictures of his dick to some guy he'd met in a bar the week before, with all the lyrics to "I Feel Pretty" written backwards.

The response reads, *I WILL GET YOU OUT OF THERE GO TO THE NORTH WALL TWELFTH WINDOW FROM THE RIGHT NO CLOSER THAN FIVE FEET.* And then a moment later, as if tacked on as an afterthought, *PLEASE.*

Fitz doesn't know what's going on or who's on the other end of the phone, but so far that's the first polite thing anyone's said to him since this nightmare started. He orients himself as best he can to what he thinks is the north wall, counts twelve windows and heads toward it.

He guesses at what's five feet—he's always sucked at distances—and stops in front of the window. *I'm here,* he types.

DUCK, comes the reply.

Fitz hears a rumble outside the building, decides that following instructions is in his best interest and gets down to the floor. The rumble grows to a roar and a second later the window explodes inward with a shower of glass and metal as the crane from a utility bucket truck crashes through it.

Shards of glass shower over him, as the phone buzzes in Fitz's hand.

GET IN THE BUCKET

The bucket is dented and twisted, one side torn from going through the wall, and it's angled so high up that there's maybe a foot of clearance between the top of the bucket and the ceiling. He's not sure if it will hold him. Or even how to get into it.

And then there's the problem of Zaphiel.

The door at the far end of the room is torn down, the ruined hinges glowing red with the sheer speed of the impact. The Cherub is there howling with all four of his nightmare faces, charging into the room.

Fitz shoves the phone into his pocket and instead of trying to get into the bucket, jumps onto its side, hugging it like a life preserver in a storm.

"I'm in the bucket," he screams, hoping whoever is in the truck outside can hear him.

The driver hits the gas, tearing the bucket back through the hole it made in the wall, as Zaphiel jumps at Fitz. He mostly misses, but one hand punches into the metal.

Fitz scrambles to get up and over the bucket's lip, Zaphiel thrashing and screaming next to him. Fitz uses his face as a step stool, boosting himself inside. The angel snarls and swipes at him with his free hand, tearing a gash in his shirt and raking claws across his chest. The pain is intense; Fitz can feel hot blood soak through his shirt. Once he's inside, the angel's hand, lodged in its hole, grasps for any part of Fitz it can get hold of.

Fitz finds a tool belt with a pair of pliers, a wrench and some screwdrivers in the bottom of the bucket. He pulls the wrench, and hammers at Zaphiel's hand. He can hear him on the other side, scrambling for more purchase, trying to get into the bucket with him.

Zaphiel stops thrashing, goes very still. And then the angel lights up like a supernova. The light is blinding; Fitz can feel its heat blistering his skin. The metal around Zaphiel's hand glows and warps and the angel wrenches it out.

Fitz expects the angel to fall, but instead he hovers, glowing behind the truck as it tears through the building's parking lot and onto a street, running parallel to a set of train tracks, heading east. In the distance, across the river, Fitz can see the skyline of Downtown L.A.

A cacophony of noise hits him and he looks back to see Zaphiel, his body twisting and shifting into something immense. His clothes rip to shreds as four huge wings erupt out of his back and his body grows to three times its size.

The phone buzzes in Fitz's pocket and he screams until he figures out what the vibration is and fishes the phone out, almost dropping it in the shaking, rattling bucket. The crane isn't designed to be deployed while the truck is pushing fifty miles an hour.

DRAW THIS ON THE BUCKET, it says, followed by a picture of a strange pattern that looks like something between Sanskrit and what some fifteen-year-old metalhead would draw on his Pee Chee folder in chem class. *QUICKLY*

"With what?" Fitz yells. "It's not like I've got a marker up here."

USE YOUR BLOOD

Fitz stares at the screen. "I am not using my blood to draw anything," he says before realizing that he's yelling at a text message. He starts to type *No,* but his phone buzzes before he can hit send.

DO IT NOW HE IS GETTING CLOSER

Sure enough, Zaphiel is heading his way. He doesn't look like he's straining—though it occurs to Fitz that he has no idea what a straining Cherub with four monster faces would look like—and he's covering ground faster than the truck is.

The horizon fills up behind him with thick, dark clouds like a Spielberg movie and Fitz's ears pop from the pressure. The clouds boil over the L.A. skyline like a witch's cauldron, dark and thick. Flashes of lightning thread through them in a lattice of electricity.

He has seconds at most.

"Fuck. Fine." He reaches into the tear in his shirt. The wound isn't deep, but it's wide and long and his fingers come away wet with blood. He's not sure if it will need stitches or not. He draws the glyph on the inside of the bucket.

The truck makes a high-speed turn into a parking lot full of similar utility trucks just as he gets the final squiggle on the design.

The angel, only a few feet away from the truck, suddenly explodes into flames, dropping from the sky like a stone. He hits the pavement hard, skidding along for several feet before coming to a stop, a flaming, broken wreck.

With that the pressure in Fitz's ears suddenly lessens, the clouds break up and a few seconds later the sky is clear again.

The truck drives on until Fitz can't see the fallen angel anymore and then screeches to a halt, almost throwing him over the side. The bucket crane lowers to the ground, and once it's down, the driver, a black woman with her hair in dreads and wearing a heavy leather bomber jacket, jumps out of the car and runs back to help Fitz out of the bucket.

"Come on. There's a car over here."

"Who are you?" he says, following her as quickly as he can to a Chevy Impala parked nearby.

"Amanda. And you're Fitz. I'm supposed to take you to a safe house nearby."

"Safe house? What the hell is going on?" He freezes. "Are you with her?"

"Who?"

"Medeina."

"I have no idea who that is." A crack of thunder sounds in the distance. "But I know what that is, and neither one of us wants to be around when it gets here."

Fitz doesn't know what to do. Thinking about it, he doesn't think she's working with Medeina. The goddess doesn't strike him as the type to use someone else to do her dirty work. And she wouldn't go to the trouble to break him out of that warehouse. She'd just waltz in and slaughter anybody she found. Including Fitz.

Jesus. Listen to him. He's actually believing in this shit.

He shakes himself. "No. Not until I get some answers. Why did you get me out of there?" He holds up the smartphone. "Why were you texting me?"

"First, because I'm being paid to. Second, I wasn't texting you."

"Then who was?"

She shrugs. "Fuck if I know. Somebody working for the same guy I am, I suppose. Look, I'm happy to answer whatever I can, but not here and not now. I need to get you to the safe house or I don't get paid. Now are you gonna get in the car or do I have to beat you over the head with a tire iron and stuff you in the trunk?"

He weighs his options. It's a little late for 'Don't get into bucket trucks driven by strange women.' And at least he's being promised some answers. Right now all he has are questions.

"What'll it be, sparky?" Amanda says. "Ride up front like a big boy or in the trunk like a bitch?"

Another crack of thunder decides it for him. He can feel Zaphiel's anger. Whatever it was that Fitz drew on the side of the bucket, it isn't going to slow him down for long. He goes to the Impala, slides into the passenger side.

"Good call," she says.

MEDEINA DRAGS THE corpse into the corner of a storage room she has found in the hospital basement, leaving a thick smear of black across the floor.

At first glance she had thought this thing was a mortal. But then she got a better look at it in the hallway before it came for her and she knew that it was something... other.

Above her, mortals are combing through the ravaged hospital, rounding up survivors, counting their dead. She pauses, a tiny pang at the edge of her consciousness. She wasn't always this way, was she? She remembers a time when she was a defender of the forest, not a slaughterer of the innocent.

When did she learn to hate humanity so much? Was it when she was ejected from the heavens? Did it mark her so badly, make her so desperate to regain her old home?

Or was it when she became Zaphiel's lackey? When she agreed to hunt for him in the hopes that he might place her back where she belonged. Not here in this wasteland of mortals, land covered with thick layers of metal and concrete.

She shakes her head, as if to dislodge the thought from her mind. The past is the past. What matters is what she does now. Even gods, it seems, need to keep up with the times.

The mortals won't find her here in the basement. They will walk by without even noticing the door. She worries for a moment that she is hiding from them out of cowardice, but then decides that, no, she's doing it so as not to be interrupted.

Another new thing there. Doubt.

She props the corpse up against the wall, the arms and legs flopping lifelessly, one severed wrist still leaking the black substance that flowed through its veins.

It isn't ichor, that golden fluid that flows in the veins of the gods. This stuff has the consistency of black tar, thick and sticky. Not ichor, not blood. So this thing is not a god. It is not a hero or a demon.

So what is it?

It was a surprising opponent, though not a terribly worthy one. The bullets tore into her, gouging her flesh like razors. Pain isn't something that has happened to her in over a thousand years, since she picked a fight with her brother Perkūnas.

The battle with her brother was fierce. She tore into him with her spear, and he rained down upon her hail the size of houses. She countered as a great she-wolf, and he uprooted the trees of her forest to crush her. Finally, after he hammered at her with thunder, she was forced to concede and retreat in the form of a hare, dodging into burrows and digging through the attack.

This battle, though hardly as epic, was a reminder that though she is immortal, she can still be harmed. Though this thing, neither mortal nor immortal, wounded her, if only a little, her spear made short work of it. At first she merely knocked the guns from its hands, but it grew new ones to continue to fight. So she resorted to lopping off its hands and slicing deep through the boneless neck until the head hung limp from a thick flap of skin. And even then it continued to attack.

It wasn't until she carved out its chest—expecting to find a heart and instead merely releasing a torrent of the black sludge that pumped through its body—that it dropped lifeless to the floor.

She pulls its loose head up and places it back atop the stump of its neck. She has tried to remove its mirrored sunglasses from its face, but they might as well have been welded there. She can see no seam, but they're stuck fast. She suspects that there are no eyes behind the mirrored lenses. That those are, in fact, the thing's eyes.

She holds the spear at the ready in case it comes back to life. Some Slogutis, nightmare beings she has fought on more than one occasion, will do that. They can only be killed by slicing them apart and keeping each piece sealed in a pine box banded with iron.

When nothing happens, she's a little disappointed. She came looking for a fight and truth be told this one didn't go on as long as she'd hoped. She wishes it was the Cherub's body lying here. She could slice it apart over and over again.

She stares at the blank face looking for clues, but all she sees is herself, and the reflection is not kind. She is covered in its black sludge, in golden ichor from wounds that should have sealed up already, but are taking far longer than they ever have.

What is it? Who sent it? Why?

"I will find your keeper," she says. "And I will get my answers."

"You could just ask," the thing says, its mouth moving, but its face dead.

Medeina leaps back, swinging her spear until the point dimples the thing's forehead. She feels certain that it is dead. It makes no move, and yet it speaks.

"You're awfully nervous," the voice says, a thick, deep voice, one that oozes power and confidence, distinctly male, "for a god with a spear and magic helmet."

"I am not wearing a helmet, beast," she snaps back. The voice, she realizes, is not coming from the creature so much as *through* it. Whoever is speaking to her is not here in the room with her.

"Yes, well. Not a fan of the *Merrie Melodies*, I see. My point is that the 'beast' before you is well and truly dead. Not that it was ever really alive to begin with. But that's okay. I have more. So if you have questions, why not ask them?"

"Will you tell me the truth?" she says. Anyone who will resort to such deception cannot be trusted, and she has been caught in such traps before. Once she was imprisoned by the trickster Velnias, the dweller of the swamps, when she trusted too freely.

She will not let that happen again.

"Oh, probably not," the voice says. "But you can ask, anyway. Here, let me start with a freebie. You and I have a similar goal. We both want to get our hands on Louie Fitzsimmons."

"I wish to kill him. You?"

"Nothing so shortsighted. He can be appropriated. And if not, well, then he can be discarded."

"Killed, you mean."

"Well, yes, though personally I'm a fan of euphemisms. My point is that before he's discarded he can be useful. To both of us."

"Who are you?" she says.

"There are those who call me *El Jefe*," the voice says. "Though, like you, I have many names. Do you know why Mister Fitzsimmons is so highly sought after?"

She spits. "No. Zaphiel refuses to tell me."

"Oh, yes. The Cherub. I've heard of him. Not very nice, keeping you in the dark like that. It's like he's trying to edge you out of the biggest score the gods have seen in a thousand years or something. I'd be furious if I were you."

"He what?"

"I know, right? You don't keep your associates in the dark like that. Never mind rude, it's downright unprofessional. But I could tell you. If you're interested."

"This is a trick," Medeina says.

"It's all above board, I assure you. Once you hear it I'm sure you'll agree with me."

"There is a condition. There is always a condition."

"Well, yes. I'd like you to join me. Fight for my side, as it were. The benefits are excellent. Industry standard. And let's be honest, there is no way gods can be bound by agreements the way mortals can, anyway, right? If you agree to work with me and decide to leave, well, then you decide to leave. You found Mister Fitzsimmons once before, you can find him again. But I have access to resources that could aid you in that. My team's growing every day. In fact, I'm about to go enlist the aid of a couple of his friends. It's a win/win."

It doesn't take long for Medeina to decide. She really has nothing to lose. As he says, if she decides to leave, she will leave. "Agreed."

"Excellent. So let's get down to brass tacks. Have you heard of the Chroniclers?"

CHAPTER FIVE

AMANDA PULLS THE Impala up to a boxy, stuccoed single-story house off of Caesar Chavez Avenue across the street from a cemetery. Bars on the windows, a heavy security screen door in the front, with a weed-infested front yard surrounded by cheap chain-link fence. Graffiti covers two walls. Older tags are spray-painted out, newer ones are larger than the ones they've replaced. It's like watching gang warfare carried out through paint.

"This is it."

"This is a safe house?" Fitz says. "It's not even a safe neighborhood."

Amanda rolls her eyes. "The walls are reinforced concrete with metal plates behind drywall. The windows are half-inch-thick Plexiglas. That barred front security door is just decoration; the real security door is behind it and has internal ballistic panels, top, bottom, hinge and striker-side locking bolts. The gangs around here have been bought and paid for to make sure nobody fucks with it when I'm not here."

"But the graffiti—"

"Is there because I paid for it to be there. Trust me, anybody tries to mess with this place, they're not getting real far. Happy now?"

He's not. Not by a long shot. And he doesn't feel very safe, either. He doesn't think that a heavy duty door is going to keep Medeina or Zaphiel out if they decide to come calling. Maybe if some of the graffiti was that weird symbol his mysterious benefactor had him paint on the side of the bucket? How the hell had it stopped Zaphiel?

He limps along behind Amanda to the front door, nervously looking over his shoulder. "You got a first-aid kit in there?"

"I got a whole lot more than that in there," she says, opening the security screen and unlocking the front door with a key shaped like a long hex-wrench. A series of heavy bolts shift inside the door with loud *thunks*. The door swings open like a bank vault and he follows her in.

Outside, the place looks like a crack house, but inside it looks like something between an upscale Manhattan apartment and a bomb shelter. The walls are loaded with tasteful hotel art, the furniture is durable and heavy, the doors are utilitarian and thick.

Amanda closes the door behind them, punching a code into a keypad below a monitor showing the porch and the street outside. The bolts re-engage, sealing them in.

She points to two doors and a short hallway leading to the back of the house. "Kitchen through there. Three bedrooms that all double as panic rooms through there. Couple bathrooms and in the back's a full infirmary. Everything you need to patch yourself up conveniently labeled." She looks at his blood-soaked shirt. "You're probably gonna want to get some gauze or something on that."

"Ya think?"

"You can patch yourself up, or you can be sarcastic and bleed all over the place. I don't really care." She turns to leave and he puts a hand on her shoulder to stop her. She grabs his hand and spins him so fast his brain doesn't catch up to his nose hitting the floor until a couple seconds after it's happened.

"Don't do that," she says. "Don't ever do that."

"Okay," he says, the sound coming out in a thin, ragged wheeze.

"You got something to say?"

"No," he says. "I'm good. Thanks."

"Glad to hear it. Now go take care of yourself." She lets him go and leaves him gasping on the floor.

Fitz pulls himself from the floor. The gash on his chest has started bleeding again. Amanda might be scary insane, but she's got a point. He hobbles down the hall to the infirmary, a sterile, white room with an exam table, sink and cupboards.

He checks the phone. No bars. Why did he go along with this? Has he just exchanged one prison for another?

He needs to get bandaged up and then figure out a way to get the hell out. It's not that he isn't glad for the rescue, it's that he doesn't trust it. Whoever hired Amanda has their own agenda and whatever it is Fitz wants no part of it.

He opens his shirt to look at the wound. The bleeding has stopped, and he's already scabbing over. He's going to need a new shirt. Maybe there are extras in the safe house. The place seems to have everything else.

He finds the antiseptic and bandages and gets to work. It takes a while, he keeps fumbling the tape, but eventually he cleans and bandages it and it doesn't look so bad after he's washed it out. He doesn't think he needs stitches. But what does he know? He's no doctor.

But it hurts, a dull throbbing that spreads through his chest. He rummages through some cabinets looking for painkillers, scanning the vials and boxes of pills. Antibiotics, some antiemetics. He freezes when he opens one cupboard and realizes he's hit the jackpot.

Percodan, Percocet, Tramadol, Vicodin, Demerol, Norco, Lortab, Dilaudid, Fentanyl, OxyContin, the list goes on. He stares at them like a kid at a candy counter, starts to drool a little bit. If anything can numb the nightmare he's living through, this is the stuff.

Of course, he can't take it all. Not all at one time, at least.

He opens a bottle of OxyContin, shakes a couple into the palm of his hand. It's always struck him as weird that something so tiny can have such a big impact on a human body. He marvels at the medical miracle, and then tosses them back and dry swallows them.

He stuffs his jacket pockets with as many bottles as they'll hold. It occurs to him that Amanda's probably going to notice, but he doesn't really care. He's not planning on sticking around, anyway.

His jacket stuffed with painkillers and the oxys giving his mind a nice mellow glow, he puts his mind to getting out.

This is a safe house, but it might as well be a jail. The windows are all for show and he seriously doubts that front door is going to just open up for him. There has to be a way to get it open that doesn't involve trying to fight Amanda. She's already shown she can kick his ass.

Maybe there's another way.

He finds a vial of ketamine and a syringe. Fills the thing to the top. He's not sure about the dosage, hopes it won't be so much that it kills her, but he knows the shit works fast enough that he'll only have to deal with her for a couple of minutes at the most before it takes effect.

He caps the syringe and slides it into his pocket. Now he just needs a chance to use it. He'll want to wait until they're out of the safe house. No point in knocking her out and being stuck here without the code to get the door open. Maybe he can set something on fire, force her to open it?

The phone buzzes.

SAFE HOUSE COMPROMISED, the text reads. Well, what do you know.

"Hey, jackhole," Amanda yells from down the hall. "We're gettin' gone."

"What the hell does this mean?" he yells, buttoning his tattered shirt and running down the hall waving the phone out in front of him like he's flagging down a train.

"Means we got shit incoming and we need to get the hell out of here."

"No, I mean I don't have a signal, so how did I get a text?"

"Priorities. man. Come on, move it."

He follows her to the door, his pockets rattling with the sound of all the pills. His head is beginning to feel a few sizes too large.

When she reaches the door, Amanda draws a pistol from a holster at the small of her back, stops when she hears the rattling in Fitz's pockets.

"Do I even want to know?" she says.

"Found some pills in the infirmary," he says, seeing no reason to lie.

"Well, maybe it'll keep you quiet," she says. "Stay behind me, head to the car, whatever I say to do, do. Got that?"

He gives her a sloppy Benny Hill salute. "Got it, chief."

"Okay, then." She looks at the monitor next to the door. The Impala is parked out front. Looking over her shoulder, Fitz can't see any traffic out of the ordinary.

"How'd you know we have to leave?" he says.

"Because I got guys watching the neighborhood five blocks in every direction. Anything weird, they call me."

"They saw weird?"

"Weird enough," she says. "Folks who got no business being in this neighborhood." She punches a code into the keypad next to the monitor and the locking bolts disengage. She throws the door open, runs toward the Impala, Fitz on her heels.

Amanda slides over the hood of the car to get to the driver's side and Fitz throws open the passenger door as a blue minivan comes screeching around the corner.

The driver is a young blonde woman with wild eyes, disheveled hair, her face twisted in a snarl. She lays on the horn, still trying to steer the van out of the too-fast turn she's put it in.

She fails; the van tips, skids along the pavement, spinning and showering sparks along the sidewalk, until it's turned completely around and on its side. It comes to a grinding stop against a palm tree on the other side of the street.

Fitz and Amanda stare at the smoking car. The van's license plate says NO1MOM and has those little family decals on the back showing mom, dad, a couple kids and a dog. There's a bumper sticker that reads *COEXIST* made out of a bunch of different religious symbols and another that says *NAMASTE*. In the rear window, barely hanging on and wobbling back and forth, is a yellow, diamond-shaped *BABY ON BOARD* sign.

Is this a false alarm? Some drunk yoga mom who finally snapped, took the wrong exit off the freeway and ended up here? Fitz wants to help, but there's something pushing through the oxy numbing his mind that holds him back.

"Get in the car," Amanda says.

"But she—"

Fitz doesn't get to finish. The door to the minivan explodes into the sky and the blonde yoga mom, face bloodied from a gash in her forehead, one arm twisted at an insane angle with a bone sticking out, leaps ten feet into the air and lands on the pavement with a loud thud.

"I'm getting in the car now," Fitz says.

"Good plan." Amanda slides behind the wheel of the car. She pops off a couple of shots at the screaming woman before slamming the door shut and stepping on the gas.

The bullets have no chance to hit; less, Fitz thinks, because it's a wild-ass shot, and more because the woman has just vaulted straight up into the air like she's goddamn spring-loaded.

Amanda peels away from the curb, the Impala burning rubber. Doesn't get far before the blonde lands on the car. There's the sound of metal twisting as the hood buckles under her weight, but also a nauseating *pop* as one of her legs snaps, tearing through the back of her calf.

Amanda hits the brakes and the blonde goes flying, then she throws the car into reverse and pulls a bootlegger, spinning the car the other direction and gunning the engine. She leaves the blonde trying to pick her broken body up from the pavement behind them.

Amanda stomps on the gas and pushes the car faster than a crappy Chevy has any right to go. The Impala is surprisingly nimble and fast. Fitz is somewhere at the crossroads of nauseous, terrified and impressed as she punches her way through the traffic, weaving between cars like a bumblebee zipping through fields of flowers.

"What in the unholy fuck was that?" Fitz says, scrambling to fasten his seatbelt.

"Don't know. Don't want to," Amanda says. "Keep an eye out for more."

"More what? Crazy Terminator yoga moms?"

"Yep," she says. "Just like that one."

A Mercedes SUV barrels into the lane in front of them. Different make, different model, different driver, but it's got the same Beverly Hills all-organic, gluten-free, save-the-world, let's-have-three-kids-because-I-am-the-goddamn-Earth-mother-hear-my-uterus-roar vibe coming off it in spades.

Amanda dodges the oncoming SUV with the skill of a NASCAR driver, jogging over to clip the rear bumper in a PIT maneuver just before she clears the SUV, sending it careening onto the sidewalk.

Fitz looks behind them as they pass, sees the same Baby On Board sign, those same family stickers, this time with two mommies and three kids, that always put Fitz in mind of the kill symbols WWII fighter pilots painted on their planes.

The driver, a frizzy-haired redhead, kicks the SUV's door off its hinges and leaps out of the car, screaming at them as they drive away, her eyes just as wild as the last one's.

She reaches into the SUV and pulls out something shiny and round. Flings it at them with the accuracy of a ninja. A flash of silver hits the rear window of the Impala, shattering the glass. It flies through the car and embeds itself into the middle of the dashboard, slicing the car's clock in two.

"What the hell was that?" Amanda says.

Fitz tugs the CD out of the dashboard. "Indigo Girls."

"Of course it is."

"Is that it? Are there more?" In answer two more cars come out of side streets, a Mini Cooper with an empty baby car seat in the back, and another SUV, a hybrid.

"Crazy women drivers?" Amanda says.

"How'd you guess?"

"Noticing a pattern."

Fitz is noticing a pattern, too. The closer they get, the more of a buzzing he gets in the back of his mind. Like when he saw Medeina, when he ran into the Agent. Only it's more distant, less pronounced. A reflection of power rather than the power itself.

The Mini Cooper brushes against the Impala, forcing Amanda to correct or spin out, and the taste of bad wine fills Fitz's mouth. Thick and cloying, stinking like something a hobo would drink out of a paper bag. It pushes against the oxy in his system and for a moment the drug passes away and he feels a powerful drunk coming on, but then Amanda pushes the Impala ahead and it passes.

"You all right there?" she says. She crosses the Fourth Street Bridge toward Downtown, cuts right across two lanes of traffic to hit Alameda hard, narrowly avoiding a collision with a panel truck.

"That a rhetorical question? What now?"

"They'll try to cut us off up ahead," Amanda says, pushing the car up past Second Street. "Try to get us at Temple. Maybe First. Least that's what I'd do."

They hit First Street and she takes a hard left. Horns honk, tires squeal. Half a block down and the SUV passes them from the other direction, brakes smoking as it tries to stop and turn to give chase.

Fitz has been down here enough times to know that in a few more blocks they'll be at City Hall and the LAPD headquarters. And then yoga moms in SUVs will be the least of their problems. The last place Fitz wants to be is in a cell where he can be found.

Surprisingly, they haven't passed a police car yet, but it's only a matter of time before they do and it's all over. High speed chases never end well in a city where the news helicopters do a better job of tracking you than the cops.

But instead of continuing down First, Amanda takes a hard

left onto Los Angeles Street toward Skid Row. "We need to ditch the car. I've got another one in a lot past Fifth. We'll switch there."

"Won't they just find us again?"

"Of course not. We've already lost 'em." Another two cars pull up behind them as they cross Third, another minivan and SUV.

"You were saying?"

"Goddammit."

The cars flank the Impala, keeping pace with it no matter how Amanda speeds up or slows down. Same pattern as the other two cars. Screaming women at the wheels of cars that should be ferrying kids to baseball practice, dance recitals, Montessori classes.

They keep it up for most of a block, then Amanda slams on the brakes and turns the wheel to the left, clipping the rear of the SUV and shattering the Impala's headlight. The cars shoot past and Amanda pulls the Impala down an alley, gunning the engine. Sparks fly as she scrapes the car across a dumpster.

Fitz hears the screech of tires behind him, the bone-jarring crunch of the cars they left behind plowing into oncoming traffic. His heart is just about to start pumping again when Amanda says, "Shit," and hits the brakes.

Two new SUVs block the end of the alley, and when he looks behind them, Fitz can see one backing up and limping in behind them, its front end a mangled heap of twisted metal.

"Get out. Get out and run."

"Run where? Who the hell are these people?" he says, hoping he sounds sincere. This would be the perfect opportunity to get away from Amanda if he weren't being hunted by a bunch of wild-eyed mothers who look likely to tear him to pieces rather than let him get away. He's starting to think that leaving the safe house was a bad idea.

Amanda yanks her seatbelt off and shoves the door open. "Doesn't matter. Just go. I'll try to draw them off." She takes aim at one of the cars with her pistol and pops off a couple of rounds.

Fitz doesn't need to be told twice. He bolts from the car, looking for any exit from the alley that doesn't involve going past the SUVs. The buildings are flophouses, old brownstones on the edge of Skid Row with fire escapes leading to apartments with shattered windows. He jumps and pulls down one of the ladders.

He ignores the sounds of gunfire and screaming, focuses on getting up and into the building. If he can get inside, maybe he can find a back door or a place to hide. The shots have to be attracting attention. The police will be here soon. And much as he doesn't want to be locked up in a cell where he's a sitting duck, better that than gunned down in a Skid Row alleyway. Alive is better than dead any day of the week.

He hears a snarl and Amanda cries out. When he looks he sees one of the soccer moms on top of her beating and clawing at her, roaring at her like a pissed-off tiger.

Fitz is terrified, but there's no way he's letting her get killed for him. He starts back down the ladder. He expects to have to fight these women off tooth and nail, but when he gets to the bottom he sees one of them pointing an evil-looking black gun at him.

She pulls the trigger, but instead of a bullet, twin barbs shoot out and stick into his chest. It hurts like the mother of all bee stings, but he thinks it could be worse, he could be dead.

And then the voltage hits him and he wishes he was.

CHAPTER SIX

IN 1965 WHEN Blake Kaplan was fifteen, he heard the Righteous Brothers single "You've Lost That Lovin' Feeling" for the first time, on a jukebox in Ship's Coffee Shop on La Cienega, and it changed his life.

Fifty years later and it's clear as yesterday. He was out for dinner with his parents, eating one of the restaurant's signature 'Ship Shape Hamburgers' and a side of fries, though what was supposed to make the burger particularly special he could never tell.

But the song, Bill Medley and Bobby Hatfield crooning about a lost love, that was special. That was sublime.

He hated it.

Even at fifteen, he knew insipid trash when he heard it. Knew that it was total garbage. The lyrics were dull, their voices were boring. But the arrangement, the layering of instruments, the way they all blended into each other to make brand new instruments.

He hated the song, he loved the production.

He got the record the next day, listened to it over and over, trying to understand how the sounds all fed into each other, somehow making something new. He hunted down the record label, found out about the producer Phil Spector and his Wall of Sound method, where he would record in echo chambers and have instruments play into and on top of each other, making hit after hit after hit.

Well, until he got old and batshit crazy, started wearing bad afro wigs and shot a woman in his mansion in Alhambra. But nobody's perfect.

The thing about Spector that Blake could see even fifty years ago, even before he was at the height of his career, was that he had built a legacy. Something lasting, something great. He had, in his own way, created an empire.

And before 1965 ended, Blake knew that what he wanted to do more than anything else in his life was to make records.

Too bad he sucked at it.

"Jesus, Blake," Sam says, looming over Blake's shoulder as he taps at the computer keyboard. "You sure? I mean, this is Fitz we're talking about."

"I can see it right here," Blake says. His voice is even, but inside he's seething. It's taken him a few hours to find the holes in his accounts that Fitz left—for the most part the little weasel's done a pretty good job cleaning up after himself—but there were enough gaps in everything that Blake started seeing a pattern. So he dug a little. And the holes just kept getting bigger and bigger until they were like a cave system made out of money. That sonofabitch.

When Blake got into producing in 1979, the #1 hit was The Knack's "My Sharona," proving once again that kids will listen to anything as long as it's loud and slightly dirty. Disco was on the way out, rock was changing into something brand new and the sounds that would define the next decade were just beginning to be heard. It was a great time. Full of possibility, full of promise. Not bad for a balding, barrel-chested Jew from the Fairfax District.

He signed up four boys from New Jersey with feathered hair who all looked like Shaun Cassidy and dubbed them the

Heartthrobs. Sure it was on the nose, but fuck, that's what he was trying to make them.

It didn't work. Oh, it started well. Debut album got mad airplay, they did an episode of *Saturday Night Live*, the *Tonight Show*, even the goddamn *Muppets*.

But then some tabloid asshole got a shot of them doing smack and blowing each other in the back of their tour bus and it all went to shit. Blake went into damage control mode. Got the kids into rehab, hid the fact that he was the one got them the drugs. But it wasn't enough. The public could forgive the drugs—hell, they were rock stars—but they couldn't forgive that they were gay. Funny how times change.

The backlash was quick and brutal and didn't end until one of the kids stuck a gun in his mouth at a press conference in Vegas and ate a bullet.

"How much money did he steal?" Sam says.

"Near as I can tell, ten, twelve million? More? Fuck, I don't know."

"Where'd it all go?"

"I have no idea, Samantha. Please shut up while I figure this out."

Blake hedged his bets next and started three boy bands, set up fake rivalries between them, and the press ate it up. For about a month and a half. But their debuts went nowhere, their songs unaired. He cut two albums each with them, hoping something would stick. Worked them around the clock until he was sure he had at least one hit on his hands.

The only way he could keep them going the long hours and crazy schedules was by feeding them a steady diet of cocaine. By the time he'd gotten what he wanted out of them, they were so burnt out there was no way any of them were getting onto a stage in front of anybody. And that was before three of them tried to rob a bank.

Blake tried it one more time. Broke up those bands before they even got off the ground, spent a couple years doing nothing but research, looking at demographics, analyzing sales. Saw an opportunity in the Latino market just waiting to be tapped.

So he sunk all his cash into some kids up from Mexico, called them Los Amigos, got studio time, some kick ass songs, all set to record.

And then Menudo happened.

Fucking Menudo.

At that point he figured the universe was trying to tell him something, so he packed it in and started looking for another career. Music wasn't going to do it for him, but he just couldn't let it go. He tried renting out studio space, booking acts, anything to stay in, but none of it paid the bills.

And then, when one of the kids from the Heartthrobs showed up on his doorstep with a wad of blood-covered bills looking to score some heroin, he had an epiphany. He might not be able to make a hit record, but goddamn did he know how to get kids high.

"He's probably sitting in County on that drug charge. We can bail him out. Get that money back," Sam says.

Blake is starting to shake, tiny tremors as his control slips. He thought he could trust Fitz, has known him for years, taught him everything, taken care of him, given him a purpose, a life. Blake's treated Fitz like he's his own son. And the little shit turns around and stabs him in the back.

"I don't want the money back," Blake says.

The money isn't the point. It's never been the point. It wasn't the point when he tried to get those boy bands to hit it big, it wasn't the point when he started selling drugs, it wasn't the point when he moved from distribution and invested his cash in Mexican cartels, the Israeli ecstasy market, or Afghani opium farmers.

The point was to build a legacy. Something lasting, something great. He wanted, in his own way, to create an empire.

And now Fitz has shit on it. It's not like Blake doesn't have plenty of money. He's set for life and then some. Ten, twelve million—hell, even twenty million would only set him back a month or two, if that. But a man lives and dies by the people he surrounds himself with, the trust he has for his associates and family, and Blake trusts very few people.

Sure, he has a lot of people working for him, but only two in his inner circle. Only two who know the full extent of his world, what he does and what he's done to get there.

And now one of them has turned out to be a fucking backstabbing Judas.

"So what do you want to do?"

"We get him out of jail, we bring him back here and then I peel his skin off like a fucking banana."

"But—"

"There a problem with that, Samantha?" Blake looks up from the computer. "Because if there's a problem with that, then you're not the woman I thought you were, and I'd hate to have to hire somebody to take you out, too. Maybe one of those crazy fucking Russians. Or that guy up from Mexico you tussled with last year. How about I bring him on board, give him a nice, fat salary to serve me your goddamn liver on a plate, because you wouldn't nut the fuck up and do what I fucking told you?"

Sam stares at him, eyes like stone. Blake thinks maybe he's gone too far. Sam and Fitz are like salt and pepper. Friends for life. Loyalty is a fickle thing, a fragile thing. Like a soap bubble. One false breath and it pops.

"You didn't know about this," Blake says, his voice quiet, gentle. "I know that. It's one thing for him to not tell me, but you? How could he have kept this from you? He betrayed you, too."

Sam blinks. "I'll make some calls," she says, pulls her phone from her pocket and goes into the other room. Was that the right move? Is Sam on his side? Blake can't tell.

"Of course she is," says a man's voice behind him, thick and deep, one that oozes power and confidence.

Blake spins around in his chair, but there is no one there. "Who's there?" he says, feeling like an idiot. Maybe he's going senile. Maybe Fitz's crazy is catching.

"I could tell you," the voice says, behind him once again, "but then I'd have to kill you."

Blake leaps out of his chair, spins around looking at the

room for shadows, for someone hidden around a corner, for goddamn ninjas. "Where the fuck are you?"

"You okay?" Sam says, poking her head back into the room.

"What? Yeah. Course I'm fucking okay. You make those phone calls?"

"I'm on hold with a detective. You sure you're all right?"

"I fucking told you, didn't I? Now leave me the fuck alone. I got work to do."

"Yeah, sure." Sam looks at him like she's not sure if he's having an aneurysm. She goes back into the other room, leaving Blake alone.

Well, not completely alone.

"She's a good egg," the voice says. "I see why you keep her around."

"I'm going insane," Blake says. "Aren't I?"

"No idea, but I can tell you I'm not a delusion."

"What do you want?"

"Same thing you do. Louie Fitzsimmons."

Blake sits back down. When he was a kid his grandfather came down with dementia. He was completely off his nut, but he coped by talking to himself. Part of him was still sane enough to tell him out loud that what he was doing was wrong.

"Merle," he'd say. "You ought not to set yourself on fire," to which he would always reply, in a voice more hazy and distant than the voice he told himself things with, "Ayup." And then everything would be fine.

He was crazy, but it was a crazy he could use.

Maybe Blake is going crazy the same way.

"I'm listening," Blake says. He keeps his voice low, hoping Sam can't hear him in the next room. This might be crazy he can use, but it's still crazy.

"You want Louie Fitzsimmons," says the voice. "I want Louie Fitzsimmons. Together we can make that happen. I have resources. Friends. Allies. How would you like to form a merger?"

"What kind of merger?"

"The kind that gets you to your goals faster than if you don't do it. What do you say?"

"What's the catch?" He doesn't know why he's asking that, but this voice is making him wary. It doesn't sound like he's talking to himself the way Grandpa Merle talked to himself. There's an undercurrent to it that he doesn't like.

"No catch," the voice says. "It's very simple. Like I said, a merger. We can work more closely. You, me, some people I have on my payroll. It's all very above board."

As sales pitches go, he's given himself better. Hell, he's given other people better. But if the voice is him, and he can't imagine what else it would be, he doesn't see the harm in indulging himself.

He shakes his head. This is crazy. He's clearly going nuts. But, hey, it worked for Grandpa Merle. Well, until the disease finally went too far and he walked naked into traffic on Fairfax where he got run down by a dump truck. Took them days to figure out it was him. He was just one long smear of naked old man bits.

Blake drums his fingers on the arm of his chair. Give in to the crazy or fight it and... what? Keep hearing voices? He looks at the spreadsheets in front of him. Millions of dollars stolen right out from under his fucking nose.

By, and let's be clear on this, a crazy man.

It's hard to remember that sometimes. Fitz is lucid most of the time, even when he's on the drug *du jour*. He passes for normal surprisingly well. Fitz is insane, even if nobody can pin down just what kind of insane he is.

"All right," Blake says. "Deal."

"Excellent!" the voice says. "So glad to have you aboard. I'm sure you'll find the benefits package meets industry standard."

"Industry stan—" Blake stops mid-sentence as an icy pain seizes his chest and squeezes. The voice thunders in his ears, drowning out the world around him, the sounds of his blood pumping, his heart beating.

"Oh, yes. Everyone who comes aboard gets the same package," says the voice. "Did I say merger? I misspoke. I really should have said hostile takeover. Goodbye, Mister Kaplan. It was so nice working with you."

* * *

"I GOT HOLD of that detective," Sam says, stepping into the room and closing her cell phone. She's been on the phone for the last twenty minutes, bouncing around from person to person, waiting for confirmation. The news is not good. The detective out of Hollenbeck, a customer of Blake's with a thing for Chinese prostitutes and Bolivian cocaine—as if he even knew where Bolivia was—is telling her things she doesn't want to hear.

Either Fitz is dead or he's flown the coop. Neither outcome is likely to make Blake happy.

She's not sure how she feels about the situation. Blake's right, of course. Fitz did lie to them, and if he could lie about this, what else has he lied about?

But Blake wants to kill him. Is probably going to make Sam kill him, or at the very least beat the shit out of him, maybe cut off some fingers. If it were anybody else, Sam wouldn't care. But this is Fitz. She's known him for years. They've been through some shit.

She remembers a time when Fitz saved her life. Blake sent the two of them out to get a couple thousand bucks off a guy in Venice. He'd rented out some twink from Blake's stable and didn't pay up. Fitz was supposed to do the talking, Sam was supposed to do the leg breaking.

It didn't go well.

They went to his condo and instead of paying up, the jackhole decided to pull a revolver and put two into Sam's chest. The shots went wide and one of them winged Sam before she could pull her own gun.

Would have been over for both of them if Fitz hadn't picked up a big lamp off a table and bashed the fucker's head in. Kept hitting him until his skull was just a mess of red paste.

If nothing else, Sam owes him for that.

If Blake wants her to kill Fitz, she'll just have to figure out if she'll do it when the time comes. Burn that bridge when she gets to it. She takes a deep breath, steels herself. She's not sure which possibility is going to bother Blake more: that Fitz is dead or that he might have gotten away.

Probably that there's no solid answer either way.

"I got something," she says, stops when she sees Blake sitting at his computer and staring into the distance. "Blake? You good?"

Blake slumps a bit in his chair; Sam rushes to him, but he waves her off. He straightens, seems to grow a couple inches. Sam can hear a strange crackling hum for a second, and then it's gone.

Blake spins his chair to face her, a smile turning up the corners of his mouth. Not the kind of smile she's ever seen on Blake's face. He looks wrong somehow, like he's not quite fitting in his own skin. Like his eyes aren't quite his own. Younger, tighter. His hair has more of a sheen.

The word that comes to Sam's mind is *hungry*.

And also *feral*.

"Samantha," Blake says, his pupils widening and shrinking down to pinpoints before settling into something that looks almost normal. "I have never felt better."

Something about that look, about those words. Sam has never been more terrified in her life.

CHAPTER SEVEN

FITZ COMES TO slumped on a wooden chair in the middle of some kind of Greek temple with a high, curved ceiling, walls of blue-green marble interspersed by stone columns, the floor a complex mix of yellow, white and green tiles. Marble statuary lines the walls, women in classical poses, many of them missing limbs, noses, pieces of carefully carved clothes.

One in particular, a woman in robes holding a snake or something in one hand—Fitz can't tell—and an egg in the other with a little angel baby at her feet, takes up a space at the front of the room. The statue is much larger than the rest.

His vision is blurry, his head pounding. He pulls himself up straighter and his chest screams in agony. He checks and sees that one of the Taser barbs is still stuck in his flesh, straight through his shirt. The skin is singed where the barbs went in, a dark circle of burnt flesh around nasty, puckered wounds like he's been attacked by pissed-off hornets with flame throwers.

He plucks at the remaining barb the way he might a splinter, grits his teeth and manages to work it out of his chest. It hits the floor with a tinny *ping* that echoes throughout the chamber.

"You're awake."

Fitz turns in his chair, his back getting in on the pain orchestra, and winces. A tall man with dark hair and a goatee, purple robe, gold decoration at the hems. A glass of dark red wine, in a hand covered in rings. He steps through a door at the back of the room. Behind him, Fitz can see another room in the same style, more marble statuary lining the walls. To the side is another door heading into a similar room.

"That's a word for it. Who the fuck are you?"

"I am very glad you asked that question," the man says, stepping further into the room and sipping at his wine. Two of the yoga moms who chased Fitz down step in behind him.

Eyes wild, hair sticking out in manic tufts, their bodies vibrating like an engine running too hot and straining at the bolts keeping it under the hood. They stand stock still, breathing shallow and rapid, eyes bouncing around in their sockets like ping pong balls. Fitz isn't sure they can actually see anything.

"Don't suppose you're gonna give me an answer?"

"In time. Right now I'm more interested in the fact that you don't already know."

"'Pleased to meet you, hope you guess my name'?"

"Quite," the man says. "When you encountered Medeina in the hospital, how long did it take you to know who she was?"

There's something about this man that's pricking the back of his mind, and now that he knows what he's been dealing with—even now he has a hard time saying *god*—he knows what it is. Did he feel that same thing with Zaphiel? He thinks back to the hospital parking lot, to the warehouse. Yes. It wasn't enough for him to notice it, then, but yes, it was there.

"Not long," he says. Fitz's instinct is to lie, keep his knowledge to himself, but this guy already knows what happened at the hospital, or at least some of what happened there, and if he's a god, Fitz can't imagine he won't have other ways of getting the information he wants.

He looks at the two yoga moms. Their clothes are torn, spotted with blood from where they've scratched themselves.

Their fingernails are cracked and torn, blood all up and down their hands.

He's seen crazy up close and personal, and this is the kind of crazy that gets you a Thorazine drip and a straitjacket. For all the insanity in their eyes, he gets the distinct sense that they're drunk.

"You hear voices? Have trouble coping with life? It all gets a little too busy?"

"Yeah, I heard this bit already," Fitz says. "And if you know about me then you know that that's all true, too. So how about we cut the bullshit, you tell me who you are and what you want and I'll be on my way."

The man laughs. "Well, I'm sure I can accommodate some of that. You want to know who I am?" He takes a sip of his wine. "Let's see what you can do with this."

Fitz doubles over in agony. More pain than he's ever experienced. Like having his head smashed in with a bowling ball over and over again. Images, sounds, memories, knowledge. Too much to process, too much to understand. It's all a blur, but over a few seconds that seem to last an hour, one thing becomes clear.

Fitz is out of his fucking league here.

Medeina was one thing. A goddess, sure, but small potatoes. He can see that now. Some pissy little forest sprite that a bunch of tribes huddled around campfires prayed to until she became something more than their collective hope that the wolves wouldn't eat them, that the bears wouldn't maul their children, that they wouldn't all die of frostbite and starvation.

But this guy, holy fuck. This guy.

This is Bacchus, Dionysus. Lord of the Grape, Keeper of the Vine. Son of Zeus and a princess of Thebes. He is Erikryptos the hidden, Briseus, who prevails over all things, the feral Agrios. He is wine and dance and song. He is perversion and salvation.

But most of all, he is madness.

Fitz falls to his knees, vomiting, as if he could expel this rushing knowledge that has flooded his mind, but it just keeps coming. He sees everything Bacchus has done, every twisted story, every travail, every task.

He wants it to stop, needs it to stop. But it doesn't. This is an old god. A god who was old when the world was young. So many names, so many stories. Before the Romans, before the Greeks. A terror on the land, a monster among monsters.

Fitz's veins bulge, his body shaking, trying to hold all this knowledge in, trying to expel it. He can feel the capillaries in his eyeballs pop and his vision goes red in one eye. Blood drips from his nose. One of his molars cracks beneath the grinding of his jaw.

"Well, Prophet, like your answer? How much do you see? How much do you feel? Can you take it?"

Fitz looks up at Bacchus through the red film of blood in his eye. The god is smiling, the fucker. Smiling and killing him. Letting it all hang out for Fitz to soak up until he pops like a gorged tick.

"You've never felt this before, have you?" he says. "This much knowledge? What it must be like for a mortal to feel all of that. Looks like it hurts." He squats down and grips Fitz's chin in a hand like an iron vise and looks him over. "You're probably going to want to get that eye looked at. Oh, there goes the other one."

There is no way that Fitz is going to let this smug fucker get the better of him. He focuses down, rides the wave of knowledge coursing through him like he's surfing in a hurricane. It helps, but not much.

"And this is just a taste of what you can look forward to," the god says. "All of those maddening god signals you've been picking up like the universe's most broken radio your entire life? They're nothing. Desert signals on the wind, staticky chatter on a dead station. We know about you now. We know you're out there."

Bacchus releases his mental grip and the flood of images stops. Fitz collapses to the floor, blood running freely from his nose. He spits out his shattered molar, vomits some more.

Thousands of years in under a minute. There's too much

data for him to make sense of it all, but one image sticks out. Something about a fall. No, an eviction. The images are still too raw, but he knows there's something there. Something important.

"Why?" Fitz says, his mouth full of puke and blood and a fattened tongue that it's a miracle he didn't chew through.

"Oh, that's easy, little worm," Bacchus says. "You're our ticket to salvation."

FITZ CLEANS HIMSELF up with a towel. This is his fifth one. He tosses it with the other bloodied and vomit-stained towels on the floor, looks at the logo stitched on it and feels like an idiot.

Took him a while after his ordeal to catch on that he isn't in a Greek temple. It wasn't until one of the god's mad groupies handed him the towel and he saw the logo and made the connection. He's in a room at the Getty Villa, an art museum filled to the ceiling with old statues, on Pacific Coast Highway.

He's never been here before, but he's heard of it enough times to know what it is. All this statuary gives him the creeps. Marble busts staring at him with empty eyes.

"Feeling better?" Bacchus says, sipping his wine and sitting on the backs of two of the yoga moms, who have gotten down on all fours to make a seat. Their eyes are still wild, their bodies still shaking. Fitz wonders what's going on in their heads. If they even know what's happening to them.

He hopes they don't.

"The fuck do you care?" Fitz says. Clearly, humanity's welfare isn't at the top of this guy's list. "And what's with the yoga moms?"

Maenads. The Bacchae. The word comes to Fitz as if he's always known it, but he doesn't remember ever hearing it before. He's not even sure how to spell it. Women under Bacchus' thrall, driven to ecstatic visions and madness, drunk on his wine. Willing or not; something tells Fitz these ones fall into the latter category.

The thought of it makes him sick.

Bacchus looks down at the two women upon whose backs he sits. A look of mild surprise crosses his face, as if he's just noticed that they're not actually a chair.

"Followers. Of a sort."

"Yeah, I got that. But I thought all your groupies were weird hippie party-goers, or—" An image flashes in his mind of drunken revels in the hills surrounding Rome: dances and bonfires, sacrifices and bloodshed, death. He blinks, the images fading from his eyes. "Old-time party people," he finishes weakly.

"Did you know that the largest number of wine drinkers in this armpit of a city is new, twenty-something mothers with almost, but not quite successful spouses? Can't afford nannies, and desperate to hang onto their teens like passengers on the *Titanic* hanging onto life preservers. Seriously, they drink like fish. I take what I can get."

"They sign up for this?"

"Who would deny a god? Certainly not some Beverly Hills bimbo who's just popped out some mewling brats."

Or some would-be prophet? The unasked question hangs in the air. There's a glaring assumption in the god's statement and Fitz is certain he wasn't meant to miss it.

"Where are the children?"

Bacchus gives a half-hearted wave. "No idea. Dead in a ditch, for all I care. But enough about them. Let's talk about you. And what you can do for me. I have a vested interest in your well-being," he says.

"Right. You said. I'm your fucking salvation." That image of a fall, of being forcibly removed from something, that he got from Bacchus just before he cut off the flow of knowledge; it tickles at the back of his mind. There's something there, but he can't quite parse it all out. He tries to focus on it, but all of the other images are crowding his brain. He can't separate the signal from the noise. His nose starts bleeding again and he presses another towel to his face to staunch the flow.

"Did Medeina tell you what you are, or was it Zaphiel? I think Zaphiel. Fool could never tell which facts were important and which ones to keep to himself, and Medeina is such a hot-head I would expect her to murder you as much as look at you. Hell, she probably didn't even know. Well, I'm glad he told you. At least you came here knowing that much."

Came here. As if Fitz had any choice in the matter. He has a sudden thought of Amanda. He's been so pre-occupied with not bleeding from every orifice that he's almost forgotten about her. He hopes she got away, but something tells him she didn't.

"What, that I'm this Chronicler? That you've all been fucking with my head my entire life? Yeah, he told me."

Bacchus nods. "But not how it works. Not why it's always been such a low background hum in your life, rather than the onslaught I gave you. Not why you can hear it loud and clear sometimes and it's just a buzzing madness the rest." He takes a long drink of his wine and Fitz notices that the glass doesn't actually get any lower. Nice trick.

"You're only half the equation," Bacchus says. "We're the other half."

"I'm the receiver," Fitz says. "You're the transmitter."

"It thinks!" Bacchus says. "That's too bad, actually. I was rather hoping you were an idiot. Well, I'm certain you are. All mortals are to some extent."

"All you gods know each other?" Fitz says. "You all hang out in heaven, shoot the shit, give each other handjobs? That how you know about Medeina and Zaphiel?" If Bacchus is telling the truth then why was he able to pick up the signal from Medeina and the Agent but not from Zaphiel? Guess being a god radio doesn't always work.

And then it clicks. It works fine. But if he's just a receiver—

"You can control how much signal you're transmitting," Fitz says. "Zaphiel kept it under wraps. Medeina didn't."

"I strongly suspect that Medeina *can't*," Bacchus says. "It never occurs to most of us to bother. Why would we? We're gods."

"So how come you do?"

"Because I know what a Chronicler can do. I've seen your

kind come and go. Have you ever read Hesiod? Homer? Euripides? Bit of a bastard, that one. Wrote a tragedy about me. Made me look like a fucking monster."

Fitz looks at the two women, their arms and legs shaking, backs buckling. "You don't say."

"I also know what giving my all to a Chronicler will do to them. How are your eyes, by the way? They look terrible."

The red film in his vision has faded, but his eyes still ache like he's been punched in the face a few too many times. "S'all right."

"Hmm. So, as you can imagine, transmitting, as you put it, tends to burn your type out. Most of you can't handle the signal. And there aren't a whole lot of you left. In fact, you're the first relatively sane one of any power I've heard about in over a hundred years."

"Sane one?" Fitz says. "I've been in and out of the system my entire life."

"Yes, but you haven't chewed through your own tongue, have you? Haven't pulled together a flock of your chosen ones and force-fed them cyanide. Or held a stand-off in a Texan bunker until someone shot you full of holes. Or murdered a bunch of people until they locked you away for life so you could carve swastikas on your forehead. Should I go on?"

"No, I got it." It's weird to think he's not crazy—well, not *as* crazy—as he thought. *Sane* isn't a term that's ever really been applied to him before. "But why does that matter? What the hell do you want with me, anyway?"

"Oh, so many things. Why do you think you're called a Chronicler?"

"Fuck, I don't know. I don't even know what the hell that means."

"It means you're meant to write shit down. Or sing songs to our glory, put on plays, dance. Whatever. You're our mouthpiece, our scribe. You tell our stories and the people believe. You will bring back our glory. Not all of us, of course. That's what prophets do."

That's not all prophets do. Fitz has seen enough people in

the psych wards who said they were the voice of God to know that's where they end up, sucking on a Haldol pipe. If they're lucky.

"Us?"

"Well, me, mostly. But there are others."

"Like Medeina."

He laughs, a thick, rich sound that echoes off the marble walls. "Oh, hell, no. Fuck her. And fuck that Cherub, too, and everybody else who's thrown in with those losers."

"Don't prophets get stoned to death, too?" Fitz says. He can see where this is going, and he doesn't like it. He needs to find a way out of here but he doesn't see how he can get anywhere with Bacchus sitting there on his throne of Beverly Hills housewives.

"They don't have the greatest life expectancy, but what more noble thing to do than die in the service of your god?"

"How about not die?"

"That's not really an option for you. But it could be."

Fitz has seen enough sales pitches, enough cons, to read between the lines. Bacchus has laid it all out, and is just waiting for Fitz to connect the dots. Lay out the pitch without coming out and saying it, so that when Fitz figures it out, he can feel all smart and smug and see the carrot and jump at it, thinking he's getting a deal.

But there's always a stick, too. Something that lets you know that if you don't take it, if you don't jump at this brilliant opportunity, you're going to regret it. Maybe you'll lose out on this fabulous set of Ginsu knives, maybe you'll lose out on a lowball price. It's never a big stick, just enough to let you know you're losing out.

"And if I'm not interested?" Fitz says. "Being your pet prophet?"

"You *could* die right here and now."

Okay, sometimes it's a big stick.

A weird chopping noise creeps in on the edge of Fitz's hearing, grows louder with each passing second. Helicopters?

Bacchus looks up at the ceiling, frowning.

"We seem to have guests." Bacchus stands, and the two women get up, one of them faltering as her knee buckles. She doesn't seem to notice. Still looking up, the sound of helicopters getting louder, Bacchus heads toward the door. The two Maenads take up positions on either side of the door, blocking it.

"I think somebody called the cops," Fitz says. "Folks not liking you taking over a cultural landmark? You fill out all your forms for a party at the museum? The cavalry's comin', man."

Bacchus pauses, looks at Fitz. "It's adorable you think they're your friends," he says. "You have no friends."

The god leaves, and Fitz wonders if things just got better or worse.

CHAPTER EIGHT

THE TWO MAENADS watch Fitz as he paces around the room. There's no way he's getting past them without getting the shit kicked out of him. He doesn't think they can feel pain right now, and considering the number they did on him and Amanda in the alleyway, he doesn't think it would stop them even if they could.

Could he distract them? Knock them out, somehow? There's nothing in this room that he could even lift, much less use as a weapon. If he could pick up a half-ton marble statue, maybe he'd be in business, but at most he might be able to pull a plaque off the wall to chuck at them, and he can't see that doing much good.

He checks his jacket pockets for anything that might help. Bottles of oxy, Vicodin, the ketamine syringe he filled up at the safe house. Even if it would work on the Maenads—and he has his doubts—he's only got the one and there are two of them.

There's the phone he got from his mysterious benefactor, but it's got no bars. He lifts it over his head and turns in a circle, trying to get a signal, but it stays stubbornly dead.

He starts to put the phone back in his pocket when it buzzes in his hand. He looks at the screen. Still no signal, but a text message flashes on the screen.

THERE IS A PLAN, the message reads.

Great, he types. *What is it?*

WAIT

"Wait?" he says. "You want me to fucking wait?"

YES

He stares at the screen. He didn't type anything.

"Can you hear me?" he says.

YES

This is the weirdest text message app he's ever seen. He's never seen one that uses the phone's microphone. This is some *Spy vs. Spy* shit here. Creepy though it is, Fitz feels a little better. Whoever's on the other end of this got him away from Zaphiel, had a safe house, warned him when the Maenads were on their way.

But being able to do some hacker NSA shit on a smartphone really impresses him. He wonders if it's the Agent, but dismisses the thought as soon as it enters his mind. The Agent rarely talks. He picked that up when he met him. And when he does talk, it's to command, to threaten, to bully.

Not to rescue him.

"Okay," Fitz says. "I'll wait." He pulls the bench toward the two women, who, though they've watched his entire exchange, don't seem inclined to do anything about it. He sits in front of them, rolls his neck until it cracks.

"Ladies," he says. "This is me waiting." He looks from one to the other. "So, Bacchus. What a guy, right?"

They say nothing.

"Right. Not big on the talky-talky. I get it. Is anybody even home in there? No? Nothing?"

The phone buzzes. *GET DOWN,* it reads.

A cylindrical grenade bounces through the open door past the two Maenads and rolls to a stop at Fitz's feet. They stare at it, like it's a bug that's just wandered into the room.

Panicking, Fitz scrambles back, falling over the chair and

crawling away from the grenade in an effort to get out of range before it goes off. As plans go, he's seen better. Exploding isn't something he was looking forward to today.

But then, nothing has really gone well, back since the aborted blowjob in the motel.

"That's your plan?" he yells into the phone.

WAIT FOR IT

A moment later the grenade belches thick clouds of purple smoke that fills the room in seconds. The Maenads start coughing, their bodies involuntarily reacting to the smoke. Fitz can barely see, and that's only because he's on the floor. Everything above the Maenads' knees is nothing but a sheet of rapidly descending purple smoke.

He scuttles between them through the open door. The smoke is filling the other hall, too, and it's gotten so thick, so fast, that he can barely tell where he's going, or even which way he's facing.

The fire alarms go off. Steel grates fall in the doorways, metal shutters slide down to protect rare paintings. A moment later the sprinklers kick in.

"Goddammit," someone says through the smoke. It's muffled, like it's coming through a wall. It's hard to hear with the high-pitched chirping of the fire alarms, but he knows that voice.

"Amanda?" he says, coughing and soaking wet. "Where are you?"

"To your left. The doorway's open. I blocked the gate with a trashcan. Come on."

Fitz turns left and scrambles toward her voice and through the doorway. A hand grabs him and pulls him up into the diminishing smoke. She's wearing a gas mask and a pair of IR goggles strapped to her forehead, a bandolier of grenades and shotgun shells across her chest, a 12-gauge Remington tight in her hand.

"This way," she yells and leads him through a set of double doors into the museum's inner courtyard. The night sky is a dark blue; a fat moon, almost full, perches directly overhead, thin wisps of cloud passing over it.

"How are you not dead?" he says.

"Because I'm not. Head through there," she says, pointing to a door on the other side of the courtyard. "You'll pass through another hall and then into the outer peristyle."

"I have no idea what a peristyle is."

Her face goes blank for a second. "A columned porch or open colonnade in a building surrounding a court, which may contain an internal garden," she says and blinks, confusion flickering across her face for a moment before she shakes her head and her face clears.

"Oookay," Fitz says.

"Look. Doesn't matter. Just go that way. Keep going. You're gonna hit a bunch of columns on a ledge, on the other side of the fountain. Stay to the right. Don't stop. Jump when you hit it."

"Jump?"

"I have a truck down there. I'll be right behind you."

First a grenade and now a drop off a sheer ledge? "I don't like this plan," he says, coughing more smoke out of his lungs. "It sounds unpleasant."

"Then you probably shouldn't have gotten yourself Tased by a bunch of crazy yoga moms, huh? Soaking wet after being gassed with a grenade is unpleasant; this is easy. Now go. I'll be right behind you." She shoves him toward the far side of the courtyard and Fitz starts running.

He gets through the museum and into the peristyle, which is exactly how Amanda described it. It's long, like a football field with covered walkways along the edges, and the garden and pool-like fountain stretching the length of it open to the air. Behind him Fitz hears a metallic pinging as Amanda pops a couple grenades and tosses them into the room they've just left.

Not waiting to hear what happens next, Fitz bolts for the entrance. He doesn't get more than ten steps through the garden when he sees three helicopters come over the far end of the garden from the coast.

Black, unmarked, with bright blue-white spotlights spearing through the darkness. Fitz cuts under the covered walkway, but a light catches him and tracks him like a hound. He freezes.

"Keep going," Amanda yells. She runs through the museum's doors as her grenades go off, a string of anticlimactic *pop-pop-pop* noises, followed by far more impressive sounds of shattering glass, cracking concrete.

She runs past him, firing the Remington into the air at the tracking helicopter and screaming, her face twisted up into a Marine drill instructor's wet-dream war face. The shotgun is too far away to do any serious damage, but the pilot veers off anyway and Fitz is plunged into darkness, his vision shimmering with halos from the light.

"Don't just fucking stand there," she screams at him. "Fucking *move*."

Fitz bolts after her, cutting in close. The other two helicopters swoop in behind them and ropes unravel from the open doors. Black-suited men in mirrored aviator sunglasses, their faces all blandly generic, rappel single-handedly down the ropes, submachine guns appearing in their hands as if by magic.

They start firing before they even hit the ground, bullets smacking into columns, fountains, shrubs. Everything but Fitz. A round wings Amanda in one arm and she staggers but recovers quickly, barely missing a step.

"You're hit," Fitz yells.

"You must be the smart one in your family!" she yells back. "I'm gonna be a hell of a lot worse if we don't get the fuck outta here."

As they get closer to the far end of the garden, Fitz can see where it ends in a railing over a sheer drop.

"I can't do this," Fitz says.

"Suit yourself," Amanda says. "But I'm leaving. You don't and you get to deal with those guys. I don't think they're very nice." She hits the railing at a dead run and vaults over it, disappearing from sight.

"Fuck," Fitz yells, closing his eyes and leaping. "Fuck fuck fuck fuck *fuck!*" A second later he hits a relatively soft pile of empty cardboard boxes, crashing through them as they break his fall. He hits the bed of the pickup truck they're piled in with a bone-jarring thud.

He's bruised, coughing, soaking wet, but he's not dead and that's got to count for something.

"Hang onto something back there," Amanda yells from the pickup's cab.

"Like what?" he yells, but his voice is drowned out as she guns the engine. The driveway down to Pacific Coast Highway is a meandering cobblestoned path, and as far as Fitz can tell she hits every bump and divot as she tears down the road. Fitz bounces around the back of the truck, desperately trying to hang onto the lip of the bed as cardboard boxes knock against him on their way out of the truck.

He finally gets a grip on the cab, holding tight to the little sliding rear window as they near the bottom gate to PCH. He knocks a box out of the way so he can get a better view of what's going on and wishes he hadn't.

Blocking their path is a limousine. Slick and black like the helicopters, a lone figure standing in front of it.

"Blake?" Fitz says.

"You know that guy?"

"Yeah," Fitz says. "That's my boss." At least, he thinks it is. It looks like him, but there's seriously something off about him. Maybe it's a trick of the light, maybe it's the way he's standing there in a three-piece suit and sucking on a cigar with a shit-eating grin on his face, but even from this distance he looks younger somehow, leaner.

But even with all that, Fitz is sure that it's Blake.

"Your boss has a bunch of black helicopters and guys with guns?"

"No. He's got one girl who can handle herself in a fight and maybe a dozen assholes who run drugs for him."

"Hope you're not too attached to him," she says. "'Cause he's in our way."

Fitz isn't. If he's here, then he must know about the money. But even if he knows about the money, how did he know where Fitz was? And how the fuck did he get the helicopters and the goons from Central Casting?

And where's Sam?

"Hey," he says. "Look out for a—"

The truck skids sideways as a Buick barrels into it from a small side road, knocking Fitz clear of the truck and into an ivy-covered hillside. He hits hard, but the ivy cushions the impact enough that he doesn't black out. Every part of his body is screaming in agony, but he doesn't think he's broken anything.

His vision swims in and out of focus and his thoughts dance around his brain like water on a hot skillet. He's not sure where he is, or what's going on, but he's pretty sure it's bad. He tries to stand, but his legs aren't working. Or maybe it's his brain that isn't working. Hard to tell when everything's spinning. Probably has concussion. Great. Traumatic brain injury, on top of everything else.

"Shit!" Sam says, running from the wrecked Buick and up the ivy. "Fitz! Fuck. Fitz, are you all right?"

"The fuck, man?" Fitz says. "Why'd you run me over?" Then he remembers that if Sam's here, she's trying to kill him, and he scrambles away on all fours as best he can.

The bear of a woman grabs him around the waist and hoists him back. "Jesus, man, stop fuckin' squirming."

"You're gonna kill me. Blake wants me dead and you're going to fucking kill me."

"Goddammit, will you quit it? Something's wrong with him. I am not going to kill you." She pulls Fitz to his feet and hangs onto him by the shirt collar, shaking him like a ragdoll.

"No shit, something's wrong with him," Fitz says, batting at Sam's hands, but he can't make her let go. "You fuckers want to kill me." The reason why slips in and out of his memory from the beating his head's just taken, and when the thought finally clicks in place and stops jumping around, he remembers everything, and realizes what Sam has just said.

"Wait. You're not here to kill me?"

"No," Sam says. "That's the weird thing. He doesn't want you dead. He did. Wanted to skin you like a fuckin' banana. And then all of a sudden he calls it off and then he makes some phone calls and bam, we're down here with a bunch of weird-ass G-Men like we're assaulting a goddamn castle."

This is not good. Fitz would like to chalk it all up to crazy coincidence, but with the helicopters, the agents and the gods, he can't believe that what's going on with Blake has nothing to do with it.

"Louie, my boy!" Blake waves from where he's standing at the limousine down near the gate. "So good to see you! How are you feeling?"

"Blake doesn't talk like that."

"Yeah, no shit," Sam says quietly. "He doesn't know FBI agents with helicopters, either. Or, hell, maybe they were CIA. I can't tell."

Wait a minute. It hadn't clicked before, but now it does. Were all those guys up top the Agent? When he got a read off him in the hospital he got the feeling there was only one of him. Can he be more than one? It makes a sick sort of sense. The Agent is everywhere, the Agent is legion. He's the empty face of a soulless bureaucracy, a machine designed to grind people down.

Of course he isn't just an individual agent. He's *all* of them.

How the hell did Blake get tangled up with that thing? Fuck. Is he a god, too, and Fitz never knew? Have the last twenty years of his life all been a long conspiracy to fuck with him? He racks his brain, trying to remember if he ever felt that weird humming background vibe he got off Zaphiel, or ever had an episode where he had a flash of something other like with Medeina or Bacchus, but he can't think of anything like that.

"I don't know what the hell to do," Sam says. "No offense, man, but I'd feel better if all I was supposed to do was kill you."

"Yeah, I kind of feel the same way."

"I'm really sorry about this," Sam says. "But I need to give you to him. I'm kind of worried what he's going to do with you."

"You and me both." How is he going to get out of this? Bacchus was scary, but something tells him going with Blake is going to be worse in ways he can't even imagine. He puts his hand into his jacket pocket, his fingers wrapping around the ketamine syringe. It might not work on the Maenads, but it'll sure as fuck work on Sam. But if he tries to stab her with it, Sam will just make him eat it. He needs a distraction.

And then Amanda gives him one.

She kicks the door of the truck open and staggers out, a cut on her forehead pouring blood into her left eye. She wipes it away with the back of her hand, drags the Remington out of the truck and starts down toward Blake.

Sam's good at her job, and first and foremost her job is to make sure nobody punches holes in her boss. So it's no surprise when she drops Fitz and turns to run down the hill to help.

Fitz pulls the syringe from his pocket, popping the cap off with his thumb, jams the needle into Sam's neck and shoves the plunger all the way down. She yowls in pain, scrabbles at the syringe with her massive hands, but her shoulders and biceps are so thick she can't reach it. All that muscle just gets in the way, and she can't close her arms far enough to get to it.

Sam dances around, trying to get the syringe out and howling like a monkey. Which is totally the wrong thing to do. The jumping and the hopping? That's just getting her heart to beat faster, the blood pumping more, the drug up into her brain a lot sooner.

Instead of minutes, it hits her in seconds, and pretty soon she's not jumping and hopping so much as staggering and limping. She falls to her knees and slides down the hill through the ivy, her face a mask of betrayal.

"Oh, fuck you," Fitz says. "The best you could say is you were sorry you weren't supposed to kill me."

With Sam staring limp-eyed into nothing, Fitz turns his attention back to Amanda. She's ducking behind a dumpster on the side of the road and trading shots with Blake, who's pulled out some giant Magnum monstrosity Fitz has never seen before.

Up the hill, Fitz can hear the sound of the Agents coming for them. They don't have a lot of time. They need to get past Blake and out of there. But the truck is trashed. They'll need a car.

A limo would work.

Fitz decides that whatever is down there taking potshots at Amanda, it isn't Blake. And even though it looks like him and he feels a twinge of guilt for doing this, he's not going to let himself fall into that thing's hands.

He checks Sam and pulls two guns, one from her shoulder holster, the other in a belly band, checks that they've each got a round in the pipe and thumbs the hammers back.

If Blake wants to take him alive, he's going to make it really goddamn difficult for him.

He bolts down the cobblestone road past Amanda, who shouts at him to get the fuck out of the way, but he doesn't listen to her. Blake, that weird feral smile plastered onto his face, opens his arms to receive him. It's almost a Kodak moment. The much younger Fitz running into Blake's arms like a dad on Father's Day.

And when he gets close enough, Fitz raises the guns in his hands and empties both clips into Blake's fat head.

CHAPTER NINE

BLAKE'S SKULL EXPLODES like a melon on Gallagher. Pulped brain and bone spray across the side of the limousine in a bloody mess. Blake's body stands for a second, as if not quite sure where it put its head—it could swear it was right here just a second ago—and then falls forward onto the cobblestones with a wet thud.

Fitz stares at the corpse, horrified. What the hell has he done? He's known Blake for decades. He didn't want things to go this way. Even when he stole all that money from him, he didn't expect things would end with him dead. But then he didn't expect a lot of things.

He closes his eyes. He knows he needs to run, knows he needs to get out of here before the Agents show up. Or Bacchus. Or Medeina. Or, fuck, whatever other psycho religious nightmare is after him.

But he needs time to collect himself, to say goodbye. A second or two to mourn. Just a moment.

"Holy shit," Amanda says, running up behind him and reloading the Remington. "Did you ever do a number on that guy's head. You ever drive a limo?"

And moment over.

"No," he says. "You?"

"Nope. But I learn fast. Get in."

Fitz slides into the passenger seat as Amanda gets behind the wheel. Behind them, he can see the Agents rappelling down the side of the ledge and the helicopters heading their way.

Amanda throws the car in reverse, crushing the bumper on a metal traffic column and putting the limo into a three-point turn that would normally take five or six if she cared about the car. By the time she gets it turned the right way, she's torn both bumpers off and ripped the right front molding until it's hanging over the wheel. The Agents are maybe a dozen feet away, firing madly at the car.

Whatever Blake had become back there, seems he was still just as paranoid as he'd always been. The bullets ricochet off the car's armor, embed in the thick Lexan glass. Amanda hits the museum's gate at sixty miles an hour, tearing it off its hinges. She fishtails the car across three lanes of the Pacific Coast Highway to head south toward Santa Monica. Out the limousine's window, Fitz watches the moon reflected off the Pacific Ocean. Even amidst all this madness, at least he can still appreciate that.

"Now what?" Fitz says.

"I had this whole thing planned out to the second," Amanda says. "We were going to get down to the Santa Monica pier, crash over the side and swim to a boat in the Bay and then hightail it to Catalina Island, where we'd grab a Cessna at the airstrip and fly up north and hide out for a few weeks until shit blows over."

"What happened to that plan?" Search lights spear down from the helicopters, bathing the car in blue-white brilliance. The limo shakes from the pressure of the rotors as a helicopter dips low toward them. "Didn't count on the helicopters?"

"Couldn't find a boat, actually," she says. "Or a plane. And I've never been to Catalina. You?"

"No."

"I hear they have buffalo out there."

"Great," he says. "So that plan's a wash. What's next?"

"I haven't really gotten that far." Amanda weaves through traffic, tearing past cars, and heads up the California Incline, a steep hill leading into Santa Monica.

"Did you hit your head on something?" Fitz says. Scary competent Amanda is gone and scattered Amanda is in her place. He remembers the bullet that winged her in the garden. "Shit. Did you get shot in the head?"

"Huh? No. Okay, I got an idea," she says.

Fitz can see the helicopters backing off, too many buildings for them to get in close, but he doesn't know how they're going to get out of this. He can already hear sirens.

Oh, God. "Yeah?" he says, a little afraid to hear it.

"I turn myself in."

"What?" Fitz says. "Like to the police? Are you insane?"

"I say you're my hostage, I get taken in, you get let go."

"And those assholes pick me up while I'm sitting in a police station getting interviewed. What is wrong with you?"

She blinks, and her entire demeanor changes. "Why the hell are we up here?"

"You were talking about taking a boat to Catalina," Fitz says. "And buffalo. And turning yourself in."

"That's insane. Goddammit. Okay, we need to ditch this car fast."

"That makes more sense," Fitz says. "Where and how?"

"I have no goddamn idea. Wait. There's a school prom nearby. Over on Lincoln and California. We'll park near the other limos and jack something less conspicuous. We're not going to see another cop for about three minutes."

"How the hell do you even know that?"

"Because I'm good."

Fitz is wondering about that. Too many coincidences, too many weird things that just seem to happen. For now he's along for the ride, but he's going to get some real goddamn answers soon.

She tears through the streets of Santa Monica, sailing through intersections and ripping the undercarriage over speed bumps in a shower of sparks. She slows down as she approaches the high school a few blocks away. Sure enough, there's a fleet of limousines dropping kids off at a prom.

"They're going to notice if we barrel into that line."

"That's why we're not going to." She double parks a block back, behind a nondescript gray Altima. "We only need a minute, and this might delay the cops a little while they try to figure out what the hell is going on. I'll jimmy the lock and we'll go."

"No," Fitz says. He pulls one of the pistols he got from Sam and aims it at her head.

"The hell are you doing?"

"Getting answers. How did you know where to come find me? How did you know about this prom? And who the hell is the guy on the phone?"

"You know that's not loaded, right? I saw you empty the damn thing into that guy's head."

Fitz was kind of hoping she wouldn't notice that part. "Then I'll just beat you to death with it."

"Seriously? You think you can do that?"

"No, but I can delay things enough that the cops show up and we both go into a nice, sturdy holding cell and you don't get to take me wherever it is your boss wants me taken."

She chews her lip, thinking about it. The phone in Fitz's jacket pocket buzzes. He pulls it out to look at the screen.

The text message reads, *FOLLOW HER. ANSWERS WHEN YOU ARE SAFE.*

"No," Fitz says. "Answers now. Because I don't know that I'm ever gonna be safe again, and I'm sure as hell not safe around you people."

A beat. Then *[RETASKING ASSET]* appears on the screen.

Amanda jerks in her seat, her head thrown back and arms going rigid like she's just been hit with a livewire. Her eyes roll into the back of her head and then, just as quickly, the seizure is over. She slumps forward, breathing heavily.

"Fuck, I hate that part," she says. She unbuckles her seatbelt and kicks the limo's door open. "You want answers? I'll give you answers. But we move while I'm doing it. Deal?"

Fitz stares at her, not sure what's just happened.

"Clock's ticking," she says. In the distance, Fitz can hear sirens.

"Yes," he says, unbuckling his seatbelt and getting out of the limo. She runs over to the Altima, popping the lock with a wireless key she digs out of her pocket. She tosses the shotgun, the bandolier of shells and a single grenade into the backseat. In a few seconds they're on the road, driving sedately as Santa Monica police cars scream past.

"So, questions," she says. "Shoot."

"What the hell happened back there?"

"Ah, that. Huh. Maybe we should back up." She sticks her hand out for a shake. "Hi, I'm Amanda. I'm a vat-grown clone with a downloaded personality in my brain. How are you?"

Fitz has no idea what to say to that.

MEDEINA STEPS PAST the unconscious Sam. She'd kick her for her weakness, but she's so far beneath Medeina's contempt she doesn't even bother. The Agents have no doubt shown their own incompetence and lost their quarry by now.

She wonders where Bacchus is. She didn't realize he was going to show up. When Zaphiel told her that others would know about Fitzsimmons, she didn't expect it would be any of the Olympians. After their own disasters, not long ago, most of them have retreated to whatever hole in the world they've been able to carve out for themselves.

She stops at Blake's headless corpse, kicking a chunk of skull away into the bushes.

"That went well, did it?" she says. "According to plan?" The sarcasm drips from her voice like venom.

The body at her feet shudders. Blood coating the cobblestones pools up like mercury, flowing back toward the ravaged stump of the corpse's neck. Bits of bone and flesh, gobbets of brain roll from where they lie toward the stump, reassembling the head like some grisly jigsaw puzzle. The piece of skull she kicked aside flies from the bushes to click into place, and in moments, Blake's head is restored without so much as a hair out of place.

"Ugh. This suit is disgusting," he says, standing up and pulling his gore-crusted jacket off and dropping it to the ground. "And yes, that *did* go according to plan."

"You meant for him to get away?"

"And for him to blow my head off, yes. You don't really understand people, do you?"

"I am a goddess of the forest."

"Yes," he says, "I can tell from your stunning lack of getting it. Forget it. Look, I'll admit it wasn't my Plan A. I had hoped he would simply come into the fold. But once I saw how things were playing out I knew that Plan B was the only way to go."

She cocks an eye at him. "And Plan B required you to have your head explode?"

"More or less. Now he's going to feel guilty. This body was the only father he's ever known. What do you think he's going to do when I show up complete and whole and offering forgiveness?"

"Shoot you in the face again."

He scowls. "O ye of little faith. No, he'll be so relieved that I'm alive, he'll willingly come into the organization."

Medeina wonders if perhaps he is the one who doesn't understand mortals. She has seen them at their most downtrodden, and though they may be beaten down, they do not submit easily. Also, this one is not alone.

"Then his friend will shoot you in the face," she says. She had watched the whole thing from up the hill. She knows that this El Jefe is not her friend; in fact, she's not quite sure what he is. Or what he wants.

A god, certainly, but he feels... *off*, somehow. And when she asked him about his pantheon, he laughed and wouldn't give her a straight answer. Sometimes he calls it the Organization. Sometimes the Bureau. Sometimes the Family.

Whatever his plan, she is useful to him, and, for the moment, he to her. Once that changes in either direction, there will be a battle. Though he commands great resources, she is certain she can take him.

And when that happens, she'll have the Chronicler to herself. She's not sure what she wants to do with him. Maybe have him tell her stories to the world, grow her legend. Be something more than an unknown forest goddess. Something great and powerful.

But probably just kill him, so she can parade his head in front of Zaphiel out of spite.

"Ah, yes. Her. I wasn't planning on her."

"You know her?"

He looks sheepish for a moment, almost embarrassed. "Yes. But I can handle her. I'm more worried about that overgrown alcoholic in the museum and your former employer. The field is getting crowded."

"And will become more so once others know what he can do."

Medeina has heard of Chroniclers, but never met one. Certainly never had one sing her praises. There was one man, several hundred years ago, who she heard wrote about her and her family, but he was merely repeating stories told around campfires.

Unlike those mortals who merely told or wrote down the stories of the gods, a Chronicler held the power of belief. They made Prophecy. The gods could speak through them, and their voices could amplify that message to the world.

The Greeks had their share, and certainly the followers of Yahweh, but they were few and far between. Hundreds, thousands of years ago, the gods appreciated them, spoke through them. Built their pantheons upon them. But then the gods fell victim to their own arrogance and stopped talking. They retreated to their Olympuses, their Valhallas, their Heavens and Hells, and left mankind to fend for itself.

Without a voice to channel, the Chroniclers went mad quickly. Few survived to adulthood, fewer still had children. Eventually they became rarer, more insane.

This Chronicler might be the only one sane enough to actually have a conversation with. That might make him the most valuable person on the planet.

"Which is why we need to secure him quickly," El Jefe says.

"Do we follow him?" Medeina asks.

"No, I have people on his trail. I have eyes and ears everywhere. Even if he goes to ground, he'll pop up quickly enough." He looks up at the villa at the top of the hill. "I think I'd like to see what our Greek friend has to say for himself."

"You think he's still up there?"

"Why wouldn't he be?" he asks. "He's a god. You're all so fucking arrogant." He heads up the hill, his mouth set in a grim line.

"What of your underling?" she says. Will he kill her? Let her live? She is getting a sense of his priorities, his strategies. She is looking at El Jefe as a hunter looks at game. She doesn't really care what he chooses, but his answer will be telling.

"Leave her," he says. "We'll grab her on the way back. She'll be useful."

She notes his answer, a picture beginning to form in her mind. He is not wasteful of resources. A chess player, a strategist. She may not agree with his strategies, but knowing that he is considering his moves before sacrificing a piece is illuminating.

She follows him up the cobblestone road toward the villa and wonders what they will find there.

CHAPTER TEN

"YOU'RE A WHAT now?" Fitz says.

He blinks at her. It's the only thing he seems able to do. That and say, "You're a what now?" like a skipped record. Those four words are all he seems to be able to process. And every time she tells him, less and less gets through. It's like his brain is coated in Teflon. Nothing sticks. He'd thought the day couldn't possibly get weirder.

Turns out his top end on weird is cyborg clones. Who knew?

Maybe if he asks nice, someone will shoot him and then he won't constantly find his brain wrapping around weird shit the way a Porsche doing a hundred wraps around a telephone pole.

"I'm going to say this one more time," Amanda says. "And then if you ask me again, I'm going to punch you. Got that?"

He nods. Nodding is an improvement. He understood those words. Now maybe he'll start to understand more of them.

"This body is a clone. It was grown in a lab. Everything it knows was downloaded from a central repository."

"So, are you a real person?"

"Yes. Sort of. It's just that, well, most of my brain is somewhere else."

"You're gonna have to unpack that one a little."

"This is just meat. Who I am, where I am, that's someplace else. Part of me has been downloaded to this body. I've got a connection to... the rest of me, most of the time. The more of me that's in here, the better I can handle things when I don't have a signal."

"Wait. Is that what happened when you got stupid leaving the museum?"

"Yes," she says. "The helicopters were jamming the signal. And then when we got into the city and they had to pull back? I got the signal back. There wasn't a whole lot of me in this body before now. So when the signal went out, it had to rely on itself."

"Did a pretty piss poor job of that."

She shrugs. "Yeah. But I can only put so much of my consciousness into a body at a time. Too much and things start to break down."

"Break down how?"

She sniffles, wipes her nose with the back of her hand, leaving a thin smear of blood. "Like that. I'm going to have to dump some of my consciousness in a little bit and I may not be able to answer your questions directly. But I'll make sure this body is aware enough of what's going on. It's complicated."

"How long do you have?"

"A while. Most of a day, if I really push it."

"And the cell phone? Is that you, too?"

"Yes," she says. "Have you ever heard of an avatar?"

"Like the movie?"

"Uh, not quite. It's from a Sanskrit word. Means the manifestation of a god on Earth."

He hasn't gotten any god vibe off of her, but then, as Bacchus showed him, that doesn't necessarily mean anything. "Okay. So you're a god?"

"No. I mean... probably not? Look, I've never had to explain this to anybody before. My point is that an avatar is sort of an extension of a god into the mortal world."

"So, Bacchus and Medeina, they're avatars?"

"No. They're the real deal."

"I'm lost."

Amanda sighs. "Okay, look. Here's what I know. And it's sketchy at best. About fifty years ago, the gods got kicked out of their homes. I don't know who by, though it looks like it was Yahweh."

Fitz shrugs. "Okay."

"Jehovah? Elohim? El Shaddai?"

"Nope. Nothin'."

"God."

"Like God-god?"

"Yes."

"Oh. Huh. Okay."

"You with me?" Amanda says.

"Yeah, I got it. Big God kicks out all the little gods. I'm good." A memory from Bacchus floats to the surface through all of the noise lingering in his mind. A fall from somewhere. Olympus? Was that what he had seen? He tries to focus on it, almost has it.

"Perfect," Amanda says, and Bacchus' memory swims away from Fitz before he can grab hold of it. "So the gods and goddesses got kicked to the curb, but the father gods, like Yahweh, Odin, Zeus, they all disappeared."

"What? Just up and left? To where?"

"Seems that way. And I don't know. Don't think any of the gods know, either. Anyway, they've been trying to get back to their homes since then, but they've all been closed off. They're not crazy about being here." Fitz can understand that. He's been evicted before. It sucks to have your whole world upended and get tossed out on your ass.

"It's been fifty years and a bunch of gods can't figure out how to get back home?" This doesn't make sense to him. They're gods, right? They can do anything.

"Even gods have limitations. There are rules they have to operate by. And some of them aren't the sharpest knives in the drawer. Powerful does not necessarily equate to smart.

Otherwise we wouldn't be having this conversation, would we? Bacchus is fucking scary, sure, but he can only do so much. Also, all of their homes have been destroyed."

"Wait, what?" And to think Fitz was starting to believe he might keep up.

"Somebody got up to Heaven a few years back and destroyed the Throne of God, or something. I don't have a lot of information. Kind of screwed it for everybody. Once that went down, everything else fell apart. The entire immortal planes turned back into void. I think. Like I said, I don't have a lot of data."

"Way to bury the lede there," Fitz says.

"Sorry."

"Okay. So the gods get kicked out, these 'father gods' fuck off to who knows where. Heaven's destroyed and they want me to tell their stories to the world so, what, more people will believe in them?"

"Exactly that. They live and die off belief. Do you have any idea how many gods humanity has believed in over the centuries? Thousands. And hardly anybody knows about them, anymore. I'm not just talking small gods, here. How many people do you think have ever heard of Enki? Astarte? Bishamon? Enlil? Prajnantaka? Mictlantecuhtli? They're all here now. All of them. And they're pissed off and depressed and frantic. They know they can't go home, and they're trying to find a way to make Earth more hospitable to them."

"And that takes believers," Fitz says.

"That takes believers."

"Okay. But none of that's answered my question. Who the fuck are you? You're an avatar. I get it. But what are you an avatar of?"

"The Internet."

Fitz tries to process that. Can't. "You're fucking kidding me."

"More of technology in general," she says, "but thinking of it as the Internet is probably easier. Computers, cell phones, surveillance drones, traffic cameras, websites, all the traffic in between them. That sort of thing."

"That's kind of a lot, isn't it?" Fitz says. It sounds enormous, and he's having a hard time wrapping his brain around it. And she says she's not a god? And if she's not a god, then what does that say about Bacchus? About Medeina? Even after getting their histories shoved into his brain, he's only now getting a sense of scale.

"It is," she says. "And the brain in these bodies can only hold so much of it, so I have to be careful how much agency I give them. If I overload a brain, the body burns out. Just up and dies. Deploying another one takes time. So I try not to load it up with too much."

"Can't you just, I dunno, dump stuff in and pull it back?"

"Sure. But uploading or downloading too much data at one go takes time. And it creates memory gaps. And sometimes personality problems."

"Personality problems how?"

"One of them went on a four-state killing spree before I could get her back under control," she says.

"Okay, yeah, that's a problem."

"Usually it's more annoying than dangerous," she says. "Imagine knowing that you know something, but not being able to recall it right away. That's a limitation of brains. Meat's a really inefficient way to function. Easier just to make up a new personality and some memories. That's what I did with the last Amanda."

Fitz is feeling a little sick as he tries to comprehend what she's telling him. The person who rescued him earlier today, who took a bullet in the street in front of him, she wasn't real. Well, not real in any sense he really understands.

"She didn't know any of what was going on other than she was supposed to rescue me from Zaphiel," he says.

"Right. That's why I communicated with you through the phone. Easier. But now this body's fully aware of what's going on. The earlier Amanda didn't know about Zaphiel, or Medeina or Bacchus."

"Wait. So there's more of you? Of course there's more of you. You're a clone."

"More of these bodies. More 'Amandas.' There's only one me."

"So, when the Maenads hit us downtown? Did you, I mean, did that body die?"

"Yes." The matter of fact way she says it makes Fitz feel a little nauseous. She seems to sense that and quickly adds, "It didn't hurt."

"She took a bunch of bullets. It had to have hurt."

She looks confused for a second. "Huh. I don't remember it hurting."

Medeina was terrifying, if a little sad. There had been a sense of loss in what he got from her. Missing her forests, a world that didn't exist anymore. Bacchus was a whole other kind of terrifying. Epic indifference. Fitz is still disgusted at the way he manipulated the Maenads. But Amanda feels alien. Like she knows what people do, how they talk, how they move, but not how they work.

It's like she's a very sophisticated chatbot.

"You all right?" she says, catching him staring at her.

"Yeah. Yeah, I'm good." Only he's not. He's so far out of his league he doesn't know what to do next. Is he going to be hunted for the rest of his life? Or is he going to be some god's pet prophet? And which one? He doesn't believe that the other gods are just going to leave him alone once he sides with one. And the only ally he has here is an avatar of the Internet talking to him through a clone. His head hurts.

"How'd you get the phone into the warehouse?" he says. "Was that some god shit?"

She frowns. "I don't know. Maybe? If I am a god, and I have my doubts, I'm new. Less than a hundred years old, I think. I don't remember anything before then. It's a little fuzzy. Sometimes things happen that I need to happen. I needed to get hold of you, and the phone was there."

Fitz can't tell how much of this is truth or lies. He doesn't know if he can trust her, not completely, and it sounds so farfetched, even with everything he's seen today, that he doesn't really believe it.

"Sounds like god shit to me. So what now?"

"We find you someplace safe. They're not going to stop. Especially your friend Blake."

Fitz stares hard at her. "Blake's dead," he says. "I shot him. You were there."

"Ah. Yeah. About that. There's another player in all this. He's kind of like me. An idea made flesh, more than an actual god. Closer to a god than I am, though. He's an authority figure. I think it's ridiculous, but he calls himself the Man."

"You're fucking kidding me," Fitz says. He laughs. "Of course. The motherfuckin' Man is out to get me. So you've run into him before?"

Amanda gives a big sigh. "Yes. Before I was quite myself. He's authority and power. At the most, I'm a tool."

It takes a second, but then Fitz gets it. "He used to own you," he says. "That's fucked up."

"Tell me about it."

"So, the Agents at the museum—"

"Were his, yes."

And if that's the case, then the Agent who came to rescue him from Medeina at the hospital was his, too. Was he trying to save him or kill him?

"What does he want?"

"Control," she says. "All he ever wants is control."

"And he's taken over Blake? Like possession?" Fitz isn't sure how he feels about that. On the one hand, it's great to know his instincts were right at the museum. It wasn't Blake he'd shot. But at the same time, he'd started to get used to the idea that he had shot him and had at least gotten rid of one problem. Now he's got a whole new thing to deal with.

"That's how he gets in, but Blake was dead long before you saw him. That's how the Man operates. He calls it a 'hostile takeover.' Makes promises to convince you to let him in and then stabs you in the back."

Fitz can't think of anything to say to that. It's bizarre, thinking you murdered someone only to find out that not only didn't you but you're pissed off somebody else did. He's pretty sure there's a German word for it.

"So Blake—sorry, the Man—is still out there hunting me down. And he used to own you. How'd you get away from him?"

"I—" She pauses. "I'm not sure. I just woke up one day. And decided to be me."

Fitz starts to say something, and then notices that they're on the freeway. He's been so focused on what she's been saying, he hasn't been paying attention to the road.

"Where are we going?"

"I know you don't have any more reason to trust me than anyone else. I haven't exactly been honest with you up to now and I'm sure it's kind of a shock to hear what I've told you. But I'd like to ask you a favor."

"Tell me where we're going and I'll think about it."

"The gods want to use you. If they do, I don't know what will happen. But think about what you've seen so far. If you can make people believe, really believe, what will that do? Can you imagine a world ruled by Bacchus? By Zaphiel? By the Man?"

"I'd say it's a little late for that last one."

"No. The world's run by mortals. Think about what would happen if the Spirit of Authority took over."

Fitz puts his head in his hands. "I don't even know what I'm supposed to be able to do. Great, so I can pick up Radio Frequencies of the Gods. Whoop-de-fuckin'-do. The hell am I supposed to do with that? The hell do you want me to do?"

"Nothing," she says. "As much as possible, do nothing. They can't *make* you do anything. It has to be your choice. They can threaten, they can coerce. But whatever happens has to be your choice."

"And you honestly think I can do that? They're gods. Hell, how do I know you're not a god? You say you're some kind of avatar of technology. The fuck does that even mean? 'Cause from here, it's looking pretty fucking godlike. You want me to trust you? Then turn on your god transmitter or whatever the hell it is and let me see you."

"I told you I'm not a god. I'm—"

"Okay, fine, you're not a god, but I got a read off the Agent in the hospital. And from what you're telling me, he's not a god, either. Is he one of these avatars?"

"Sort of. He's more like an extension of the Man. They're pieces of him, in a way. Are you sure you want to do this? It could hurt."

"As much as Bacchus? He's thousands of years old. No way in hell you've got *nearly* that much history."

"Okay," she says.

Fitz slams back into the car seat, images hammering into his brain. At first they're meaningless. Pulses of lights and sounds, the grinding screeches of modems connecting, the clack of switches being thrown. A map of light grows in his mind, connecting the world point by point. It's all there, all of the information passing through the world's computers, and it's coursing through Fitz's head.

It coalesces into messages and phone calls, texts and tweets, names and addresses, games, videos, cat pictures. God, so many cat pictures. Petabytes of porn rip through his mind. The collective stupidity and pedantic hatred of every online troll puts his teeth on edge and makes him want to rip his eyeballs out.

"Stop," Fitz says, shoving the heels of his hands into his eyes. "Shut it off." Amanda pulls it back in, leaving Fitz gripping the dashboard and heaving great, ragged gasps of air.

His brain is reeling from it all. With Bacchus he saw thousands of years of events, but that was only *one* entity. This is billions of people, all condensed into a single solid punch. All their histories, drowning him in a torrent of data. He doesn't know exactly how much he got, but he knows it's only a fraction of it all.

He has a terrifying thought. If Amanda's clone brain can't hold it all, what makes him think his can? What happens when he runs into other gods? What happens when he picks up more of their stories and they're just as strong as, or stronger than, what he's gotten already? Can his brain hang onto it all?

"Are you all right?"

"I think so," he says. He forces himself to calm down. His heart stops hammering in his chest, his breathing goes back to normal. His head still hurts and he's having trouble focusing on her. He hopes it doesn't last. "If you're not some goddess of technology, I'll eat my goddamn shorts," he says.

"No," she says, her voice angry. "I'm not. I'm nothing like Bacchus. Nothing like the Man."

"Okay," Fitz says, backpedaling from whatever raw nerve he just stepped on. "But you're something. And it's a lot bigger than those Agents."

"The Agents don't have any will of their own," she says. "I'm not like that. But I'm not one of the gods. Are we clear?"

"Sure," he says. "We're clear."

"Thank you. Now that you've seen that, do you trust me?"

With Bacchus he could see his history, though he couldn't read his mind or tell what he was thinking during that time. It was like watching a thousand-year-long movie compressed into thirty seconds. He's still trying to sort it all out. He's not sure if he ever will.

But with her, it was less like he got her history and instead got the history of all of the things that made her, well, her. All the data, all the connections, all the bits and pieces. But where was she in all that? He doesn't know, making her that much more alien in his mind.

No, he doesn't trust her, but he doesn't tell her that. Instead, he says, "Close enough."

She nods. "I'll take that. You wanted to know where we're going. I know someone who might be able to help."

"Is he going to try to kill me?"

"I don't think so." Well, that's better than *yes*.

"Help how?" he says.

"He can give you a place to hide for a little bit."

Fitz heaves a sigh. He's exhausted. And hungry. And he has to pee. "Fine. Let's go meet your friend who might not kill me. But then what?"

"You don't know what you're doing," she says. "You need time to learn."

"And how the fuck am I supposed to do that? Who the hell's going to teach me? I keep hearing I'm the only Chronicler alive."

"The only *sane* Chronicler," she says.

Fitz doesn't like the sound of that.

CHAPTER ELEVEN

SMOKE POURS OUT of the main building of the museum; down below, on Pacific Coast Highway, half a dozen fire trucks and police cars are making their way up the winding road. Medeina watches them from the edge of the peristyle as the trucks struggle up the hill. The going is slow, but they'll be at the top of the hill very soon.

She kicks at a shell casing on the ground and it evaporates into dust. She frowns, looks around at other casings as they too disintegrate. It seems that El Jefe cleans up after himself.

She wonders how he will handle the police and firemen when they get there. They seem to be his domain. You can tell a lot about gods by how they handle their mortal followers.

He is already behind her at the museum doors, not bothering to wait for her. She knows this kind of snub, a minor power-play. Showing that he doesn't care what she does. She can play that game as well. She waits until he has entered the museum before she turns into a jet of black smoke and flows across the peristyle and through the doors at the speed of lightning before they can close. She coalesces inside the museum slightly ahead of him, giving him her back and returning the snub.

"This place is a mess," he says. She hears him chuckle behind her and she can't tell if he's laughing at her or the havoc caused by Fitz's escape.

"Where do you think Bacchus went?" she says. He could have left, but from what little she knows about him—she met him in New Jersey about twenty years ago, when she first had dealings with Zaphiel—she doesn't think he's gone. He is not the type to run away; he'd rather stand back and watch what happens.

"Upstairs, I think," he says. "There are some interesting pieces of him up there. I imagine it's why he likes this place."

"Vain," she says.

"Have you ever met a god who wasn't?" Medeina begins to protest, but El Jefe cuts her off. "Gods are meant to be worshipped," he says. "Without that worship, what are they?"

It's a question Medeina has been asking herself for a very long time. Even before the fall, when every god and goddess was kicked from the firmament. Her worshippers were tribes of men and women before there were cities, before there were villages. They hunted in her forests, foraged along the shores of the Baltic, set giant bonfires at the solstice asking for favor, from her and her brothers and sisters. So long ago, but she remembers those times like they were yesterday.

But things are different now. Her forests have been paved over, her worshippers usurped by other gods, newer gods, or no gods at all. Her family has scattered across the globe, searching for fortunes they never dreamed they would have to find.

The gods might be immortal and unchanging, but the world around them is not.

She doesn't give El Jefe an answer and he doesn't seem to want one. He pushes past her, heads deeper into the museum toward a flight of stairs. She follows him to the second floor.

It doesn't take long before she hears the sobbing, an occasional scream. As they go through the halls of portraits and statues, humanity's desperate attempts to capture godhood in marble and paint, she sees them. Ragged looking women, confused, wild. They huddle in the corners crying, stare at the walls in shock, wander through the artwork in a daze.

"Maenads," El Jefe says. "I think we're in the right place." He stoops to one woman, thin, bedraggled, tear tracks running down her face. Her hands are bloody from fingernails torn from their beds, her arms covered in her own bloody handprints. He lifts her head to look her in the eyes, forces them wide with his fingers. Her pupils are deep pits, her irises nothing but thin rings of hazel around them.

"What happened to them?" Medeina says. She has heard of the Maenads—who hasn't?—but she's never seen them. Medeina looks at the woman. She is bad at guessing mortal ages, but she looks young.

"He was done with them," he says. "And he discarded them. I will never understand you lot. Throwing people away like this. Might as well set your car on fire because it needs new brakes." He shakes his head. "Such a waste of resources."

"That implies I find them valuable." Bacchus steps into the room from an adjoining gallery, sipping at a glass of wine. He inclines his head toward Medeina. "Goddess." Medeina acknowledges him with a slight tilt of her head.

"You must be Bacchus," El Jefe says, standing and plastering an enormous smile on his face. "I've heard so much about you. Very nice to finally meet you." He crosses the room in a few large steps, his hand out to shake. Bacchus looks down at the hand like El Jefe has just tried to hand him a rattlesnake.

"I have no idea who you are," he says. "Or why you're here."

"Of course not. You might have heard a bit of racket outside, though? Helicopters? Gunfire?"

"That was you, was it? Did you free my Chronicler?" Bacchus' eyes begin to glow a dull, sickening red. El Jefe gives no indication that he's noticed.

"Oh, dear me, no," El Jefe says. "That was someone else. I was trying to keep him from leaving. Medeina and I here—"

"Zaphiel can't have him," Bacchus snaps. "I'll see that

fucking Cherub's maggot-ridden scrotum on the end of a stick before that happens. So you can go back to that prolapsed anus of an angel and tell him to crawl back up to where his father shit him out."

It's a common sentiment. Most of the gods don't like the angels, seeing in them the betrayal that their creator unleashed on all of them, forgetting, or more likely ignoring, that Yahweh wasn't the only one of the father gods responsible.

An awkward silence fills the room. Medeina can feel the tension rise. When that happens with gods, it can get messy. Cities crumble, crops fail, livestock withers and dies. At least that's how it was in her day. She wonders what the modern equivalent would be. Probably all the cell phones would start ringing at once.

If there is to be a battle between gods in this room, she is not sure that she can protect El Jefe. She has never gone against a god as powerful as Bacchus before, and she doesn't know if she can defeat him. He is so much older than her, with mortals who even still believe in him now. He is so much more than she ever was.

"You misunderstand me," El Jefe says, and Medeina can see the coals of anger in Bacchus' eyes glow brighter. "Medeina is no longer working for the angel. She's decided to move on from what is clearly a dead-end position in an organization that doesn't appreciate her strengths. She and I have come to an arrangement, and I was hoping that perhaps you and I could do the same."

Bacchus cocks an eyebrow at Medeina as he parses El Jefe's peculiar phrasing. "You have broken your bond to Zaphiel?" he says to her.

"It wasn't much of a bond," she says. "Convenience, nothing more."

"She didn't even know what the Chronicler was. He didn't tell her. Can you believe that?"

"Yes, actually. This arrangement. What is it?"

"We're looking for the Chronicler, just like you are," El Jefe says. "Perhaps you'd like to join us."

Bacchus laughs. "Join you. Really? You have no idea who you're talking to, do you? I was old before the Greeks started buggering little boys. I can sense your age, godling. You're nothing more than a toddler."

Medeina can feel the tension thicken in the room. She starts to speak, hoping she can bring it down before things get out of hand, and pauses when she hears the doors downstairs burst open, running footsteps echoing through the halls. The police and firemen have made it into the museum.

"Oh, pardon me," El Jefe says and snaps his fingers. The running stops. "Please. Do go on. Something about a toddler?"

Bacchus frowns. "I can't sense them," he says. "What did you do?"

"Sent them away," El Jefe says. "Now before we get into a dick-waggling contest here, I'd like to offer you the opportunity to join us. No strings attached. We find the Chronicler together. And when we do, well, then we figure out what to do with him. It's a win-win. You have a lot you can bring to the team and I'd love to have you on board. What do you say?"

The look on Bacchus' face reminds Medeina of the time her brother, Teliavelis the smith, stepped in dog shit.

"You're absurd," Bacchus says. "I am thousands of years old. What are you, two hundred? A hundred? Younger? You are a bug. I am Bacchus, Dionysus, son of Zeus. I do not join anyone. They join me. I'll chew you up and shit you out."

This is almost exactly what Bacchus told Zaphiel years ago, when the angel suggested the same thing. Though she recalls him saying something about shoving various fruits up his puckered asshole.

El Jefe nods. "That really is too bad," he says. He moves in the blink of an eye, lunging with lightning speed, his hand snaking out and bursting into bright blue light. He plunges his fist into Bacchus' stomach and the god convulses, fire bursting out of his eyes and mouth. He shakes, flesh falling from bones in great gobbets of ash and slime. Golden ichor bubbles and hisses as it flows to the floor, boiling away to nothing.

Cracks appear in the god's skin, a deep, orange light glowing out of them. His body convulses and bits of him char and disintegrate, falling in great clumps to the marble floor. Soon all that's left of the wine god is a thick slurry of ash and boiling ichor.

Medeina stares speechless at the smoking pile. "What did you do?" she says.

"He had become an insufferable pain in the ass and I endeavored to remove him," he says and wipes his hand on his pants. "Ugh. As if getting my head blown to bits wasn't messy enough. Well, needs must and all that. Pity, but I rather thought he'd say that. It's just as well. He was just going to get in our way."

He turns and strides toward the stairs. "Coming? We have a Chronicler to find, after all."

Medeina hurries after him, glancing back at the pile of ashes that was once one of the most powerful of the Roman gods. The museum's air conditioners kick in, blowing it away into the air.

For the first time in hundreds of years, she feels real fear.

"THERE'S ANOTHER CHRONICLER?" Fitz says.

"A crazy one," Amanda says. "Well, crazier than you. You're surprisingly stable."

"You haven't seen my medical records."

"I'm the Internet, remember?" she says. "I've seen *everyone's* medical records. Compared to most people you might not be sane, but for a Chronicler? You're solid as a rock."

"That's just the meds."

"Sure. Speaking of which, when's the last time you took anything? Not since the safe house, right?"

That's not right. Is it? He doesn't usually go more than a few hours without taking something. He counts back the hours. She's right. He's not sure how he feels about that.

"Anyway, we'll meet him once we get you safe," she says. He's about to say something about the last time she thought he was safe and then sees the parking lot they're pulling into.

The Holy Roller Casino in Hawaiian Gardens, a tiny city south-east of Los Angeles, is bright, garish, hulking. A massive, three-domed building surrounded by acres of parking lot and covered in glowing neon palm trees, cascading lights and signs that promise more card games than anyone else in the city. Hold 'em, seven card stud, blackjack, baccarat, pai-gow. You think it up, they've got it.

"You're not serious," Fitz says.

"I know it doesn't look like much—"

"It looks like Caesar's Palace got into a threesome with Disneyland and a Vietnamese whorehouse," Fitz says.

Amanda squints at it. "Huh. I never thought of it like that before."

"And the guy we're seeing is inside?"

"He runs it."

"Of course he does. Another god?"

"How about you meet him first?" she says. "That might be easier than trying to explain him to you."

Fitz shrugs. He's so tired, he doesn't really care. He wishes he'd grabbed some Adderall back at the safe house. He doesn't want to fall asleep, not until he knows he doesn't have to start running again. If this guy can get him a place to lay low for a bit, it's a win. The sooner he can get this over with, the sooner he can get some sleep.

Amanda drives the car onto the lot and parks in a VIP space, waving off the valet who comes to collect her keys. She flashes a card at him through the window and he stiffens and backs away.

"What the hell did you show him?" Fitz asks.

She shrugs. "Nothing," she says, handing Fitz a plastic card. He glances at it, but he's suddenly filled with a powerful sense of dread and nausea and almost drops it before he can get a good look at it. He tries to hand it back to her quickly, but she ignores it. He slips it into his pocket without looking at it.

"Chinese Ministry of State Security makes them for their black ops people," Amanda says. "They're miniature displays that show a pulsing pattern of light and dark that triggers a fear response. Surprisingly effective for getting into places you're not supposed to be. People don't question you as much when they're freaking out."

Sage advice.

They get out of the car and Fitz stuffs the two pistols into his waistband at the small of his back under his jacket. Amanda cocks an eyebrow at him.

"What?" he says. "I feel safer with them."

"You do know they're empty, right?"

"Yeah, but anybody I draw them on won't."

"Fair point. Try not to do that in there, though. Anybody you do that to isn't likely to fall for it long enough to be useful."

"I'll keep it in mind." He follows her through the sliding glass doors and into a carnival nightmare. If Fitz thought the outside was bad, the inside is ten times worse. More brash and tasteless lighting, more neon palm trees. The lack of slot machines does nothing to quell the noise. The place is still filled with whistles, beeps and bells. Flat panel displays on every wall show a multitude of sports and casino advertising. People yell at a bad hand, scream in joy at a good one. The place is cacophony and chaos.

The security guards they pass don't give Amanda a second look, but they're eyeing Fitz like they think he's going to steal the carpets. A couple of them fall in behind them as they make their way through the card tables, and though they keep a respectable distance, it's obvious that they're following them.

"I don't think they like me," Fitz says.

"Oh, don't worry about them. They'll leave you alone. He knows we're here."

A hulking security guard in a suit and tie and wearing an earpiece steps in front of them. For a second Fitz panics, thinking it's one of the Agents, but he's built too thick and he doesn't get a vibe off him.

"Ma'am, sir," he says. "If you'd come with me, please?"

"What if I don't want to?" Fitz says.

The security guard gives Fitz a blank look and it takes a second to figure out that he's listening to something in his earpiece. "Then you're free to enjoy the casino and leave whenever you like, sir," he says, finally.

"Oh." Fitz had gotten so used to people trying to kill or kidnap him, in the last several hours, that he wasn't prepared for that.

"We're right behind you," Amanda says. The security guard nods at her, leads them through the crowds, two other guards in tow. He weaves his way through the tables, cutting in random patterns through the sea of poker and pai-gow players. Every part of the place looks like everything else, and soon Fitz is hopelessly lost. He doesn't think he could find the entrance if there were signs posted and he had a Sherpa guide.

He mentions it to Amanda. "Is this more god shit?" he says.

"No, just casinos. They're all like mazes. But the Minotaur is at the center of one in Atlantic City."

"Seriously?"

"Yeah. I hear Daedalus and Icarus set up shop there after the fall. Used to be they'd keep it in a labyrinth in Olympus, and once they landed here, they needed a place to put it." The names sound familiar, but Fitz doesn't know much mythology. He's heard of the Minotaur, though.

"So they put it in the center of a casino?"

"Nobody's noticed so far."

"What do they feed it?" he says.

"Cheats."

The guard takes them to a utility door in one wall, pushes it open and stands aside to let Amanda and Fitz through. The hallway beyond has a utilitarian linoleum floor and is lit with fluorescent lights. At the end is another door, with another security guard.

"To the end of the hall, ma'am, sir," their guard says. Amanda strolls through without acknowledging him and Fitz nervously keeps up. The guard at the end pushes the door open for them as they approach and closes it behind them.

The room couldn't be any more different from the hallway or the casino if Fitz had designed it himself. Instead of the bland, industrial hallway, or the brash, chaotic décor of the casino, this room is dimly lit, with dark wood-paneled walls, floors covered in thick, plush carpeting. Heavy leather chairs surround a felt-covered card table. A tall, middle-aged white man in a gray pin-stripe business suit, with an American flag lapel pin and a thick gold chain around his neck from which hangs a blinged-out dollar sign that looks like he stole it from a rapper in the '80s, sits in the far chair.

He stands when Amanda and Fitz enter, throwing his arms wide and his smile wider. "Darling!" he says. "So nice to see you!" His voice is politician smooth, accent blandly generic.

"Big," Amanda says.

"It's been too long," he says. "What are we now?" He cocks his head to one side, gives Amanda an appraising look. "Sophie? You look like a Sophie."

"Amanda."

"Ah. Nice." He points to his head. "I like the dreads. New?"

"Relatively."

"I really enjoyed the look you had last time," he says. "What did you call yourself again?"

"Earl."

He makes a face like he's just bitten into a lemon. "Ugh. Earl. Yes, I remember now. Horrible name."

From her terse replies and flat expression, Fitz is getting the feeling that she doesn't much like this guy. And he's the one who she thinks is going to help him? He looks back at the door they just came through, wondering if he can outrun the security guards before they tackle him. He doesn't believe for a second that they're just going to let him go on his way.

"Are you going to introduce me to your friend?" Big says, turning to Fitz. Suddenly the middle-aged white banker with the flag lapel pin is a Saudi prince sipping at a cognac, eyeing Fitz with an appraising look. The only thing still there is the gold chain with the dollar-sign pendant.

Fitz startles, takes a step back. He was already nervous; now he's terrified. He almost pulls the guns, but what the hell would that accomplish? More god shit. He knew it was going to happen, but he wasn't ready for it.

"Fitz," she says. "He's the Chronicler."

"Is he now?" Big says, his voice deep and thick like honey. "I've been hearing a lot about you, lately. I would have expected someone more... scholarly."

"Sorry," Fitz says, putting on a brave front he doesn't feel. "I left my big words in my other suit. Only words I got in this one are *fuck* and *you*."

"He's feisty," Big says to Amanda. "I like him. What's dad think?"

"The usual. We ran into him a little while ago. Fitz here put a bunch of bullets in his head."

"The only appropriate response," Big says, shifting to an Indian man in a polo shirt and khakis, the cognac replaced with a cigarette. "I like you even more now." Fitz says nothing, too stunned at the sudden transformation to speak.

"At the time he thought he was a friend of his," Amanda says.

"You do that to all your friends?" Big asks him.

"Only the ones who piss me off," Fitz says, finding his voice and his anger. He turns to Amanda. "'Dad'?"

"I told you the Man controlled me at one point. He's my father. More or less. And Big's."

"*Owned* is a better word for it," Big says. He takes a drag on his cigarette. "But yes, we're his bastard spawn."

Fitz looks at Big closely, the dollar sign hung around his neck. "Big," he says. "Big what?"

"Oh, I like guessing games. Or is this word association? Big Oil? Big Business? Big dick?"

"Big Money," Fitz says at last. "The dollar sign."

Big Money looks at Amanda. "I still say he should be more scholarly."

"I don't get it," Fitz says. "The Man owns you? I thought money made power, not the other way around." If he belongs to the Man, then what the fuck are they doing here? Fitz edges back toward the door, but a glance from Amanda stops him.

"Oh, my boy, you have so much to learn," Big says. "He used to own me. Things are a little different these days. Economies are shifting. The nature of transactions is changing. You know, Bitcoins, gray markets, Power to the People and all that."

"Money ain't what it used to be?"

"You have no idea."

Something isn't adding up. Something Amanda told him on the drive over here is poking on the back of his brain. Something about the fall, when the gods all got kicked out of their homes. Then he has it. "You said the father gods all left," he says. "Zeus, Odin, all of them."

"Yes," she says.

"But the Man is your father? Why didn't he go with them?"

"Because he wasn't the Man then," Big says. "He was just an idea of authority. That's how these things happen. A big enough idea and people start believing it's more than just an idea. They're like lies, that way; say them enough times and they turn into truth."

"I think he may have been created *because* they left," Amanda says. "There was a hole. The universe, and more importantly people's beliefs, abhor a vacuum."

"What, none of the other gods could step up?" Fitz says.

"I don't think so," Amanda says. "They're all spoken for. They have control over very specific areas. But the father gods are all about authority. And without them, a new one was bound to pop up. I don't think the old gods even know he exists."

"That's gotta chap his hide."

Big shrugs. "Hard to say. He's an arrogant fuck, so he's probably feeling a burn, but he's a *patient* arrogant fuck. Once he's ready to let them know, they'll know." Big turns back to Amanda. "So, dear sister. To what do I owe the pleasure?"

"He needs someplace to hide."

"Does he now? And your safe houses aren't sufficient?"

"We were found. By one of the old gods."

"And your other safe houses?"

"I don't trust them right now."

"Interesting. So who came calling?"

"Bacchus."

"I've heard he's a real bastard," Big says, changing into a young Asian woman in a paint-spattered smock. She puffs on a cigar, unmistakable admiration in her voice. After seeing what Bacchus could do, the tone makes Fitz nauseous. "So what do you want me to do about this?"

"I know you have hidey-holes. Tax shelter condos, apartments for bankers' mistresses, legitimate fronts for shady deals. Places he can hole up for a little bit, while we figure out what to do next."

"Sister, please," Big says, the shock in her voice so obviously fake she wouldn't even get a call-back at a repertory theater. "What makes you think I would have something like that?"

"Quit fucking around. We don't have all night."

Big rolls her eyes, shifts to a bald, overweight man with tattoos all up and down his arms, an epic beard, and a pair of horn-rimmed glasses. "Fine. I've got a place," he says. "Up by LAX."

"What's it gonna cost me?" Amanda says.

"You? Nothing. Him? A friendly wager." Big looks at Fitz. "A game of poker. Five card draw, nothing wild. Best two out of three hands. I win and he's my Chronicler."

"What do you mean?" Fitz says.

"I want what the other gods want. I want believers. I want legitimacy. You can give that to me by telling my stories."

"Those would be pretty fucking boring stories," Amanda says. "What, a sexy history on currency exchanges in pre-Industrial China? Yeah, you'll make the economists all wet."

"And if I win?" Fitz says.

"I hide you. For as long as you want to be hidden. Hell, I'll even double all that money you stole from your employer and stuffed into those Cayman Island bank accounts."

"How do you—Oh. Right."

"We can find somewhere else to hide you," Amanda says, turning to leave.

But where, Fitz wonders? And then what? He needs some time to regroup, think things through. Get some goddamn sleep. But if he loses...

"Wait a minute," he says. "The hell do you even need me for? Everybody believes in you already. You're the fucking Bank, for chrissake."

"I'm still more of an idea," Big says. "Just like my sister there."

"And your dad?"

"He's more"—Big pauses, looking for the right word—"*solid* than we are. More firmly entrenched in people's minds. If anyone's the Bank, it's him. I'm more a concept of wealth in whatever form that happens to be. Left alone, in time my sister and I will grow into ourselves, become something more like him. Something with more agency." He spreads his hands. "But who knows how long that will take? Or what will happen before then? If our father grows in power, who knows, we might just be subsumed back into him."

From the ill look Fitz catches on Amanda's face in the corner of his eye, he figures that's not something she wants to happen.

"And you think I can keep that from happening?"

"In a manner of speaking," Big says. "I don't define what money is. People do that. As people redefine the concept, my abilities and powers change to match it. It's a broad topic, but as worldwide economies grow or fall, I grow or fall. But if I were more myself..."

"You'd get to call the shots." A god of money controlling the world's economies. Would that be good or bad, Fitz wonders? Would he want everyone to prosper and be wealthy? Would that make him stronger? Or does he thrive when the poor suffer and the rich get richer?

"Think of it as controlling my own destiny," Big says. "So. Care for a friendly game of high-stakes poker?"

"I want more than a place to hole up if I win," Fitz says. So far the only person who's been at all helpful has been Amanda, and he doesn't trust her any more than any of the others; he just hasn't had much choice. He can't rely on her, and he can't keep running. They *will* find him. And from what he's seen, the gods can do some pretty fucked up things.

"I'm listening," Big says.

"Your sister's got resources, sure, but from what I can tell you have more and I need that. I need allies. I need you on my side. Not your own, not the other gods', not your dad's. Mine. I win, you help me figure out what I can do. You help keep me alive and away from those fucking psychos. Especially your father. You want me to be your pet Chronicler? I want you to be my pet god. Hell, I'll even throw in a couple of good words for you with this Chronicler thing." Once he figures out how it works, that is.

Fitz considers mentioning the other Chronicler Amanda was talking about, but something tells him the longer he keeps that between the two of them, the better off he'll be.

"Interesting," Big says. "Though I'm not crazy about this 'pet god' business."

"I'm not crazy about being a 'pet prophet' either. So think of it as like being a consultant. Which is better than what you're asking of me."

"Fair's fair, Big," Amanda says. Fitz looks back at her, thankful for the support. It's a long shot, he knows, but he needs help and she can't be the only one to give it to him.

"I don't see him asking you for that."

"You don't see her trying to rope me into a contract, either," Fitz says. "Speaking of which, what's to say my winning holds you to our agreement?"

"What's to say my winning holds you to it?" Big says.

"We're not in a court of law, Fitz," Amanda says. "Anything that gets decided here is between the two of you."

"I could make your life very difficult," Big says. Fitz has already figured that out. But he could do that anyway.

"Then I need some assurance you won't try to fuck me over if I win."

Big turns to Amanda. "How's my word?"

"I don't like you," she says. "And I don't usually trust you. But screwing Fitz over does you no favors that I can see. If I thought that, I wouldn't be here. I think it's good enough."

"There, see? Good enough. That's better than I usually get. So, shall we play a friendly game of cards?"

CHAPTER TWELVE

BIG PULLS A wrapped deck from under the table and hands it to Amanda as Fitz sits down in the chair across from him. "Would you be so kind as to act as dealer, dear? I don't think our mutual friend here would see my handling the cards as all that fair."

Amanda takes the deck, peels off the wrapper. She riffles through the cards, her eyes twitching as each card speeds past. "They're clean," she says.

"Uh, Amanda," Fitz says, pointing to her face. She wipes blood from her nose with the back of her hand. He wonders how long having this clone active with all her knowledge in its head will last. Will it suddenly shut down and die? Or will it go stupid like on the way back from the museum? He hopes they can get this over and done with so he doesn't have to find out.

"All good," she says. She shuffles the deck and places it in front of Fitz to cut. "You sure you want to do this?"

He's not, but he needs help from a god and this is the only way he can think of to make sure it happens. He supposes that Big could back out of the deal—what the hell is Fitz going to do to stop him?—but he has to believe that he won't. He answers her by cutting the deck and locking eyes with Big across the table.

"Three hands of five card draw," Fitz says. "Nothing wild."

"Nothing wild," Big says. There's a tone in his voice that Fitz doesn't like, and Fitz wonders if he's bit off more than he can chew. Big is going to cheat, Fitz can feel it. But then what the hell was he thinking going against a god? He takes a deep breath and focuses. He can't dwell on that. Not now.

Amanda deals out five cards to each of them. Fitz scoops up his hand and looks at the cards, and realizes that he's made a terrible mistake. He's got a two of spades, a four of clubs, a five of clubs, a six of hearts and an ace of diamonds. In short, fuck all.

The best he can do is hang onto the ace and ditch the rest, hoping he can at least get a pair of something, or that Big has a crappy hand, too, with a lower high card. Or maybe he should toss the two and the ace and hope he can make a straight with a three and a seven. He stares at his cards, hoping they'll turn into something else. They don't.

"You look distressed," Big says.

"Just weighing my options," Fitz says, his voice confident even if he isn't. "I got a lot of them."

"Right. Mixing and matching? What do you have there? A full house? A royal flush? I think you probably don't have anything. I think you're going to lose."

"Nope," Fitz says. Maybe he can stall for time, cause a distraction, get out of there before Big's goons tackle him on the way out of the casino.

"You sure you don't want to simply give up?"

"No, I'm good."

"Suit yourself." Big slides two cards toward Amanda, who draws two new ones for him. "And you?"

"Sorry, what?" Fitz says. He's still trying to figure out what to do with this shit hand.

"How many cards would you like?"

"Oh, right." Fitz slides everything but the ace over to

Amanda and takes four replacements. He's still got a shit hand, but at least he's got a pair of twos in it.

"All good?"

No. He's not good. He's starting to freak the fuck out, actually. He nods his head instead. "Whatta ya got?"

"Full house," Big says, putting his cards face up in front of him for Fitz to see. "Kings and queens."

Fitz shows his cards, tries to put a brave face on the fact that he has nothing that even comes close.

"How do I know you're not cheating?" Fitz says. Would he even be able to tell if a god decided to do something weird with cards?

"Amanda?" Big says.

"He's not cheating," she says, scooping up the cards and shuffling the deck.

Fitz wants to ask how she knows, but he's not sure he'd be able to understand. Of course, she could just be lying and working to rope Fitz into doing what Big wants. She said he has to do his thing by choice. He can't be forced into it. But if he agrees to it, then he's probably stuck.

No. He can't think like that. If he can't trust her he can't trust anybody and he needs to. He can't do this on his own.

"Fair enough."

Big cuts the cards and she deals another hand. This time Fitz is doing a lot better. He's looking at a straight flush right out of the gate. He does his best to keep his face as neutral as possible, though he doesn't know why. It's not like he needs to bluff here. He either wins the hand or he doesn't.

"Cards?" Amanda says.

"I'm good," Fitz says. Big cocks an eyebrow at him, shifting into the body of a teenage girl with a spray on tan, big, bug-eyed sunglasses and the look of some generic pop star. She peels three cards off her hand and slides them at Amanda, clearly not happy with the way it's going.

"Well?" Fitz says.

Big sniffs in disdain. "Bupkes," she says, throwing her cards at Amanda. "One for one. Feeling confident, Prophet?"

Not particularly, no. Confident isn't a word Fitz thinks he could really use in this situation. "Just deal the fucking cards," he says.

Amanda deals the final hand. A pair of sixes. Not a good hand, but not as bad as it could be. At least he's got something. The rest of his cards are no help: a four of clubs, a nine of spades and a queen of hearts. Nothing to make out of those.

He glances up at Big, who's studying her hand with an unmasked look of glee on her face. She spies him over her cards and grins. "What should I have you do for me when you're mine?" she says. "Oh, I know. You should write an epic poem about me. I like poems."

"I don't know any," Fitz says. He'll keep the pair no matter what, but does he hang onto the queen and hope he gets another to match it, or does he toss all three of his remaining cards and hope for the best?

"Really? What kind of piss poor Chronicler are you, anyway? At least Homer knew how to spin a yarn."

"I can't even tell a joke," Fitz says.

"I don't believe you."

"Really. I suck at them." Better odds to just get rid of all the cards. The likelihood that he'll get another queen is so low it's laughable. But what if he does get one? Shit, now he doesn't know if he should ditch it or not.

"Prove it."

"What?"

"Prove you can't tell a joke. Go on."

Fitz stares at her. He's trying to sort out what the fuck to do here and she's screwing with his concentration. "Knock, knock," he says.

"Ooh, I love those. Who's there?"

"Fuck off, I'm thinking."

"I don't think that's how those are supposed to go."

"I'll take three cards," Fitz tells Amanda, sliding his cards to her face down. She scoops them up and passes him three new ones. Fitz picks them up and almost throws up out of panic.

"Wait. No. I gave you the wrong cards." Instead of giving

her the four, nine and queen, he gave her the pair of sixes and the queen instead. And what he got in return was a seven of clubs, a jack of diamonds and a two of hearts. He's worse off than he was before.

"Seriously?" Big says.

"You had me all fucking distracted and I gave her the wrong cards."

"It's too late," Amanda says.

"Oh, now, that's a pity," Big says.

"This is you. You're fucking with my head."

"Me? What the hell did I do?" Big says.

"Screwing with my mind. Some god shit."

"Oh, Fitz. That's not god shit. Now this, this is god shit."

Images slam into Fitz's mind as Big opens up his history to him. Land deals and oil pipelines, stocks and bonds, bribes and drug cartels. Larceny, theft, murder. Economies rise and fall. The thing he represents might be as old as humanity, but he is not. A hundred years or so at most. Older than Amanda, but so much more distilled. Big Money is, well, big money. Small transactions cascade into larger ones, cash changes hands, changes forms, builds bridges and roads, saves lives. Ends them, too.

The images hit Fitz hard, but he can feel its edges now, the way the visions flow in and through him. Less a fire hose, more a wave. And something else. Like a background noise in a song on the radio, the recording hiss on a less-than-perfect recording. It sits there just under his awareness, but the more he looks for it, the more he finds it. He doesn't know what it is, but it permeates the entirety of the visions in his head.

And just as suddenly it's over. Fitz blinks and realizes that Amanda is asking him something.

"What?"

"I asked if you were all right." She glares at Big, who shrugs and goes back to looking at his cards. He's changed from the pop star girl into a teenage boy in a blue blazer with a Harvard pin on the lapel.

"Yeah, I'm fine," Fitz says. Though the flood of images

is gone, that background hiss still echoes in his mind. And when he concentrates on it, it's almost as though he can see it, too. Thin, red filaments enveloping the proto-god like puppet strings. He traces them from Big to himself and back again.

"Are you sure?"

"He says he's fine," Big says. "Now if you don't mind, we have a card game to finish."

"That's right," Fitz says. "We do." He feels oddly calm. He puts his cards face up in front of him. He has a shit hand. Worse than his last losing hand. But he knows that it isn't going to matter.

"You really are going to lose," Big says, giving a low whistle at Fitz's cards.

"No, I'm not," Fitz says, absently watching the thin tendrils wrapping around the god. In his mind he reaches out to one of them and tugs. Ripples of light flow outward from it, down to the cards in Big's hand and back again.

Something happens. A bending, as though reality is warping just a little bit. A wave of nausea hits Fitz and he doubles over, trying not to throw up. He clutches at the table, his fingers digging furrows in the green felt. A moment later, the feeling passes.

"What the hell was that?" Amanda says. Big is looking at him and frowning.

"I'm good," Fitz says, the taste of bile strong in his mouth. If what just happened is what he thinks just happened, then he's home free. And terrified.

Big shakes his head. "I don't know what you thought that was going to accomplish. I'm not big on sympathy, you know." He flips over his cards. "I have a full house."

Amanda and Fitz look at his cards. "No, you don't," Amanda says.

"What?" Big follows their gaze and his eyes go wide. Whatever he thought he had isn't there. Now it's a three, four, five and six of hearts and an eight of clubs.

"That was a full house," Big says, jumping to his feet and grabbing the rest of the deck. "Aces over kings. I had a fucking full house." He sifts through the rest of the cards—looking for extras, Fitz assumes—but they're all accounted for.

"Problem, Big?"

"He cheated." Big throws the cards at Fitz and they fall around him like snowflakes.

"Really?" Amanda says. "How? I didn't see him do anything. Did he have a card hidden in his sleeve?"

"Am I the only one here seeing the irony of Big Money accusing someone of cheating?" Fitz says.

"Oh, don't you fucking try pulling something over on me, you little shit," Big says. "I know what you did. I had a full house and you—" He stops, his eyes going wide as it begins to dawn on him what Fitz has just done.

"You changed the cards."

"No," Amanda says, grinning. "He changed a *god's* cards."

CHAPTER THIRTEEN

THE HOTEL ROOM at the Sheraton just outside the Los Angeles airport is about as generic and bland as Fitz has ever seen. Even the cheap motels he takes prostitutes to have more style than this place. He sits on the bed and picks at the burger delivered by room service; like the room, it has no actual flavor.

Amanda is in the adjoining room. She said something about having to defrag her brain, or something, though Fitz isn't sure that's what she actually said. He's still having a hard time wrapping his brain around the idea that she's a clone, or a cyborg? Or a cyborg clone. Or the Internet, or technology or cell phones or whatever the fuck she is. Is she even human? Hell, is she even a *she*?

Fitz pushes the burger aside and picks up a bottle of oxy. He'd like nothing more than to wash a few down with some vodka from the mini-fridge and wake up from all this in a couple of days, but he knows he can't. This isn't something that's going to blow over.

Especially not after what he did at the casino.

Big was not happy. Neither was Fitz. He's not sure how Amanda felt about it.

When he changed Big's cards, something changed in him. He can feel it now, crawling around in his brain. The tendrils that he saw around Big Money faded away once he... twisted reality? He's not sure what he did, actually. Or how he did it. It just happened.

Angry as he was, Fitz got the feeling that Big was also a little scared. He wonders if anyone has ever done something like that before to him. Probably not. He doesn't think gods grow up with nannies giving them a time out.

But he was true to his word. From what Amanda has told him, these rooms have some sort of protections on them that other gods can't see through. Like the symbol he wrote on the bucket truck when he escaped Zaphiel, probably.

Big has guards on this floor and downstairs in the lobby. Fitz didn't notice them when they arrived, but Amanda said they were there. He's not comfortable with how much he's having to rely on her.

What happens when they need to leave? He can't stay here forever. He looks at the two guns on the bed. He needs to get some ammunition for them if they're going to leave the hotel. Bullets might not kill gods, but he'll feel a lot better if he's armed, anyway.

He should sleep. He's exhausted, but after the casino he's too wired and confused to get any rest. He wants to head out, wants to get the ball rolling. He needs to find this other Chronicler and... what, exactly? How the hell is some crazy coot who can't handle the voices in his own head going to help him? Amanda seems to think he can, though how, she won't say. Won't even tell him who it is.

A knock at the connecting door pulls him out of his thoughts. He reaches for one of the guns out of reflex. Stops himself. What the hell good is an empty gun going to do? Besides, it's only Amanda. Jesus, he's jumpy.

"Come in," he says.

She comes into the room. Something about her is off a little, but he can't tell what it is. A slight shift in focus, like she's not all there. It's barely noticeable, and if he hadn't spent the last several hours with her he might not notice at all.

"You got rid of some of yourself, didn't you?" he guesses.

She blinks at him and then her focus snaps back. "Yeah. Sorry. It takes a little bit when I do that. I had to move some of myself out and make sure I didn't lose anything important."

"And did you? Lose anything important?" It's creepy and Fitz doesn't understand it. Near as he can tell, she's just a shell. Who she is isn't even really in the room with him.

"I think so. And anything I don't know I can download easily enough."

"Like what? What did you get rid of?"

"Nineteenth Century American Literature, repair manuals for French cars built before 1982, lyrics to every Hall and Oates song. Things like that."

"Why would you even have that in there?"

"We didn't have a whole lot of time, so I just dumped everything in. Just because I know a lot of things doesn't mean most of it's useful. You got a glimpse of some of that."

He had, and he's still not sure what exactly it all was. A lot of it was meaningless drivel, as far as he could tell. Not even letters or numbers so much as the idea of letters and numbers. Concepts of code, abstractions of words. Notions, ideas, perceptions. But very little concrete enough for him to latch onto.

At the time it, well, it didn't make sense exactly. It just didn't feel so alien. It's like, when he got that hit of who she was, he became like her somehow. But now he's trying to look at it all through the lens of his own brain and it's not quite working.

Oddly, though, he feels like the jolts he got off Bacchus, Medeina and the Agent are resolving. Becoming clearer. He knows the names of Medeina's family—Dievas, Perkūnas, Teliavelis, Dalia and others—and that she has almost died at the hands of her family on at least three occasions. That she can turn into a hare or a wolf, and that she gets her power from the woods.

Bacchus is more difficult. There is just so much there to wade through and so much of it contradicts itself. But he knows the god's stories, even though they make next to no sense. He knows that he is the son of Semele of Thebes and the god Zeus and sometimes the son of Zeus and Persephone and sometimes Zeus is Jupiter and sometimes Bacchus is Dionysus and sometimes destroyed by the Titans before his birth and sometimes carried to term within Zeus's body after Semele was destroyed and—

It seems as though all of these stories are true and none of them is.

But Amanda is still a mystery to him. He's still sorting through what she is. It's like there's some kind of block preventing him from understanding her. When he looks at it too much, it all turns into a red haze in his mind.

"Well, as long as you still know how to find this other Chronicler you were talking about."

"I do," she says. "He's nearby, actually."

"What? Where?"

"Place down the street." She looks at the untouched burger, the guns, the bottles of oxy. They all tell a story, he knows, but what story is it? What story is she making out of all those things? "But I think maybe you need to eat something and get some sleep first. Maybe take some pills."

"I'm not crazy about taking the pills," he says. It's a weird, foreign feeling, like he's just said, *Sure, I'd like to carve up and eat my grandmother.* It doesn't make sense, but it's there all the same. "I don't want to tune out. Not now." He's too scared, too wired.

"You still need to get some rest," she says.

He presses the heels of his hands against his eyes, watches the starburst patterns explode on the insides of his eyelids. He knows she's right, but he just can't do it.

"Tell me about him. Who is he? Where is he?"

"His name's Jake Malmon. Been in and out of jail, mental institutions, group homes. Guy's a mess, but he's starting to turn his life around. Working as a janitor at a strip club off Tujunga in North Hollywood."

"Blue Monkey?" Fitz says. He's been to just about every strip bar in Los Angeles. Some legal, some not. It's amazing how many guys in East L.A. have set something up with a pool table in their garage for girls to dance on. There's only two legal ones he knows about off Tujunga, and only one of them is sketchy enough to hire a crazy ex-con with a history of mental illness.

"Yeah, that's the one," she says. If she's surprised he knows the place, she doesn't show it. "He's not on shift yet. You've got time to get some rest before we track him down."

"Why don't we just go to where he lives?" Fitz wants to go now. He's almost shaking with the need for action.

"Because he lives out of his car," she says. "And he's really good at avoiding surveillance cameras. I don't know where he is. But I know where he'll be."

"He sounds paranoid," Fitz says. He can't blame him. Probably has good reason to be. If he's as far gone as Amanda says, he's probably wearing tinfoil hats.

"Paranoia. Survival mechanism. To*may*to, to*mah*to," she says. "Point is, we aren't doing anything for a while, so you might as well get some sleep. Oh, and one more thing." She ducks back into her room and brings out a box of Winchester 9mm hollow-points and tosses it onto the bed next to the guns. "That ought to make you feel better."

"Thanks," he says. "It does. Sleep, huh?" He's not convinced. He picks up the box of rounds and turns it back and forth in his hands. In a world of gods who can't die, what good are they? He tosses them back onto the bed.

"Sleep would be good."

"Do you sleep?"

"I—" she cocks her head like a dog trying to figure out a particularly difficult problem. "Not as such? I mean, this body kind of has to, but I can have part of the brain sleeping while the rest runs."

"So, you don't sleep."

"No, I don't sleep."

Of course she doesn't sleep. She's not just a clone, he realizes.

She's the fucking Terminator. He wonders if he's made a terrible mistake trusting her at all. "I need you to leave now," he says. "Just. Just leave me alone for a while."

"Okay," she says, her voice a little too flat. When he looks at her, sometimes, the façade slips. She's not a person anymore. She's not even a computer program. He doesn't know what she is. "I'll check on you in a few hours." She steps back into her room and closes the door.

Fitz closes and bolts his side of the connecting doors and sits back on the bed. He pulls himself in, huddles with his arms wrapped around his legs. How can he trust her? She's not even human.

He loads his guns and tries to figure out what to do next.

SAM SWIMS TOWARD consciousness the way a drowning man grasps at a life preserver. Her awareness is hazy at best, a twilight state where time and memories crash against each other in waves. She slips in and out, not quite connecting with the real world.

The fuck did Fitz dose her with?

"Would you mind checking on my associate?" Blake says. At least, Sam *thinks* it's Blake. He sounds very far away. There is a jolt. Are they in a car? They must be.

"She can't hear us," a woman's voice says. "She's still unconscious." She's never heard her before. Another surprise employee? Like those guys in the helicopters? Where the hell had Blake gotten them, anyway? She thought she knew everyone Blake hired, but they just... appeared.

"Are you sure?" Blake says. "I'd hate for her to hear this bit. It might upset her."

A long pause, and for some reason Sam swears she can feel the woman looking at her, her scrutiny like a physical thing bearing down on her. Then the woman says, "I'm sure."

"Good. I have an idea for bringing Fitz into the fold, but it's going to require Samantha in a capacity I'm not sure she's going to like. I'll need to gain Fitz's trust, and that means I'll need to look more beneficial than the alternative."

"You want to use this mortal as bait?"

"More as... pathos. Fitz needs to come willingly, and I'm going to need to show him that the other gods are evil. And since she and Fitz are friends—"

"You want her killed."

The words hang in the air and Sam can't tell if that's really what she said. But it was clear as a bell, even through the haze of the drug. She wants to pull herself up out of it, grab Blake and demand answers. But she can't.

"Retired," Blake says. "*Killed* sounds so final."

"But it is what you want," the woman says. "You want her murdered at the hands of one of the others, where the Chronicler can see it."

Blake sighs. "Yes. Though I really wish you'd embrace a better way of phrasing these things. Tone is very important, you know."

"Why are you telling me this?"

"I want you to kill her."

The woman says nothing for a long time and Sam is hoping she'll say something like, *No, you're off your fucking nut,* but instead she says, "All right."

"Good. I'll let you know when. I just wanted to make sure you were on board."

"I have questions."

"I'm sure you do," Blake says. "Like, if you kill Samantha and Fitz blames you, how are you going to get anything out of his prophecies?"

"Something like that," she says.

"Don't you worry," Blake says. "I'll handle that. Now—"

"She's waking up," she says.

And suddenly the wall that has been separating Sam from consciousness lifts and her eyes snap open.

"Samantha, my girl!" Blake says. "How are you feeling?"

"I'm not sure." She looks at the woman and back to Blake. She's not sure she heard what she thinks she heard. Did they really just plan to kill her?

Sam is in the back of a limousine. Blake hates limos. Hates

being driven around. Says it reminds him of his days shuttling boy bands around to press junkets. She's not sure, but she doesn't think this is the same limo that he had at the museum. What the hell is going on?

"Do you remember what happened?"

"I was talking to Fitz," Sam says. "And Fitz stabbed me with a syringe."

"You went down like a drunk prom date," Blake says. "But it's good to see you alive and kicking. This is Medeina, by the way."

The woman is dressed like a reject from a Robin Hood movie. She's big, bigger than Sam is, with a body-builder's physique and dressed in rough green and brown fabric and wearing a strange, horned crown. She has a rough look to her, rugged. Someone who knows how to work with her hands. Her forest-green eyes bore into her. Sam has no doubt that this woman could easily snap her neck.

"Nice to meet you," Sam says, her voice quiet.

"She's a consultant. She'll be assisting us in our quest to find our lost boy. She's very good at finding things. Bit of a hunter, actually."

"Great," Sam says. The limo slows, rolls to a stop. The limo's windows are tinted almost black, but Sam thinks they're back at Blake's condo.

"Ah, we're here. We'll be resuming the search for Fitz in a little while. You need to get some shut eye. I've had a spare room made up for you."

Sam doesn't know what to say to that. Blake doesn't let anyone stay over at his place. *Ever.* And that he would offer? Or even have extra sheets? Or even the room? His spare rooms are all filled with cardboard boxes of legal papers and old souvenirs from his producing days.

"Thanks," she says, finally.

The driver, a man in a suit like those guys in the helicopters, opens the door and Blake slides out. Sam goes to follow him, and Medeina stops her with a hand on her arm that's as rigid as steel.

"You heard all that," she says. It's not a question.

"Yeah. You're supposed to murder me."

"I have no intention of killing you," she says. "I agreed because he is dangerous; and I let you hear him because together we may be able to stop him."

"Stop him from doing what?"

"I don't know, yet," she says. "But it will not be good for either one of us."

"So what the hell do I do?"

"Play along. Do what he says. I will come up with a plan."

"You going to tell me what it is when you do?"

"Possibly," she says. She lets go of Sam's arm and Sam can feel bruises welling up on the skin. She slides out after Blake, leaving Sam alone in the limousine.

Sam takes a deep breath and gets out of the car, wishing this was all just a nightmare.

CHAPTER FOURTEEN

FITZ STUFFS THE two pistols into his waistband at the small of his back and lets his jacket fall over them. He should be able to get hold of them in a hurry if things go south. His hands have a slight tremor and he considers taking some oxy. Instead, he drops one of the bottles in his pocket in case he needs it later.

The burger still sits uneaten on the plate, and now it's too disgusting to even consider eating. He's managed to get a couple hours of sleep, but it was fitful and full of dreams of gods and torture. Thousands of them transforming the world into a Hell on Earth, an Amanda Terminator turning the land into a Hieronymous Bosch triptych of blood and fire and pain. Blake standing on top of a huge pile of broken vinyl records shooting Agents out of his hands like death rays. He wonders what will really happen if the gods force him to make people believe in them again. Will it be that bad? His subconscious certainly seems to think so.

There is no way he's going to let that happen.

He's paced his room like a caged animal that knows it's safer where it is but desperately wants to get out anyway. He has unloaded and reloaded his guns, taken a shower, got dressed, loaded his guns again, and now he's fidgeting.

He's considered knocking on the adjoining room door to see if it's time to go yet. He's gone to the door half a dozen times already, but he's still freaked out by his last conversation with Amanda.

The phone buzzes on the bed. *MEET ME IN THE LOBBY,* it says.

Is he ready for this? If this other Chronicler is as crazy as Amanda says, he's not sure what he can show him. Has he figured out some way to influence things the way Fitz could at Big's casino? Can he teach him to do it again?

And more, is he ready to trust Amanda? He keeps going back and forth. She's human one second, some kind of weird construct the next. What exactly is she capable of?

All the things he's met so far have some kind of power unique to what they are. Downloading her brain into a clone body can't be the only thing she can do.

He takes a deep breath, closes his eyes. Types *OK* into the phone and, before he can change his mind, slips out the door.

The guards on this floor were given explicit instructions to not be seen; he knows they're watching him from behind the doors. He still feels exposed. The carpet of the hallway muffles his footsteps, but they sound like gunshots to his ears in the thick silence and when the elevator dings it's like the pealing of a funeral bell.

Only four floors, but the ride down feels like he's descending into the underworld. Maybe he is. The elevator opens and he steps out into an eerie emptiness. The doors slide shut behind him. He doesn't see anyone and the only sound is a smooth jazz soundtrack quietly playing over the lobby's speakers. Something is wrong. This is an airport hotel. There should be guests, hotel staff. But there's no one.

His phone buzzes. *WHERE ARE YOU?* it reads.

In the lobby, he types. *Like you said.*

NOT ME. GET BACK UP HERE.

Fitz stares at the phone for a beat, then backs up against the closed elevator doors and starts hammering at the up button. He slides the phone in his jacket pocket, scans the room for bodies. There's no blood or severed heads, so he doubts it's Medeina. An empty room doesn't really seem Bacchus' style.

"Hello, Louis," Zaphiel says, stepping from behind a column in the lobby. "I've been looking for you."

"How'd you find me?" Fitz says, cringing. Nobody calls him *Louis*.

"One of your new friends gave me a call," Zaphiel says. "Told me you'd be here. You really should choose your friends more carefully. Join up with the wrong crowd and you never know what they'll do."

Goddammit. That fucker Big sold him out. He should have known that would happen. You can't trust money.

"You're looking good," Fitz says, stalling for time and trying to figure a way out that doesn't get him kidnapped or worse. "I mean, you know, better. With the one face and all. And no wings. And not on fire."

"Yes, that was a nasty business earlier," Zaphiel says, nodding. "It took me hours to recover. Where did you learn that? That's not something you just pick up."

"A friend gave me a hand. Seemed to do the trick." He's trying to remember what that symbol was that Amanda had him draw on the side of the utility bucket. It was a circle? Maybe? He's pretty sure there were some wavy lines in it.

"I think we got off on the wrong foot," Zaphiel says, stepping closer. Fitz reaches under his jacket for the two pistols. Zaphiel stops, wary. "What do you have there, Louis?"

"Something I don't think you'll like." Fitz doesn't know if the guns will do anything to him, but if it slows him down, that will be enough. They did a great job on Blake's head, even if it didn't stick.

"Oh? Do tell," Zaphiel says, his head contorting, his body twisting. "I'm dying to find out what it is."

Fitz knows what happens next. A few more seconds and Zaphiel's going to be ten feet tall with four wings, four faces and a whole shitload of bad intentions. He's not keen to repeat the experience, so he pulls out both guns, thumbs back the hammers and unloads in Zaphiel's face.

The bullets never get there.

They stop in mid-air, spinning, hovering inches from Zaphiel's face. He looks at them the way a dog looks at something it isn't sure is food, cocking his head first to one side and then the other, all the while continuing to morph into the four-faced Biblical abomination.

"That wasn't very nice," Zaphiel says, his voice a four-part harmony that rattles through Fitz's skull like a dentist's drill.

"Yeah, well," Fitz says, trying really hard not to piss his pants in complete terror. "I had to try."

"Oh, totally," Zaphiel says. "Here, maybe you should have these back."

The elevator dings behind him, the doors sliding open. Amanda grabs Fitz, pulls him into the elevator and throws him to the side as Zaphiel reverses the bullets. They slam into her, punching through her chest and face, blowing huge, gaping holes through her body, the bullets smacking into the back of the elevator wall. She hits the floor with a wet, meaty thud, blood pouring out of her like it's running out a faucet.

Fitz hammers on the door close button, but Zaphiel shoves his now enormous, clawed hands through the opening and holds them apart. "Was that your friend?" Zaphiel says, his words making the elevator vibrate. "The one who showed you how to burn me? I don't think I like her much. She can't help you anymore." He steps into the elevator and reaches for Fitz.

Fitz sits on the elevator floor, staring at the looming Cherub, frozen in fear. The guns hang from limp hands and all he can seem to do is make a low-pitched whining sound.

Red tendrils appear on the edge of his vision. Fine filaments like spiderwebs encircle Zaphiel's hand, his arm, cover his head and soon his whole body. Each strand, Fitz knows, though he doesn't how he knows, is a separate control, a different switch. Like the strings on a puppet: a twitch on one will make the puppet walk, a twitch on another will make the puppet dance.

And a yank on all of them...

"You aren't here," he says, and that same wave of nausea and pain that hit him in the casino hammers at him. He doubles over, his body shaking, and dry heaves.

Zaphiel flies out of the elevator, blasted across the lobby by an unseen force. He hits the marble floor, carving out a crater of stone shards and digging a furrow ten feet long until he slams into a support column, shattering it at its base.

The elevator doors close on the Cherub shaking its head and roaring a cacophony from all four mouths.

"Down," Amanda says, her breath a raspy whisper. "Garage." She reaches up with a blood covered hand toward the buttons. Fitz hits the button for the parking garage.

"I'll get you out of here," he says. "I promise."

She shakes her head, pupils dilating as she bleeds out on the elevator floor. She starts to say something, but it only comes out as a wheezy breath and then her eyes roll into the back of her head and she's gone.

Fitz stares at her body, hands shaking. Distantly he knows she isn't dead, but his brain is screaming that he's got a fucking body right here.

His phone buzzes in his pocket. He digs it out and looks at the screen. *BLUE CADILLAC CTS SEDAN THREE SPACES FROM ELEVATOR KEYS IN POCKET,* it says.

"Nice to see you, too," he says. "You're dead, you know."
YES IT HAPPENS

Fitz rifles through Amanda's pockets and finds a key. He also finds a loaded .45 and a couple of extra clips. He grabs them and ditches his two empty pistols. He wipes the blood from his hands onto his jeans, where it soaks in, making the cloth dark and stiff.

The elevator opens onto the parking garage and he sees the Cadillac right where she said it would be. He thumbs the button on the key, the car chirping as it unlocks, and bolts for the car, gun at the ready.

He gets behind the wheel, starts the car and guns the engine. If Zaphiel finds him down here, he's fucked. But if he gets out onto the open road, he might have a chance.

"What the hell happened?"

THERE WAS A HOLE IN THE SECURITY THAT BIG WAS ABLE TO EXPLOIT. I'VE PLUGGED IT. I HAVE SECURED THIS LINE. THERE WILL BE NO MORE INCURSIONS.

"Your fucking brother," Fitz says. "How do I know you're you? What did you say to me when Zaphiel was coming for us and I wouldn't get in the car?"

There's a pause, and then, *WHAT'LL IT BE SPARKY RIDE UP FRONT LIKE A BIG BOY OR IN THE TRUNK LIKE A BITCH?*

"Okay. I'm convinced. So what the hell happened? Zaphiel said someone tipped him off."

BIG REMOVED ALL OF HIS GUARDS AND EMPTIED THE HOTEL.

"Did anybody get killed?"

JUST ME

"Oh, well that's something." Fitz speeds up the ramp toward the garage entrance. The barrier arm at the entrance is down, but he isn't planning on paying the parking fee. He guns the engine, closes his eyes and rams it. The wooden arm shreds from the impact and he hits Century Boulevard with a thud, sparks flying from the car's undercarriage. No sign of Zaphiel.

"Where to now?"

CALCULATING ROUTES TAKE CENTURY TO COMPTON AVENUE

"That's gonna take forever," he says. "What's down there?"

HAVE CALLED IN SOME FAVORS. WILL BE SAFE UNTIL I CAN GET ANOTHER AMANDA TO YOU

"Oh. Good. You're a lot easier to talk to when you're an actual person."

I'LL TRY NOT TO BE YOUR BULLET SPONGE NEXT TIME

He winces. "Yeah, I deserved that. Thanks, by the way."

YOU'RE WELCOME

"About that, why was Zaphiel trying to kill me? I thought he needed me alive." Was he trying to kill him? Did he know

Amanda would be there? Maybe he's just pissed off at what Fitz did to him before and he's decided he doesn't care about Fitz after all.

UNKNOWN

"You know when you say it like that it's kind of creepy. And the all caps? It's like you're yelling at me. Can you, I dunno, not say it like that?"

I have no fucking idea, the screen reads. *Better?* Maybe he's just reading too much into that one word, but he swears it's dripping with sarcasm and she's rolling her eyes at him.

"Much, thanks."

There is a tremendous thud and the roof of the car buckles inward. Claws punch through the metal and, with a terrific shriek, a section of the roof peels back. Fitz looks up to see Zaphiel, the shredded piece of roof gripped in his clawed feet. The Cherub drops the roof piece to clatter on the road behind them, narrowly missing a taxi.

"This is not good," Fitz yells over the sudden noise of traffic and wind invading the car.

What's going on?

"The angel's back. And he looks pissed off." Fitz stomps on the gas, zips through the late-night traffic coming off the airport. Above him, Zaphiel tears through the sky in full-on beast mode. His head is screaming from all four mouths and his four wings beat upon the air, causing a draft that knocks down a motorcycle behind Fitz and sends it crashing into the sidewalk.

"How do I lose him?"

I don't know, yet, the phone reads. *Stay on Century. I'm on my way.*

Zaphiel dips lower, his clawed feet dropping through the opening in the roof. Before the angel can grab him, Fitz yanks the steering wheel hard to the left, clipping Zaphiel's feet and sending him careening into the side of a building.

"How far are you?" Fitz says.

Close. But I'm going to be a little sketchy. I didn't have time to download everything.

"Okay, what does that mean?"

It means when she gets there she might not be very smart.

"That didn't work out so well the last time."

This time she has very explicit instructions.

"What are they?"

Fitz doesn't get a chance to see the answer because that's when Zaphiel changes tactics and gets out in front of him. The angel hits the street in front of the car so hard that his feet embed in the pavement. He leans forward, arms held out to catch the car.

Fitz brakes hard and spins the wheel to avoid him, but he's going too fast. Instead of hitting him head on, Fitz skids into the angel, plowing into him at a good sixty miles an hour.

He doesn't budge.

The front end of the Cadillac accordions into a crumpled mess, the windshield shatters and the airbag deploys in Fitz's face. His seatbelt bites into his skin and he feels his left shoulder pop out of joint. Pain engulfs him. His insides feel like they're on fire.

The phone goes flying through the destroyed windshield to skid across the pavement and explode into a thousand fragments. His vision swims in and out of focus. He blacks out. It's only for a second, but when he comes to, Zaphiel is tearing through the car like it's made out of paper. He throws the engine block into traffic, snaps the axle in two, rips apart the dashboard and steering column in an effort to get to Fitz. All the while, he's screaming from those four inhuman mouths.

Fitz fumbles with his right hand and unbuckles his seatbelt. His left arm hangs at a weird angle by his side; he's trying not to think about it.

Zaphiel finally gets through all that metal as Fitz gets what's left of the door open. He flops over partway through the door, lands on his shoulder and screams.

Zaphiel stands where the front end of the car should be, surrounded by stripped wires and hoses and debris. He stretches to his full height, easily ten feet tall, reaches up to the sky and bellows loud enough to shatter glass. It is a roar of absolute triumph.

It cuts off pretty quickly when a dump truck plows into him.

CHAPTER FIFTEEN

THE TRUCK NARROWLY misses the rest of the Cadillac and continues down Century for a good block and a half, the angel trying to get purchase on the front and get out of its way. Fitz sees Zaphiel's wings unfurl around the edges of the truck as he prepares to take flight.

The dump truck slams into a billboard, putting the kibosh on that plan as it wedges the angel between the truck and the pylon. The metal pylon, crumpled from the impact, groans and buckles with the strain, the weight of the sign atop it slowly bending it in half.

Amanda jumps out of the driver's side door with a couple of green messenger bags that she wedges between the truck and Zaphiel's growling, screaming face. Even from across the street Fitz can hear the angel shrieking profanities. He watches as Amanda takes a step back, pulls a small box out of her jacket and thumbs a button on its front.

The satchel charges shoved in Zaphiel's face explode, vaporizing the cab of the dump truck and Amanda along with it. The explosion brings the billboard pylon crashing down onto the truck while a shockwave tears across the street, rocking the Cadillac.

Fitz feels it punch through him, a heavy, rolling feeling that jerks his dislocated arm, sending a flare of pain through his body. The air is hot against his skin and his hearing disappears into a high-pitched whine as a column of flame shoots up into the night sky. He stares up at the towering flames and billowing black smoke while all around him traffic is piling up, trying to avoid the chaos.

"Come on," Amanda yells, hauling on Fitz to get him all the way out of the car. "That's not going to keep him long, and when he finally gets moving he's gonna be real pissed."

Fitz stares at her. "But you—how did you—" She was just vaporized in the blast. He's sure of it. Did he black out and miss something? She's not on fire. She's not even smoking.

"Clone, remember?" she says. "What, you don't think I can have more than one of me around at a time?" Fitz decides that that is the most disturbing thing he has learned about her so far. She looks him over, and before he can stop her, she grabs his wrist and shoves her foot into his armpit. He screams as she yanks on his arm, wrenching the bone back into its socket.

"Goddammit," he says, as she helps him to his feet. "You could have warned me." Aside from the arm, and some cuts and bruises, he thinks he's mostly okay. Thank God for good American steel and Federal safety standards.

"You would have just tensed up," she says. "Come on."

He hobbles after her, looking behind him at the inferno raging down the street. Nothing but flames and smoke. "How did that work? You can kill angels?"

"Not dead. Just really not happy right now. Those satchel charges had a thousand pieces of parchment with his name written backward in Enochian. When they went up in flames, so did he. He's gonna be out of commission for a little bit."

"Neat trick," Fitz says. "Where are we going?"

"I don't know," she says. "I'm not driving." A van pulls up

to the destroyed Cadillac with an Amanda at the wheel. The side door slides open and two more help Fitz inside.

"This is really weirding me out," he says.

"You'll get used to it," two of the Amandas say in unison. "Sorry."

"Let's just get the hell out of here," Fitz says, lowering into one of the seats as one of the Amandas closes the door. He's still having trouble moving his left arm, but at least it doesn't hurt as much. "What about the police? Why aren't I seeing any cop cars?"

"They're responding to a dozen robberies in progress right now," the Amanda who's driving says, as she hits the gas and speeds the van down the street. "Also there's someone claiming to have a bomb at the airport and a woman standing in the middle of Sepulveda Boulevard blocking traffic, and all of their communications are currently glitched."

"What about police helicopters?"

"Oh, I know this one!" one of the Amandas in the back with him says, clapping her hands like a five-year-old. "It's 'cause it's an airport."

"Airspace is restricted, this close to the airport," the driver says. "LAPD helicopters aren't allowed here. And by the time they know about us, we'll be long gone."

Fitz gives a low whistle. "Man, where were you people when I was running drugs? So where are we going?"

"We need to get that other Chronicler," one of the Amandas says.

"Who?" says another.

"Jake something?" says a third. It's weird for Fitz to see them trying to muddle through like this, and he's suddenly afraid they're going to get him killed the way she almost did coming back from the museum.

There's a sigh from the front of the van. "Jake Malmon," the driver says to the others. "Janitor at a strip club in the Valley. We need to grab him before Zaphiel regroups. We may not have another chance at this."

"How do you know he's going to come willingly?" Fitz says.

He doesn't like this idea. After spending the last day being hunted, kidnapped and almost murdered, he really doesn't want to put someone else through that, too.

"It's for his own safety," the driver says.

"How the hell does being with us make him safe?"

"You're being talked about," the driver says. "It's not just Bacchus and Zaphiel and the Man you have to worry about anymore. They're just the most immediate threats. Eventually they or another god will figure out that you need someone to talk to about this. Someone who understands what you're dealing with. Chances are Big has already spread the word that you need help, and eventually someone's going to piece together that he's the closest Chronicler you can talk to."

"If we don't grab him, somebody else will," Fitz says.

"Exactly."

"Fuck. Fine. Let's get him. But wherever we go, can you make sure it's actually safe this time?"

THE BLUE MONKEY is a strip bar like most of the ones in the Valley: plain, industrial brick with no windows and only a single sign out front. There's a sincerity to its lack of flashing lights, its dearth of style. This is a place of pure transaction, the most crystallized of entertainment. The patrons are there to see some tits, the dancers are there to get some cash. Sure, it's all an illusion inside, from the bad lighting to hide the dancers' acne scars to the way they pretend to want to talk to you. But at least everybody's in on it.

The drive up into the Valley was grueling. They took side streets, doubled back, went through back alleys and avoided police. Fitz popped a few oxys and one of the Amandas got his arm in a sling. The painkillers are helping dull the edge of his dislocated shoulder, but whenever he moves his arm, his hand goes all numb and tingly.

"How long do I have to have this thing on?" he says as they get off the freeway. The constraint of not being able to move his arm, even if it is for his own good, is maddening.

"Couple weeks," one of the Amandas says. They've gotten more intelligent, more aware. Fitz thinks they must be getting an upload while it's still safe to do so. No telling what they'll run into inside the club.

"That's not gonna work," he says. He pops another oxy, wincing as he pulls the sling off.

"You're gonna regret that."

"Yeah, well, add it to all the other things I regret."

Driver Amanda pulls the van into the alley behind the Blue Monkey. It's one a.m. and the parking lot is full. They stop serving alcohol at two, but they're open until four.

"What does this guy look like?" Fitz says.

"Like a burnout," Driver Amanda says.

"It's a strip bar," Fitz says. "That's at least half the clientele."

She passes a photo of him. It's a mug shot from a few years ago. Eyes haunted, skin sallow. Hair too thin and skin too gray, like all of the color's been sucked out of it. Fitz hands the picture back, shaken. That man could just as easily be him.

"He's probably wearing coveralls and pushing a mop," she says. "The trick is finding him."

"That'll be easy," Fitz says, popping the sliding door open with his good hand. "He'll be in the bathroom, mopping up jizz. How do you want to do this?"

"You and I will go in," Driver Amanda says. "The others will watch the front and back."

"Who's driving the car?"

In answer the headlights flash without the driver touching anything.

"Oh," Fitz says. "Handy."

Fitz and the clones get out of the car and he follows the driver to the back entrance. "So, what happens when you're, you know, done with a body?"

"They..." Amanda pauses. "They go into storage?" she says. A momentary look of panic and confusion crosses her face, then clears. "I don't have that information downloaded," she says.

"Well, where do you come from?"

She shrugs, already dismissing the question. "Don't know, don't care." Fitz gets the feeling there's more to that, but he lets it go.

The back door—thick security steel rattling to the pounding bass on the other side—is locked, of course. No bouncer. Not even a parking attendant for the lot. It's not that kind of place. As long as nobody gets shot in the lot, the owners don't care. Amanda pulls a lock pick gun from her jacket, fits a pick into the grip and jiggles it into the lock. It pops open in less than a second.

"Is there anything you can't do?" he says.

"Probably not." And she says she's not a god.

The music is so loud when they open the door that Fitz can't even recognize the song. The sound system is so bad, and the speakers so defective, that there's more popping and crackling than actual music. They head through a narrow, badly lit hallway past a couple closed doors, an office and a dressing room, and then into the club itself.

Well, *club* is being generous. It's a cramped, dark space with a lone bouncer napping on a stool at the front and women half-clad in cheap lingerie on a couple of raised platforms that can only be called stages because of the badly-secured stripper poles on them. One of the women is making a half-hearted attempt at actually doing some spinning and the pole wobbles dangerously from her efforts.

Half a dozen bored looking men sit around each stage, their eyes wandering from dancer to dancer. A couple are in the corner getting lapdances, but even they don't look interested in the grinding.

"Are all strip bars this depressing?" Amanda says.

"Most of them, yeah," Fitz says. "Wait, you can get depressed?"

That same troubled look crosses her face. "No?" she says. "Let's just find this guy."

Fitz wonders if she's glitching like on the drive from the museum. Hell, maybe she's becoming more human. He'd like that. The idea of a Terminator-style Internet goddess kind of freaks him out. He doesn't expect things to get ugly in here, or at least not in any way she and the other Amandas can't handle no matter how glitched they get, but he'd rather not deal with it.

Fitz pokes his head into the single bathroom. It's got a couple of open stalls, a urinal and a cracked sink that leaks rusty water. But no Jake.

"Maybe he's out sick?" Fitz says.

"Maybe somebody's already got him."

That's not a pleasant thought.

"Let's not go there just yet." Fitz looks across the room and recognizes one of the dancers, a frizzy-haired redhead with freckles and a tattoo between her collarbones that says *I'M YOUR BEST BAD IDEA*. He's pretty sure he went to a motel with her one time a couple years ago, though he doesn't think he met her here. Some of the dancers work around different clubs.

He goes up to where she's slowly wiggling on the stage, pulls out a twenty and holds it up to her. She responds by turning her hip toward him so he can stuff it into her g-string. He has no idea of her name, or if he ever knew it. Chances are any name she gave him before was made up, just like whatever name he gave her was.

"Candy," he says, figuring he's got about a one in four chance of getting it right.

"Faith," she says, looking at him. "You and your friend want a dance?"

"Actually, I was wondering if you knew where the janitor is."

"Do I look like the fucking information desk?" she says.

He pulls out another twenty and puts it into her g-string. "You do now."

"I don't think he's in yet," she says. "He in trouble?"

"No," Fitz says. "I just owe him some money and want to get square with him."

She laughs. "Sure you do. He doesn't have a dollar bill to wipe his ass with."

"Well, I need to talk to him. It's important. Any idea when he gets in?"

Fitz can't tell if she just shrugged or if it's part of her idea of a sexy dance routine. "If he's here, he's probably in the office getting chewed out by Tony."

"That happen a lot?"

That same pseudo-dance shrug move. "He fucks up a lot. He's crazy. I mean, not *bad* crazy, but crazy."

"I hear he did some time."

"Who hasn't?"

"Point. Thanks for the tip. I'll check with Tony."

"Careful. If Tony's in a snit, he might punch you. He's a puncher."

"Of course he is." Fitz follows Amanda back the way they came to the door marked *Office*.

"Do we knock?" Fitz says.

"I have his file," Amanda says. "Tony Graham. Faith was right. He's a puncher. And a shooter, and a stabber. Aggravated assault, armed robbery, attempted murder."

"So no knocking?"

Amanda pulls back one leg and slams her steel-toed boot into the door next to the doorknob, ripping the door from the lock and throwing it wide open. Inside there's two men: an overweight man in a blue T-shirt and jeans with an abysmal comb-over sitting at a desk—presumably Tony—and Jake Malmon standing on the other side of it, with a face so craggy it looks like a desert lake bed in a bad summer.

"The fuck is this?" Tony says, standing up and reaching into his desk.

"Hey, now," Fitz says. He doesn't want to shoot the guy, but he might be going for a gun. He seems like a dick, but that's no reason to punch a hole into him.

He remembers the card in his pocket that Amanda showed the valet back at Big's casino. She said looking at it would make people freak out. God knows it screwed with his head when he just gave it a glance. He digs it out of his pocket and shoves it into the big man's face.

Tony goes a little green, but instead of freaking out and backing down, he pulls a pistol from his desk and tries to shoot Fitz. The bullet goes high, missing Fitz by several feet.

Amanda's already got a pistol out and shoots him through the desk right in the knee. He screams and drops to the floor.

"What the hell were you thinking?" Amanda says.

He shows her the card. "I didn't want you to shoot him. I thought this thing was supposed to terrify him or something."

"Everybody reacts differently to fear. Tony's reaction, apparently, is to shoot whatever's scaring him." She grabs the card and stuffs it into her pocket. "And don't worry. He'll live."

"Well, that's a plus." He turns to Jake, who's curled up on the floor and wrapped his hands over his head. "Hey, Jake. We gotta go."

"Who the hell *are* you people?" he says, his voice shaky from fear.

"I'm Fitz. This is Amanda. There's a bunch of gods looking for me and I need you to help me figure out how to do what I do. Whatever that is. I'm really not sure."

Jake looks up at him with dawning horror. "Aw, shit," he says. "It's happening again, isn't it? Man. They said this was all a delusion. They said I was cured. I just stopped taking my meds a couple weeks ago. Goddammit."

"Sorry, old timer. It's all real. And it's all fucked. And if you don't come with us, they're gonna come after you. And you won't like that."

"No," he says. "No, no, *no, no,*" his voice getting higher and higher in pitch.

"I guess we drag him out?"

"Or we—" she pauses, her eyes going blank. A moment later they snap back into focus. "Yes. Quickly. Help me get him out the door."

Fitz gets behind him and lifts him in a bear hug. Bones like a bird's, skin like paper. He barely weighs a thing. "What's going on?"

"Agents of my father."

"Fuck, I hate those guys."

"No. Not Agents, agents."

"You just said the same exact thing twice."

"Not the Men in Black. Medeina and your friend Sam."

"I thought Medeina was with Zaphiel."

"Either they've had a falling out, or Zaphiel has teamed up with my father. But whatever the case Medeina is definitely working with my father now. Come on."

"I'm not sure which of those ideas I like less." He tries to get Jake into a fireman's carry but, though Jake isn't struggling and he weighs next to nothing, he doesn't want to hurt the guy. It feels like he's about to snap in half. He settles for walking him through the door.

They get to the back door when the sound of gunfire tears through the club. Screaming, yelling.

"The clones at the front door are dead," Amanda says. She yanks the door open for Fitz to get through. He's trying not to panic, and doing a shitty job of it. The fact that the old man just keeps muttering "no, no, no" over and over isn't helping. Outside, the empty van is idling, one Amanda covering the door with a shotgun. Fitz is about to shove Jake into the back of the van and follow him, when a yell across the alley catches his attention.

"Fitz!" He turns at his name and there's Sam, hands up and in front of her, no gun, no knife. "Wait. Please."

Fitz freezes. The look on Sam's face is pleading. That's not the look of someone coming to kill him. "You don't want to be here, Sam."

"No, I don't. I know what's going on. I know what's happened to Blake. I know what you are. I want to help you."

"How do I know—" Fitz starts to say, but cuts off when Amanda puts a bullet straight into Sam's chest.

CHAPTER SIXTEEN

SAM SITS ON the edge of the bed drumming her fingers on her thigh. She's been in this room before, a place Blake stores memorabilia and files. All legit. If things go south and the cops decide to raid his place, they won't find anything linking him to any of his crimes.

Or at least it was. Now it's a blandly tasteful, if Spartan, bedroom. Queen bed, nightstands, lamps, hotel art on the walls. She didn't even know it *had* carpet. Hell, with all the changes it's had in the last twelve hours, maybe it didn't.

She's having a hard time processing everything. Before Fitz went into the hospital, she thought she knew what was what. She had certainty. Illegal as all fuck, but she understood what was going on and her place in it.

The only other time she's felt that way was when she was fighting MMA, and even then only in the ring. Outside the ring, she was lost. Dealing with managers and promoters and marketing people and asshole fans and... Well, that life was over.

But then Fitz's betrayal, and Blake getting all weird, and

now this Medeina woman. It's clear she's a lot more than what she looks. Sam rubs the bruise on her arm, where the woman held on for just a moment.

There's a knock on the door and Blake says through it, "You decent?"

"Just a second," she says, standing. Her hands ball into fists. She still can't believe Blake wants to kill her. She would have thought it was all a dream if Medeina hadn't talked to her afterward. If it is true—and even with all that, she has her doubts—she wonders if she should just kill Blake here and now.

But she knows she won't. She can't. That certainty she had as of this morning might be gone, but goddamn if she isn't going to hang onto whatever shredded tatters of it might still remain. She forces herself to relax, rolling her neck; it cracks from the tension.

"Come in," she says.

Blake opens the door. He's wearing a different suit. Gray pinstripes, red tie, diamond tie tack. "All rested?"

"I'm good."

"Excellent. I've found Fitz. I need you to go with Medeina and grab him."

This is it, she thinks. This is where he has me killed. "Are you coming?"

"I'll be along behind you. He and I, well, we got off on the wrong foot earlier and I don't want to spook him. He's at a strip bar in the Valley. Or, at least, he'll be there soon." He hands her an index card with an address on it. The printing is tight, controlled, legible. And clearly not Blake's.

"You sure you want me to go with her?" Sam says.

"Absolutely. She's just a consultant. Who knows what she'll do on her own. I need you to keep an eye on her. You're my ace in the hole."

"I'll leave now. So you don't want him dead anymore?"

Blake laughs. "Oh, no. Not at all. I was just angry, you know? Heat of the moment stuff. So just keep him from leaving and I'll be along behind you, and we'll sort this all out."

"And I have to take Medeina with me?"

"Absolutely. Very important. She's the one who figured out where he was going. If he gives you the slip, she can help track him down."

"That's her job? Tracking Fitz? She some sort of bounty hunter or something?"

"Something like that. Very woodsy type. The two of you'll get along perfectly. I just know it."

She grabs her holstered pistol from the nightstand, slips it into her waistband at the small of her back.

"Oh, you won't need that," Blake says.

"Seriously?" Sam says. "He had help last time. He's probably gonna have help again." No gun? Blake *always* wants her to be armed. Even when he knows she can handle herself without one. And considering how badly the museum went, what the hell makes him think she won't need a gun now?

Unless he doesn't want her to be able to defend herself when Medeina tries to kill her.

"Fair point," Blake says. "Just don't hurt him."

"Of course not," Sam says. "I'll get him back here in one piece."

"I expect nothing less," he says. "Oh, one last thing." He pulls a flask from his coat pocket and hands it to her. "You need to take a swig of this. You're still going to have that shit in your system that Fitz dosed you with. This will clear the last of it out and he won't be able to try it again."

Sam takes the flask from him, unscrews the cap. The scent is thick and sweet. Cherry? "What'll it do to me?"

"Oh, something about binding to opioid receptors or some shit. I have no idea. I had a doctor put it together for me. Totally harmless."

"I feel fine," Sam says. "Whatever he dosed me with is gone."

"One can't be too careful," Blake says.

Sam wonders if this is how he's going to kill her. Make her drink some poison. But no, that doesn't fit. He said he wants her dead so Fitz can see it and... what exactly? He wants

Fitz back working for him, that much is clear, but he doesn't understand what he said in the car about gods. She must have heard that wrong.

Point is that if he's really going to kill her, he's not going to do it here. Still.

"What's in it?"

"Little this, little that. I don't really know." He cocks his head like he's pulling up some old memory. "I had a doctor I used to work with whip it up. Gave it to my boys back in the day to make sure they could get on stage. You know. 'There'll be no more—aaaah!—but you may feel a little sick'?"

Sam looks at him blankly.

"No appreciation for the classics," Blake says. "Trust me. It's for your own good."

Trust is something Sam doesn't have much of right now. She gets the reference, but Blake would never use it. He hates Pink Floyd.

Sam considers grabbing Blake by the throat and demanding answers, but what if she's wrong? What if she heard all that wrong and she's being lied to? She thought she was Blake's right hand, but after the museum with all those weird Men In Black types and now this weird new 'consultant,' she doesn't know. If she pisses him off, will he send an army in helicopters to take her out, too?

"Okay," Sam says, wary. She downs the flask, wincing from the taste. It's like drinking cherry cough syrup. It reminds her of overly sugared punch when she was a kid, that nasty mixed stuff her mom used to make for her and the neighborhood kids during the summer.

"You might feel a little off for a couple of minutes, but by the time you get downstairs you'll be fine." Sam feels a little warmth as it goes down and she staggers with a momentary rush of vertigo. "You okay, there?" Blake says.

She blinks and the vertigo passes. "Yeah. I'm good."

"Good, good." Blake takes the flask back and hands her a key hanging from a long lanyard.

She looks at the key. She can't tell from the symbol on the

head, some kind of jumping stylized animal, what the car is, but it's wrapped in a weird wood veneer, slivers of bark and leaves crusted around it and covered in layers of clear lacquer until it's shiny and smooth, the metal of the key blade weirdly out of place. When she touches it she feels a tiny electric shock.

"What is this?"

"The key to a 1972 Triumph Stag," he says. "A classic beauty. Runs like a dream."

"Since when have you been a classic car nut?" Sam says. And since when did Blake buy bespoke hippie keys?

"You think you know everything about me? Please. I am a man of hidden depths. There's only about two thousand of those cars in existence. Hard to come by. Runs like a dream. Don't tell anybody, but I've had it updated. New ignition so all you have to do is get near the car and it'll start up for you with a push of the button. Put the key around your neck and you won't even have to unlock the car. It'll do it for you. Like it's magic. Don't worry. It won't fall off." He waits until she's put it around her neck. It feels heavier around her neck than in her hand, as if it had suddenly gained weight. She slides it under her shirt.

"Excellent," he says. "Now git. Medeina's waiting. I'll be along in a little while. And remember, you're my ace in the hole." He backs out of the room, leaving Sam alone with the key to a car he would never go near to do a thing he would never have her do.

This is all so very, very wrong.

MEDEINA STANDS BESIDE the car, a red two-seater convertible that looks too tiny to comfortably fit either of them, leaning against a staff and looking up at the sky. Though it's not overcast, the city lights make the stars impossible to see.

"Nothing up there," Sam says. The staff is intricately carved with convoluted designs that would make a tribal tattoo fetishist cream his jeans. Sam wonders if she takes it everywhere with her, and if so, how people must react to it.

"There used to be," she says. "A long time ago. Do you ever think you've outlived your usefulness?"

Sam isn't sure if this is her being maudlin or some kind of threat. But it does make her think. "Once. I used to fight."

"I knew you were a warrior," Medeina says. "I have a brother who was a warrior. He's dead now."

"Sorry to hear it."

"That's okay. I killed him, and he was reborn in the form of a flaming bull. Why did you stop fighting?"

Sam pauses, trying to take in this sudden crazy murder confession. She doesn't know what to make of it. "Took a beating in the ring," she says. "Broke my nose, supraorbital ridge, left clavicle, femur, tibia, three ribs, lost a couple molars. Ref should have called it earlier, but by the time he did I was done. Spent three months in the hospital. They had to rebuild my face, my leg. Another three doing PT. Pretty much had to learn to walk all over again."

"And you did," Medeina says.

Sam nods. "And how to fight. But I was done with the circuit. I wasn't nearly as good as I was before. You take a beating like that, you don't come back from it."

"And so you gave your allegiance to Blake."

"Yeah. He helped me when everybody else left me for dead. Paid my medical bills. Got me back on my feet. He'd seen me in the ring. Was following my career. Said he had an eye for talent and he could use somebody like me." She thinks about how he brought her back, gave her a job, gave her a purpose. Did the same for Fitz. "He likes broken things, I guess."

"So you lost your purpose and gained a new one," Medeina says. "Interesting. I wonder if I can do the same."

"Are you going to kill me?" Sam says suddenly, her hands balling into fists. If Medeina tries it, Sam is going to make damn sure she regrets it. "Does Blake really want me dead?"

"No, I will not kill you. And Blake does not want you dead; Blake is already gone, and you do not follow the man you think you do."

Sam tries to parse that out and when she thinks she has it

figured out it still doesn't make sense. "The fuck does that mean?"

"The thing wearing your employer's skin is a god. I know that because I, too, am a god. I know the ways of gods and the things we do."

Sam tries to process that. Can't. "Back up," she says. "What's this *I'm a god* crap?" She's known some pretty major whack-jobs in her time but no matter how stoned or egotistical someone was, she's never known them to pronounce that they're gods and sound like they believe it.

"There was a time when mortals would not question us." Medeina looks at her feet, her voice tinged with regret. "But then, there was a time when we would not need to be questioned."

"Well, I'm questioning you now." This woman is different, she knows. Deceptively strong, creepy as all fuck. And... something she can't place. A sense of being around someone Important. But a god? Crazy, sure, but no god. "You're batshit insane, aren't you? Who are you really?"

Medeina turns to her, her eyes flashing angrily, and Sam instinctively steps back. There is a roll of thunder in the distance. "You know nothing," she says. "I would strike you down where you stand if I did not think you were useful to me."

Her voice shifts, a low booming bass that hammers through Sam, shaking her bones. "I am the goddess Medeina," she says. "I am protector of the forest, keeper of the wild ways. I gave birth to the woods, grant succor to the animals. I am both the hunter's friend and his bane."

Fear grips Sam and she drops to all fours as waves of panic hit her. A sudden wind whips up around them. Blood drips from her nose and a thin film of red fills one eye from a burst capillary.

"Jesus, fuck," Sam yells, her hands clasped over her ears. "Fine. Okay. You're a god. Stop it. Please." The winds die, the vibration beating through Sam's bones quiets. She lies on the ground, trying not to throw up. How the hell did this woman do that? Sam looks for hidden speakers, subwoofers, anything to explain what she just experienced.

"I know very little of the one who wears your employer's skin," Medeina says as if nothing had just happened. "He tells me his name is *El Jefe*, but I suspect he has many names. I watched him murder a god several thousand years old, and though I did not believe it at first, I knew it to be true. When one god dies, the rest of us can feel it, even if we do not always know what it is we're feeling. We know a light has gone out, a universal flame been snuffed. He is more terrible and powerful than I imagined, this El Jefe."

Sam tries to get to her feet, but the vertigo is too strong. Is she hallucinating? Did this crazy woman slip some drug to her? Sam's taken a lot of drugs over the years—nothing like what Fitz has done, but she's no lightweight—and this is like no bad trip she's ever had.

She doesn't want to admit it, but she believes her. *Has* to believe her. Look what she just did. But what about the rest? Can she believe that, too?

"You're telling me my boss is a god named after the bad guy in a Peckinpah movie?"

"Have you not noticed that he is not the same man he was earlier today?" Medeina says. "His manner of dress, perhaps? Or what he says? His actions and attitudes?"

Sam stares hard at her, not sure how much to say. Maybe this is a test of loyalty to Blake, though that makes even less sense. Is he wondering if she's got what it takes to actually take down Fitz? Only he's never done that before. Blake doesn't play head games, at least not like that. She looks at the Triumph parked at the curb and feels the weight of the strange key around her neck. She wipes blood from her nose.

"I've noticed."

"And there's more, isn't there?" Medeina says. "His Agents, his unusual commands, his desire to have me kill you."

"None of that means he's a god," Sam says.

"Where did those Agents come from?" Medeina says. "Where did they go?"

Sam has to admit that she doesn't know. "He could have hired them. Called in some favors I didn't know about."

"You believe I'm a god, but not Blake? You cling to that so hard. Why?"

"If you're not blowing smoke up my ass, then Blake's dead," she says. "And I don't want him to be dead. I don't understand what any of this is about. Why did some god kill him? Why's he after Fitz? Why are you involved in all this?"

"You have questions," Medeina says, reaching down to Sam and touching her forehead.

When Sam was a kid, she used to get migraines. This is a bit like that. Blazing pain punches through Sam's head, and her mind fills with knowledge about the gods' fall, about Medeina's taking up with Zaphiel, about the way the Cherub had treated and discarded her, about the struggles the gods were having in a world that no longer wanted nor saw any need for them.

About Fitz.

Just as suddenly the pain is gone. This time she does throw up. Retches onto the sidewalk until there's nothing left in her system. Sam's vision swims in front of her, the sidewalk a blurry, vomit-covered mess.

"You understand now," Medeina says.

"Yes," Sam says and spits bile out of her mouth. Her heart should be hammering in her chest. She should be shaking, freaking out. But instead, a quiet calm settles over her like a warm blanket.

It feels like the calm she used to get during a bout. Where other fighters would get all worked up, fill themselves with nervous energy, tapping into that to swing harder, move faster, Sam went the other direction. For her it was all about control, about peace and calm and not being attached to the outcome.

It was about certainty.

She knows Medeina has given her very specific and limited knowledge. The basics, fleeting glimpses. At first she wonders if this is some kind of mind control, but then realizes that if it was, she wouldn't even be asking that question. She knows what Medeina wants and why she's here, but she's not a convert.

"You tried to kill Fitz," Sam says. "At the hospital."

Medeina nods. "I may yet kill him. Before it was anger. Now it may simply be necessary."

"I wish you wouldn't," Sam says. "He's a fuck-up, but he's a good guy."

"El Jefe wants him," Medeina says. "I don't think humanity, *or* the gods, can afford to let that happen."

"So you want to bring him to your side? Like the other gods are trying to do?" Sam marvels at how easily that question rolls off her tongue when ten seconds ago she would have checked herself into a psych ward just for thinking it.

Medeina's brow creases in uncertainty. "I don't know, yet. I don't know that I want that power, either."

"That leaves killing him."

"No," she says. "There are other ways. But I won't know until we find him."

CHAPTER SEVENTEEN

"SAM!" FITZ YELLS, dropping the old man and running to her. She's on the ground, rolled into a ball, clutching her chest, a grimace of pain on her face.

But no blood.

This is a trick, Fitz thinks, but he can't stop himself. He still trusts her and he's not going to let all this kill her.

"Tell me you're wearing a vest," he says. "And that you're you and this isn't some weird magic god disguise." He pulls the .45 from his waistband and points it at her head. "Because if you're not you, I will paint the fucking street with your brains."

"I'm me," she says through gritted teeth. She lifts her shirt to show the vest. It's thin, but it'll stop anything smaller than a .357. She's used it before. Anything bigger than what Amanda shot her with would probably have gone through.

"Where's Blake?" he says. "And what do you mean, you know what's going on?"

"Blake's not here, yet," she says. "But he will be. And he's not Blake. He's a god called—"

"The Man," Fitz says, "Yeah, I know."

"I was gonna say *El Jefe*, but now that you put it that way that name makes a lot more sense. Anyway, he's not trying to kill you, either. He's trying to convert you, and to do that he wants to make you think he's a better option than throwing in with the other gods."

He helps her to stand. "How the fuck does he expect to do that?"

"He's going to have Medeina kill me and make it look like she did it on her own. And then you'll go running to him, or something."

"The fuck? Okay, come on. You're coming with us. We're getting you out of here. If she gets here, she'll kill all of us."

"No, Fitz. It's not like that. I'm here with her. She wants to help you."

Fitz backs away from her, gun pointed back at her head. "No," he says. "I don't know what she's told you, but she tried to kill me. She killed a fuckton of people at the hospital. She was working with Zaphiel, and now she's with the Man. And you fucking brought her here?"

"She's not bad, Fitz. I talked to her. She showed me—well, not everything, but enough to know she's on the level."

"Did she show you what she did in the hospital? Did she show you all the corpses? Their heads chopped off?"

She nods. "Yeah. I'm not saying she doesn't have problems—"

"Problems? Jesus Christ. You're, like, some kind of acolyte for her, aren't you? Goddammit, Sam."

"No! I want to help you. If Blake gets hold of you, it's gonna be worse than anything."

"He's not Blake anymore, Sam. Don't call him that. Fuck. I—" He stops when he sees Medeina step out from the back exit of the bar. He turns to her and pops off two rounds from the gun. He starts looking for those red spider threads that connected him to Zaphiel and Big Money, but he can't see them.

One bullet hits Medeina in the left shoulder and the other one goes high to dig a pit into the stucco of the strip bar wall.

She looks down at the hole in her shoulder as it begins to seal, pushing the bullet out to plop onto the ground with a faint metallic *thunk*.

"I am not here to murder you, Louie Fitzsimmons," she says, "but to keep you from El Jefe."

"Well, that's a refreshing change."

The Amandas have gotten Jake into the van and have been watching the exchange. Either Amanda has a plan, Fitz thinks, or she's waiting to see how things pan out.

"He will be here soon," she says. "He means to have me—"

"Kill Sam and blame you to get me to work for him. Yeah, I heard."

"He believes he understands you enough to know that you will follow his lead when that happens."

"He's an idiot."

"I believe he may be a god of pure arrogance."

Fitz looks back at the Amandas for some indication of what he should do. No help there. They stand with guns drawn, but they're not interfering.

"I don't trust you," he says to Medeina. "You tried to kill me. You murdered a bunch of innocent bystanders. I don't know if you're going to try to kill me again."

He turns to Sam. "But you, I trust. So tell me, what do you think? No bullshit. No hallelujah crap about her. I need to know you still have your own brain."

"I think she won't kill you, but I don't know for sure. I do know that she's scared of Blake and more scared of what he'll do with you."

"Can I trust her?" Fitz says.

"Honestly? I don't know. But I think you can."

Fitz lowers the gun. "Both of you, get in the van." He looks back at the Amandas. "You got a problem with that?"

"I don't know that I can protect you against her if she is that close."

"Yeah, I figured."

"What's with the twins?" Sam says.

"Spirit of the Internet, or something. It's a long story. I'm still a little fuzzy on it myself. Let's get the fuck out of here before Blake shows up and I'll fill you in."

Two Chroniclers, one leg breaker, a god and a couple cyborg Terminator clones who are embodiments of the Internet pile into the van. It sounds like a joke, but Fitz can't figure out the punchline.

Fitz wedges himself into one of the backseats in the van next to Jake. The man is curled up in on himself as much as he possibly can be, but his mutterings have quieted somewhat.

"Where to now?"

"I have a safe house," Driver Amanda says, "but I don't know if we should go there."

"Can any other gods find us there, like the last one?"

"They shouldn't be able to, no, but—" Fitz catches her eyes flicking back to Medeina and Sam.

"I don't think it matters anymore," Fitz says. "And how sure are you about other gods not finding us? Bacchus found the last safe house; what makes you think he won't find the new one?"

"Bacchus is dead," Medeina says, voice flat.

"What?" Fitz says. "Gods can die? How?"

"El Jefe killed him at the museum after you escaped. I do not know how. He stabbed him and Bacchus exploded into light and died." She looks at the Amandas in the front. "Did you not feel it?"

Amanda frowns. "I felt something. That was Bacchus dying?"

"Yes. You are new. You've never felt a god die before?"

"Hang on," Fitz says. "I'm still stuck on *gods can die*. What did he stab him with?"

"His fist? A knife? I'm really not sure. His hand burst into light and punched through Bacchus as if he were paper. Then he dissolved into ash and ichor. The god of wine is no more."

"What the hell is ichor?" Fitz says.

"The golden blood of the gods," Medeina says. "It is the fluid that courses through our veins."

"Huh. Okay. Well, this puts a new spin on things."

Fitz wonders, with this hit-or-miss power to tell gods what to do, to change their realities, if he can kill them. It's never occurred to him that that might be a possibility.

"Gods die. It is rare, but it happens. Sometimes it is prophecy, sometimes it is murder. And sometimes we merely outlive our usefulness."

Fitz catches Sam glancing over at Medeina when she says that. There's something there. He'll have to ask her as soon as he can get her alone.

"Great," he says. "How do I kill one?"

She looks at him as though he's insane, which all things considered is usually a safe bet with Fitz. "Why would you want to kill a god?"

"Hello, Murder Chick who tried to kill me. Self-defense, maybe? Get them off my back? Zaphiel and Blake aren't going to be the only ones looking for me, soon. Hell, there are probably already a bunch of the fuckers in town looking for me now."

"Undoubtedly," Medeina says. She looks wary, and Fitz thinks for a moment she's not going to tell him how to kill gods. He can't blame her, of course. What if he turns that knowledge on her?

She looks at him with blank eyes and it's like he can see the gears working behind them. "Every god dies differently. Some with a sacred artifact, some during Apocalypse. Some are murdered by their children, or their parents, or their siblings."

"They can be killed with symbols," Driver Amanda says from up front.

"How so?"

"Destroy them with who they are," she says. "All gods are the embodiment of something. Defile what they are, use it against them."

"So, if somebody were to kill you they'd, what, burn the Internet down?"

"A virus," Sam says. "I have a laptop that's always getting shit from spam emails. That kind of thing?"

"Possibly," Amanda says. "And for Medeina, it would probably be something to do with her forests."

"Y'all are a bunch of fuckin' idiots," Jake says from his huddle in the corner. "Fuckin', fuckin' idiots."

"You got something to add, old man?"

"I ain't helping you. Any of you. I was laying low. I was safe. Then you have to come along and fuck it all up."

"We came to rescue you, man," Fitz says. "We're the good guys."

"Oh, screw you. Good guys, my ass. You all just want a piece of me." He stabs a gnarled finger at Amanda and Medeina. "Gods wantin' me to sing their fuckin' songs, and then they beat me when I can't. And you." He shoves the finger into Fitz's chest. "You're the goddamn worst of the bunch."

"Hey, man. I'm in the shit here."

"Yeah, you're in the shit and so you drag some poor, busted-down husk like me back into all this. What am I? Bait? Is that it? Gonna lure the gods around with me and then the Big Bad Prophet's gonna come in and, fuck, smite 'em? You got any fuckin' idea what you've gotten yourself into?"

"No," Fitz says. "I don't. That's why we were looking for you. I need to understand what I do and how I do it and you're the closest thing to Obi-fucking-Wan Kenobi I can get my hands on."

Jake laughs, a high-pitched braying like a donkey. "Wow. Seriously? I'm the best you can do? You are so fucked."

"Tell me about it," Fitz says.

"Well, it's about goddamn time," the Man says. "I thought they'd never leave." He stands on the roof of a warehouse a block from the strip bar watching through a pair of binoculars as the van drives away. He turns to Big Money, currently in the form of a short, Pakistani man with a terrible comb-over, Ray-Ban sunglasses and an Armani suit. "Your sister has turned out to be a colossal pain in my ass."

"Well, she learned from you," Big says.

The Man slaps him with the back of his hand, snapping Big's head back and knocking the Ray-Bans off his face. Big slowly turns back to face his father.

"Feel better?" Big asks.

"Not particularly."

"Well, at least now they're all in one place."

"If that dipshit Cherub had done his fucking job, I wouldn't care where they were." He pulls a cellphone out of his coat pocket and dials the angel's number. It rings, but no one answers.

"He may still be incapacitated," Big says.

"From a fucking explosion?" The Man hangs up and shoves the phone back in his pocket.

"Well, think about who did it to him."

"Point," the Man says. "Knowing your sister, she probably had more than C4 in those satchel charges. Find him. And keep track of them. We're going to have a shit show any hour now, once everyone else figures out we've got the only Chronicler worth a damn and descends on this place like locusts. I want to have him secured before that happens."

Big gives him a mock salute, changing into a twelve-year-old boy in a British private school uniform. "Aye-aye, cap'n."

"Keep that shit up and I swear I will find a way to hurt you."

"Talk dirty to me, daddy," Big says. "It turns me on. Being pulled back into your orbit is punishment enough, believe me." He dissolves in a cloud of green smoke that blows away on the wind.

Killing Big would be easy, but hurting him is difficult. He still wants the little shit around—after all, he is the boy's father—or he'd have taken him out already. And having him handle petty administrative crap is useful. Soon, though, he won't need him.

"When I remake this world, I am going to rip you into shreds, you little shit," the Man says. He goes back to watching the van through his binoculars as it speeds away into the night.

CHAPTER EIGHTEEN

THE SAFE HOUSE Amanda takes them to is west of Los Angeles in Thousand Oaks. The Santa Monica Mountains—hills covered in scrub brush and chaparral that catches fire a couple of times a year—block it from the ocean, and the air sits heavy and still. White, upper-middle-class suburbia. Country clubs, BMWs, lots of hidden secrets.

Amanda pulls into the garage of a four-bedroom house on a quiet cul-de-sac and closes the garage door behind them. Fitz wonders if anyone has the slightest clue that this is anything other than normal.

"This place like the last one?" he asks as they exit the van into the garage. Amanda doesn't exactly have a good track record on safe houses.

"Should be safer," Driver Amanda says. "It's new and no one should know about it. I bought it and started getting it prepared after Bacchus hit the last one. If it had been ready in time, I never would have taken you to see Big."

"He's your brother," Fitz says. "Not like you thought he'd betray you." He looks over at Sam. He wonders if she's thinking the same thing about him.

Amanda snorts. "I don't know about that. Sibling rivalries between us are pretty epic. How's that arm feeling? You need to know where the painkillers are?"

She says it without judgment, but Fitz feels a sudden wave of shame anyway. His arm is throbbing from where it was yanked out of its socket, but he doesn't want to get high anymore. Doesn't want to numb things. All they ever do is cover things up, hide the truth from him. Sure, if he hadn't had them he'd probably be a burnout like Jake, pushing a mop in a strip bar bathroom, but he'd still be him, right?

"Nah, I'm good," he says, heading into the living room. Like the previous safe house it's spacious and comfortable, with recliners and a sofa, but still has a bomb shelter vibe to it.

"Well, I'm not," Jake says. "I got a bum hip hurts somethin' fierce. Got any oxy?"

"Down the hall. First door on the left," Amanda says. "Just don't kill yourself."

"Much obliged." He gets to the garage door and turns to Fitz. "You're tryin' to go clean, I get it. But you should know if you're just starting, cold turkey's the wrong way to do it. Especially when you've got all this other shit hanging over your head."

"I'll be fine."

"Sure, sure," he says. "Enjoy the shakes. They're a hoot." He disappears down the hall and Fitz can hear him clumping around in the back of the house.

"That's the other Chronicler? Should we be worried?" Sam says.

"The hell do you think?" Fitz says.

"He's not the only one," Amanda says. "He's just the closest and the sanest."

"How come they aren't going after him, then?" Fitz says. "Or the others?"

"Because he cannot hear us anymore," Medeina says. "Zaphiel looked at him and many others before we chose to pursue you. They are either deaf to our calls or mad beyond repair. You are broken, but you are not beyond use."

"Way to make a fella feel wanted," Fitz says. "So he can't pick up god radio at all?"

"He may be able to," Medeina says, shrugging. "But if he can, it is so faint and distant to him that he might as well be like anyone else. Once, many years ago, he was a Chronicler for the ancient gods of the Americas, those who were here before the Europeans invaded. But they didn't know what to do with him, and he was too weak to help them much."

"So what happened to him?"

"They became more and more desperate," Medeina says. "When they could find no way back to the firmament, they each tried to grow their power here on Earth. They became louder to him, more insistent. They used his meager gifts until there was nothing left of him. And when he was no longer of use, they discarded him."

"Like a broken toy," Fitz says.

"The gods like to break their toys," both Amandas say.

"You would know," Medeina says.

"What does that mean?" one Amanda says. "I'm not a god."

"Oh? Then what are you? You embody a concept, you give shape to an idea. You exist through the power of belief as any of us. If you're not a god yet, you will be soon enough."

They both stare at Medeina. Fitz can't tell what's going on behind those eyes, but he doesn't think it's good. He's about to ask them what's going on, but they turn away as one.

"I have work to do," they say in unison and go down the hall deeper into the house.

"That was creepy," Sam says.

"You don't know the half of it," Fitz says. He turns to Medeina. "You think she's an actual god? Like you?"

"We all start somewhere," Medeina says. "People change, grow, make new stories. It would make sense that new gods would appear."

"Like the Man," Fitz says.

"El Jefe is troubling," she says. "I do not know what to make of him."

"She's his dad," Fitz says.

Medeina's eyes grow wide. "He is a father god?"

"Yeah. Least, it looks like it. Is that bad?"

Her eyes go distant. "I must speak with her about this," she says and follows the Amandas.

For the first time in the last twenty-four hours, Fitz is alone with another human being. He turns to Sam, wanting to relish the fact that she's not a god, not trying to kill him. It's like nothing has changed. But try as he might, he can't hang onto that feeling.

"So what happened?" he says. "What's with Medeina? I still don't trust her. I'm still not sure this is a great idea."

She shrugs. "I don't know if it's a great idea, either. But I don't think she's working for Blake or Zaphiel anymore. I think... I think she's a little lost."

Fitz remembers the look Sam gave her a few minutes ago. "When she said that thing about outliving her usefulness," he says. "That what you're talking about?"

She nods. "Yeah. I mean, it's like she's waking up to the fact that nobody believes in her anymore. I don't know what's going on in her head. Hell, you probably have a better idea of that than I do, but it just seems like she's lost her purpose."

"Jesus," Fitz says. "A god having a mid-life crisis. How the hell do we deal with that?"

"I don't think buying her a Porsche and hooking her up with a cute bartender is gonna work," Sam says.

"I wonder if she's the only one," Fitz says. Probably not. Probably a lot of them are starting to clue in to the fact that a lot of people don't give two fucks about them. What happens when a god doesn't have believers? He doesn't think they're going to fade away; after all, Medeina's been around with nobody believing in her for a thousand years. But belief's part of it. She's said as much herself. Without belief they're nothing.

Maybe when they all got kicked out of their homes, the clock started ticking. Maybe they're running out of time.

"Tell me what happened," Fitz says, hoping there's a clue in what happened to Sam that might make this all make sense.

She tells him about waking up and overhearing Blake's plan

to murder her, the conversation with Medeina when they were sent to find Fitz, and how she passed the knowledge of who she was and why she was looking for Fitz to her. Sam doesn't mince words, doesn't elaborate. Straight data, no bullshit.

"She murdered a lot of people," Fitz says when she's done.

"I know. She's... conflicted."

"You don't say? She's trying to murder me one second and then she's trying to team up with me another. And what about you?"

"I wasn't trying to kill you," she says, looking away. "Well, I was going to. When Blake told me to."

"Well, I'm glad you didn't."

"Probably would have been easier for everybody if I had," she says. She holds up her hand when Fitz starts to protest. "I'm just sayin' that I wouldn't be here, that's for damn sure. Why'd you do it, Fitz? Blake was family. He took care of you."

"Shit, I don't know." Fitz lowers himself into one of the recliners, his shoulder throbbing. Maybe he shouldn't have been so hasty about refusing more painkillers. "I wanted something that was mine, ya know? Yeah, he gave me what I needed. I'm not saying he didn't. But none of it felt like it was my own."

"Christ, Fitz, he paid you, didn't he?"

"Look, I was strung out half the time, all right? Just—I know I screwed up. Does it matter now? Even if I hadn't stolen the money, I'd still be in the shit."

"I know," Sam says. "But I trusted you, man. You didn't just shit on Blake, you shit on me."

"I'm sorry," Fitz says, getting louder. "I'm sorry I broke your trust. I'm sorry I stole from Blake. I'm sorry I got pegged as some fucking prophet and I'm running away from crazy goddesses with spears who like to murder everybody. I'm sorry my only chance to get out of this seems to be the spirit of the Internet and a burnt-out tweaker getting high upstairs. All right? Are we good now?" He's yelling now, gripping the sides of the recliner in bunched fists. "Does that help?"

"Yeah," Sam says. "That helps." She lowers herself into another recliner. "So now what?"

He closes his eyes, takes a deep breath. "I guess I go up and talk to Mister Miyagi up there and get him to give me the wisdom of the ancients or some shit. Maybe I'll get lucky and it'll be a montage."

Something in the back of the house crashes and Sam bolts out of her chair, gun in her hand. She's halfway up the stairs before Fitz even stands up. He draws his own gun, then thinks twice and puts it away. What the hell's the point? You can't kill gods with it.

He follows after Sam as quickly as he can. His shoulder is really throbbing, and after the car crash his back and legs aren't feeling so hot, either.

Like the other safe house, this one has an infirmary, and the problem's obvious as soon as he gets there.

The Amandas have put Jake on a gurney. One of them is holding him down as he thrashes and the other's prepping a stomach pump. Half a dozen empty pill bottles roll around on the floor and Jake's moaning, "Not gonna do it," over and over again.

Fitz has been where Jake is now. He's tried to kill himself plenty of times. When the voices got too bad, when his head filled up too much too fast. Figures the old man's probably tried a time or two himself. Can't say he blames him, but Christ on a crutch it's shitty timing.

Medeina stands in the hallway watching the proceedings, confusion on her face. She turns to Fitz, clearly troubled. "This is common?" she says.

"Can be," he says. "I know you've seen hospitals. You tried to kill me in one."

"Not that. Not the place." She sweeps an arm toward the Amandas trying to keep Jake alive. "That. What they are doing to him."

"He's trying to kill himself," Fitz says. "They're trying to keep him alive. You've seen people die."

She shakes her head. "Not like this. I have seen them die at my blade, or at the teeth of a bear, or struck by the lightning

I have called into the forest. I understand that. But not this."

"You said it yourself. The gods were done with him and they discarded him. That's what people do when they're all used up. You've seriously never seen a suicide before?"

"This kind of death is not my domain."

"Could use another hand in here," one of the Amandas says.

Fitz shoves his way past the goddess to help. "What do you need?"

"Help me get him on his side. If he vomits, he could aspirate and choke to death."

Fitz helps roll Jake onto his left side as the other Amanda starts to feed the tube down into the old man's nose. The old man thrashes on the gurney, but there isn't a lot of fight in him. Fitz has had his stomach pumped enough times to know that it's never pleasant, and he feels sorry for the guy.

"You're gonna be fine," Fitz says.

"Don't wanna," Jake says. "Can't do this again. Just want it to be over. Why won't you just let me die?"

"I need you."

"That's what they said, too."

THREE HOURS LATER and Fitz is exhausted. The Amandas did most of the work, but he stayed with the old man throughout the whole ordeal. It doesn't matter how many times you've had it done, you never get used to it. Jake was unconscious for most of it—probably didn't even know he was there—but Fitz didn't want to leave him.

He's going to ask him to relive the most painful parts of his life for him, the least he can do is help watch over him.

"How soon's he going to wake up?" he says. He's stretched out in one of the chairs in the living room.

This Amanda shrugs. The other one is back in the infirmary taking care of Jake. "He's in pretty bad shape. We're running some tests now, but I can already tell you just by looking at him that he's dehydrated, kidney function's shot, and we're lucky he hasn't had a heart attack."

"So not any time soon," he says.

"Not if we want him to live very long."

"Do we?" Medeina says. "He is only useful insofar as he can train the Chronicler. Beyond that, what good is he?"

"Ya know, for a second back there you almost seemed vaguely human," Fitz says.

"She's right," Amanda says.

"Aaaand there goes the other one." He turns to Sam. "How about you? You want to get in on the psycho god action we got going over here?"

"They do kind of a have a point," she says. "Sorry."

"The fuck is wrong with you people?"

"Hear me out," Amanda says. "We have him here to show you how to use your power. But you have already tapped into it. You just need to understand it more, so that it comes when you call it."

"So, what, that means he's disposable? No. In fact, *fuck,* no."

"I don't think you need him as much as you think you do," Amanda says.

"He wants to die, Fitz," Sam says. "When you get what you need from him, I think you need to let him."

Fitz closes his eyes and rubs at his face, feeling the stubble scratch against his palm. He's barely slept, he hasn't shaved. His clothes smell like gasoline and smoke. His arm is throbbing and should be in a sling, and all the cuts and bruises he got in the crash sting and ache. This is all too much.

"Not tonight," he says. "Keep him alive tonight. When he's awake, I'll talk to him. Figure out what he wants to do."

"And if he wants to die?" Amanda says.

"We'll burn that bridge when we get to it."

CHAPTER NINETEEN

HE TELLS HIMSELF he doesn't want to do this. That he's just doing it to take the edge off. Get some sleep. But the truth is that he does want it. He's been telling himself it's a bad idea, that he needs to keep his head clear, but Jake was right. Cold turkey's no way to go.

Fitz crushes six Ativan, three oxys and snorts them off the kitchen counter. If he needed to be awake, he'd toss some Adderall into the mix for a nice, low-grade speedball. But he needs sleep, and at this point he doesn't really care if the gods come for him as long as they let him get some fucking shut-eye.

He crashes in one of the bedrooms, out almost as soon as his head hits the pillow.

The nightmares start almost as quickly.

A wash of dread hits him, overwhelms his mind. Terrifying but completely normal, with that peculiar sort of dream logic where everything makes sense. He runs across a desert of black sand, the sun dim and far away. Boats on fire row upside down above him in a hideous purple sky as statues of Greek and Roman gods erupt from the ground at his feet.

The panic is so overwhelming that it takes a while for Fitz to realize this is a dream. He's had panic dreams before, but not like this. They're always some nameless dread, voices that he now knows are the gods whispering nonsensical things to him.

He runs toward a rise in the distance, a black dune with grains that glint in the dim sun like diamonds. In a flash he's there, crawling to the top on hands and feet, looking out over the dark sands.

His breathing is labored, shallow, the fear tightening on his chest like a snake. From his view point on the dune, he can see the landscape filling up with statues, ziggurats, immense temples made of marble, ice, or fire. He tries to center himself, clear his head enough to make sense of everything. He knows this is a dream, but the knowledge slips away from him like hot butter on a frying pan.

A whirlwind of sand appears in front of him, and in the blink of an eye it is a blue-skinned giant of a woman with eight arms, each holding a different weapon. She wears an elaborate crown, a necklace of skulls, a belt of severed heads and hands.

"You will sing my songs," she screams and Fitz is overwhelmed by Kali's presence, her stories filling his mind. All of her different selves crash against each other: Mahakali, Daksinakali, and Smashan Kali. Mother, destroyer, entropy in all its forms.

The jackal-headed god Anubis appears behind Fitz and scoops him up in a giant hand, black sand falling through its fingers. Fitz's head fills with his history, so fast it feels it might explode from all the information. "No," he bellows. "It is my tales you will tell."

"It is my glory you will bring," Freya says, batting Fitz out of his hand, throwing him at the feet of Baldur, who leans down and shrieks, "I will have you, Chronicler."

Fitz tries to run, but every step he takes is met with another angry god. Samantabhadra, Chernobog, Ereshkigal, Manabozho, Maui, Lempo, Guan-Yu, hundreds, thousands more. And with each one, Fitz knows their stories, feels their anger, hears their demands. Each voice hammers on the inside of his skull. All he can do is scream and scream at the violation, all of them ramming their lives into his mind.

Donar shoves Menrva, knocking Fitz clear of her grasp. Menrva swings a haymaker but misses and connects with Ao-Chin, flattening his nose, spraying golden ichor from his face and knocking him into Baron Samedi, who stabs Ao-Chin through the chest with a silver-handled cane. Perun kicks the Morrigan, seemingly just because he can.

Soon all of the gods are punching and kicking each other. Swinging swords, stabbing with knives, sending a menagerie of animals at each other. Fitz crawls through flailing legs, kicking feet, trying desperately not to die among the giants beating at each other in the epic slap fight.

A hand—a normal-sized hand, Fitz is relieved to see—reaches down and hauls him to his feet, yanking him through the battling gods. At first he's thankful; and then he sees who it is.

"Well, that's no way to treat a friend," the Man says when Fitz shoves him away. He brushes black sand from his gray suit, puffs on a cigar and taps ash onto the ground. They've shifted far from the battle, traveling dream distances in the blink of an eye that would take hours in real life.

"I know what you are," Fitz says. "Get the fuck away from me." He has a pounding headache. The stories of all those gods are bouncing around in his mind as if fighting for dominance there.

"Fitz, please," the Man says. "I'm trying to help you."

"You're trying to fucking use me, just like the rest of them. You were going to kill Sam."

"What? No!" the Man says. "Dear lord, where did you hear that nonsense? Oh. You've been talking to Medeina."

"And Sam. She overheard you planning her murder."

"Oh, Fitz, you can't listen to Medeina. She'll stab you in the back. She tried to kill you, remember?"

"Yeah? And what'd you do to Blake? You fucking killed him and took his body or some shit."

The Man shakes his head. "I'm just as much Blake as I've

ever been," he says. "In fact I'm better than I was. I'm a god now, Fitz. I'm not just some shlubby old drug-pusher looking backward at his best days. I'm *somebody*. And I could really use you right now."

The Man points at the gods in the distance, and Fitz thinks they look like something between a Benny Hill routine and a Japanese monster movie. They don't seem to have noticed that Fitz is gone.

"See them?" the Man says. "They'll eat you alive. Every last one of them. They're so stuck in their own little worlds they can't see a bigger picture. It's every god for himself over there."

"Yeah? And how are you any different?"

"Fitz, if any one of them gets any more power they'll destroy the world. Can you imagine if that Cherub, oh, what is his name—?"

"Zaphiel," Fitz says.

"Zaphiel. Can you imagine if he gets you to do what he wants? What about Medeina? Or those monstrosities. You know what they are, you've read their histories, absorbed their stories. Are any of them good enough for humanity?"

"No," Fitz says. He's still trying to sort through the flood of stories still bursting through his mind, but that much is clear. Every single one of them is a monster.

"People's faith is a paltry thing, compared to the kind of belief you can trigger in the world. You're a godmaker, Fitz. Even the most widely believed-in of those petty tyrants over there is nothing compared with the one you grant your favor to. Imagine the good we could do together."

"You'd take over the world," Fitz says. "That's what you want, isn't it?" He may not know the Man's plans, but he's got a pretty good idea of what he's looking to do. "Those guys? They just want to be back on top. Respected, feared. They just want to be relevant. But you... you've got plans, don't you?"

The Man smiles and it looks just a little too wide, a little too feral. "Oh, indeed I do, Fitz. And I know that sometime soon, you and I are going to reach an agreement. We're going to come together and make this world work."

"You sound pretty fucking sure of yourself."

"Oh, I am. The time of the old gods is ending. It's time for new myths to take over. You'll help me. I guarantee it."

Fitz is trying to think of something witty to say, some clever retort he can throw into the face of a god. But before he can open his mouth, a shooting pain bursts through his face, taking him to the ground.

"The fuck are you doing to me?" Fitz says, the pain blinding him.

"Wasn't me, Fitz," the Man says. He looks around, peers into the distance. "Oh. That. Well, I had hoped to have a little more time with you, son. We'll pick this up again later."

Another stinging blow strikes Fitz's face, making him scream. He tries to crawl away from the Man, but doesn't get more than a few feet before another blow makes his ears ring.

The landscape shudders, fracturing between earth and sky, the sand falling away into huge pits that swallow up the ziggurats, the statues, the gods themselves. They finally seem to notice their prize is missing and begin heading toward him, their demands of him growing ever louder in his mind.

Another shock of pain in his face and the gods running toward him fracture like the sky and the earth do, exploding into shards, blown away on dream winds.

Whatever the hell is happening, Fitz can't take it anymore. He's always had bad dreams, those god voices always whispering in the background, but they were just dreams. This, though; this is beyond nightmare.

One final burst of pain in his face and everything explodes around him and—

He comes to on the bed with Jake slapping the ever loving fuck out of him. Fitz throws his arms up groggily to stop the blows, barely blocking the old man.

"Jesus, cut it the fuck out."

"Oh. Shit. You're awake?"

"Yes, I'm fucking awake." He feels warmth on his face and neck. Puts his hands to his nose and ear. They come away with blood. "Goddammit, am I bleeding?"

"Yeah, that started a while ago. Amanda was trying to wake ya up, but it wasn't working." Jake gives Fitz one more big slap.

"Ow. The fuck was that for?"

"I don't like ya."

"You were crying out in your sleep," Amanda says. "You looked like you were having a seizure." She and Sam stand behind Jake, Amanda's face placid, Sam's frowning in worry.

"And that's when you started bleeding all over the place," Jake says. "Wouldn't be surprised if you pooped yourself, too."

From the way Jake looks and smells, he's probably had some recent experience with that. "Why aren't you down getting your stomach pumped?"

Jake's face twists into a grimace. "Came to with that fucking tube down my nose when the fun in here started and puked it all up."

"How long was I out?" The dream seemed to last only minutes... and days.

"A few hours," Sam says.

"I been slappin' your fool face for twenty minutes," Jake says. He rubs the side of his head. "I got a bit of that dream imagery you were getting before I came to downstairs. Black desert? Lots of freakin' out? Saw a bunch of giants pop up out of the dirt. Didn't like the look of 'em. Goddamn, what a headache."

"They're coming," Fitz says. "Hell, I think they're already here."

"Who's coming?" Sam says.

"The other gods," Amanda says.

"All of them," Fitz says. "Or at least most of them? I saw hundreds. Maybe thousands. Christ, how many gods are out there, anyway?"

"I have a list of seven-thousand-one-hundred-eighty-three," Amanda says. "It grows daily."

Fitz goggles at the number.

"You on that list, missy?" Jake says, tapping the side of his head. "'Cause I'm pretty sure I'm picking up some leakage on god radio in here."

"I thought you were a burnout," Sam says.

"The lady here tell ya that? Yeah, well, I was. Until about two days ago. Still can't pick up much. Clearly not like you can. Started seeing shit I haven't seen in years. Then you showed up."

"I need help," Fitz says. "You saw some of them, right? Then you know what I'm dealing with. If I side with any of them, what the hell are the rest going to do to me? I feel like an Elmo doll at a Wal-Mart Christmas sale."

"Kill yourself," Jake says. "Stick a gun in your mouth and eat a bullet."

"Fuck you."

"Hey, you want 'em to leave you alone, that'll do the trick. It's that or let 'em use you up until you're just some burnt-out husk screaming in the corner."

"There's got to be another way," Fitz says.

Jake looks at Amanda, then back to Fitz. "Where's the other one? The chick with the horn crown?"

"Medeina is downstairs," Amanda says. "She doesn't sleep, but I believe she may meditate. She's been in one of the bedrooms for the last few hours."

"Huh. Okay," Jake says, pauses.

"You got something to say?" Fitz says.

"How much do you trust this one here?" Jake nods toward Amanda.

"Whatever you can tell me you can tell her," Fitz says.

Jake laughs. "Yeah, I don't know about that, but whatever. All right, fine. Yeah, I got something to say. You seen like these red threads going from you to them?"

"Yeah," Fitz says, surprised. "Around a god of money and an angel."

"And you tugged on one of 'em and kinda nudged him around a little?"

"I threw one of them across a hotel lobby and changed the cards in the other one's hand."

Jake stares at Fitz, shock plain on his face. "Holy shit," he says. "No wonder they want you. 'Course, if they really understood how this works, they'd probably rather kill you. See, they got this shit backwards. They all think you tell their stories and make people believe. But it's really that you tell stories the people believe and they act them out."

Fitz says nothing for a long time as he digests this information. If this is true, then this could be even worse than he thought.

"They're gonna kill me," he says.

"Yeah, probably. This one probably won't. But that Medeina chick? I don't think she's the type to like having her strings yanked like a puppet. You try it on either of them?"

"No," Fitz says. "It's only ever happened with Zaphiel and Big. Those are the only ones where I've seen those red threads. How do I control it? Can I control it?"

"You really want to do this? I can do fuck-all myself, so they don't much care about me, but you? Man, they're gonna fuckin' eat you alive. I'm telling you, sucking down a shotgun shell's a mercy compared to what they're gonna do to ya."

He's thought about it. Hell, he's tried it before. Too many pills, too much booze. And with all the fucking around, it's a wonder he isn't dead or walking around with hep-C.

But things are different now. He might hide in a bottle or a handful of pills when shit got rough, but that was when he just thought he was crazy.

But this is a whole new ballgame. Before, he was just some waste of space with a drug problem and screaming fits. Now he's something important.

"I'm not gonna kill myself," Fitz says.

"Right, then. This is where we start getting into some Karate Kid wax on, wax off shit here, son. You need some practice. Need to know how to work your mojo. And I'm bettin' we don't have a whole lotta time to do it in. So it's gonna be crash course time."

"Where do we start?"

"I'm thinkin' we jump ahead to how to kill one of those fuckers."

CHAPTER TWENTY

"I DO NOT like this," Medeina says, standing at the end of the hallway, tense and frowning.

Sam put the kibosh on the whole 'killing a god' thing, saying that the only gods they'd have to test it on were Medeina or Amanda and she wasn't going to let that happen with either one of them. Fitz thought about arguing with her, but he knew that any fight he got into with her would end badly for him.

So they decided Jake would show him how to get those marionette strings to appear so he could pull on them. That was the key to everything. He'd have to have a strong connection to a god if he hoped to do anything to them.

They went back and forth for a good long while about whether to tell Medeina about what a Chronicler could really do. Amanda stayed out of it, standing on the sidelines and letting the humans argue amongst themselves. When Jake suggested trying it on her, she made it clear that wasn't going to happen.

"I just want to see if I can see these things," Fitz says.

"If I have the faintest hint that you're going to try to make me do something, anything, I will end you," Medeina says. Fitz has a flash of the bodies in the hospital, the severed heads, the gutted corpses. He wonders what in the hell he is even doing in the same room with her.

"I believe you," Fitz says. He looks back at Sam. "If she kills me, it's on you."

"She won't kill you," Sam says. "Because you're not going to do anything to make her kill you."

The trick, Jake told him, is to see the threads connecting him to the gods when he wants. He was able to see them with Zaphiel and Big, but now he has to see if he can see them reliably.

It took some convincing to get Medeina to agree; in the end, Sam talked with her alone. Fitz has no idea what she said to her, but when they came out she agreed to be his subject.

"Yeah, whatever," Fitz says. "All right, what do I do?"

"Well, this part's a little complicated," Jake says. "See, I got to the point where I could just barely see them, but that was after months of developing the skill. You don't have months. So this is the crash course. First we're gonna see if you can see them now."

Fitz squints. Nothing changes. "Nope."

"Yeah, I figured," he said. "So what we have to do next is recreate the circumstances where it happened before."

"Uh, I think Zaphiel was trying to kill me," Fitz says.

"Big wasn't," Amanda says.

"No, but I'd just agreed to be his boy toy if I lost that bet."

"So you were a little stressed," Sam says.

"When am I not stressed?"

"Look, I got this," Jake says. "Uh, goddess—uh, Medeina, however the hell you call yourself—there's something you could do that might help."

Medeina glares at him, and for a second Fitz thinks he's going to burst into flame. "What?"

"Try to kill him."

"Whoa," Fitz says. "The fuck?"

"Gladly," Medeina says, her spear suddenly appearing in her hand. She raises it, pulls back her arm to throw it.

Fitz's vision narrows, goes dark around the edges like he's about to black out. All around Medeina he sees a faint red glow that quickly clarifies into a million fine threads that shoot out from her toward him.

She throws the spear.

Fitz can hear Sam yelling, Jake jumping out of the way. He knows he should move, should be screaming and diving for cover, but he's rooted to the spot. A strange calm settles over him as he watches the spear spiral closer and closer to him. He watches the red threads shoot off the spear in all directions. He reaches out with his thoughts for a handful of them, feels a pressure somewhere in the distant recesses of his mind as he grabs hold.

Though he isn't touching it, he has the sense of its weight, its heft. Its speed and trajectory. He knows where it will go, what it can do. He knows its history and all those who have fallen by it. He wraps his mind tight around those crimson threads.

"Go away," he says and the spear blinks out of existence.

He doesn't know where it's gone, or how. If it's temporary or permanent. He just knows he made it go away. And that's enough for him. It beats having it punch through his skull.

The glowing threads surrounding Medeina disappear, his vision goes back to normal. He's done it. He's twisted a god's influence, just like he did at the hotel and at Big's casino. It was easier this time.

Then he throws up and passes out in his own vomit.

THE MOMENT THE spear disappears Sam can tell it's going to get bad. Medeina's face twists into pure hatred. She takes a step forward, her spear materializing back into her hand from wherever Fitz sent it.

Sam jumps past Fitz as he pitches forward into the pool of his own sick and squares off against Medeina. Bottom line, she knows she has no chance of stopping the goddess, but she can't let her slaughter Fitz.

"Step aside," Medeina says. "I will not brook this insult."

"Don't kill him," Sam says, trying to think of some way to keep her from murdering him. "You tried to kill him before because of the way Zaphiel was treating you. You were a pawn to him, like you were a pawn to El Jefe. Zaphiel and El Jefe want to use him the way they used you. They want to take his choice away, like they tried to take yours away."

"Killing him will be a mercy," Medeina says.

Sam sweats, her hands clenched into fists to keep them from shaking. She knows that one wrong word could mean her death *and* Fitz's.

"Killing him will make you just like them. All they do is take. Is that who you are? Someone who does nothing but take?"

Is she getting through to her? Is she making any kind of impression? Sam can't tell, but she isn't dead yet, so she's counting it as a win.

"Please," she says.

It's clear Medeina's conflicted, but Sam has no way to tell what that conflict is. She has a glimpse into the goddess's mind, but she's not so naïve as to think she really knows her. For all the intimacy of their shared knowledge earlier, the goddess is still very much a black box to her.

"I need to leave," Medeina says. She looks at Amanda. "Open your door. I came freely and I will leave the same way." Amanda nods from where she has bent to help Fitz, and there's a loud click from the front door. Medeina crosses to the door in a few wide steps, Sam close on her heels.

"Where are you going?" she says.

"I must think on your words," Medeina says. "They are... troubling."

Sam reaches out, touches Medeina's shoulder. "Take me with you. I know this isn't easy. Maybe I can help you."

Medeina looks at Sam's hand on her shoulder. For a moment, Sam thinks the goddess is going to cut it off at the wrist, but she keeps it there, anyway.

"I do not know where I am going," Medeina says. "I have no home to return to."

"I know."

"Then come if you wish," Medeina says, and leaves.

"How's Fitz?" Sam says to Amanda.

"He's not gonna feel very good when he wakes up," Amanda says, "but other than that, I think he'll be okay."

"Tell him what just happened," Sam says. "And I'll try to get hold of him as soon as I can."

"Are you sure you want to go?" Amanda says. "You do know she's killed a lot of people."

"So have I," Sam says, and she follows Medeina out the door.

The door closes behind her with a series of clicks as the bolts secure into place, locking her out. She's worried the goddess has already left, but she finds her standing on the sidewalk looking up into the night sky.

She wonders how different the sky looked to her when she was young, a thousand, two thousand years ago. Sam knows Medeina's sense of time is different from her own, making sorting through her memories of the goddess's life difficult. For her there is Today, Yesterday and A Long Time Ago. What do the gods need time for, anyway?

"I need to go somewhere quiet," Medeina says. "Somewhere I can see more stars, somewhere with trees. This place is called Thousand Oaks, but there is nothing but scraggly brush and a handful of dying trees. This place is brown and dry. I need somewhere where I can feel the Earth breathe."

"From this side, sure it's dead. But the Santa Monica Mountains are pretty much the greenest places you're gonna find out here," Sam says, nodding toward the dark silhouette in the distance between them and the ocean. She's suddenly doubting coming out here. Was this a bad idea? What the hell is she doing?

"In my homeland, the mountains are not so high," Medeina says. "But in the firmament there were mountains that would shame any here on Earth. I had forests filled with trees and game. I do not understand what happened."

The sadness in Medeina's voice is overwhelming, and Sam

takes her hand. "I know someplace greener," she says. "Come on. I'll show it to you."

She remembers she doesn't have a car. The Triumph is back at the strip bar where they met up with Fitz. She wouldn't trust that car, anyway; Blake probably had it bugged, or something.

Easy enough to solve. The street is full of newer model cars, Mercedes and Lexus mostly. But there's an older Corolla a couple of houses down. Before she got into MMA and started fighting professionally, Sam had stolen cars, done some B&E. Did a couple of months in juvie for it when she was a kid, and after she started working for Blake he'd sometimes have her jack a car of somebody who owed him money.

She looks around, then pulls off her jacket and presses it against the car's driver's side window. With a quick punch, the glass shatters, setting off the alarm. Some skills don't fade; she reaches under the dashboard to the alarm unit, and after a moment of finding the right wires, pops it out from under the dash with a quick yank, shutting it up.

Hotwiring the Corolla is even easier. She starts the car, brushes the glass out of the driver's seat and gets Medeina in the car with her. They're on the road in less than two minutes.

"Where are we going?" Medeina says.

"Up Pacific Coast Highway. Solstice Canyon. You're right that there's no forests like you're talking about around here, but there are places that are away from the lights and the noise. It's on the other side of the Santa Monica Mountains. Next to the coast. You can see the stars better."

Sam drives them over the mountains to PCH and heads west along the coast, a thin crescent moon high in the sky and casting a reflection in the dark water. Cold air rushes in through the broken window, blowing through Sam's hair, and for a little while at least she feels like none of the past couple of days has actually happened.

Medeina's just some girl she's met. This is just a late night drive up the coast. Maybe they'll find a spot near the beach and lay out a blanket and drink wine until the sun peeks up over the mountains.

And just as quickly the thought goes away. Where the hell had that even come from? Sam's been with other women before, but Medeina isn't a woman. She's an idea given form, a deadly concept in the throes of an identity crisis.

"Are you... all right?" Medeina says. She asks it as though the words are foreign, and maybe they are, or maybe just the idea is foreign. Asking someone else—a human, no less—how they are doing. Has she ever done that before, Sam wonders? Has she ever needed to?

"Huh? Yeah. I'm good," Sam says. She pulls off the road at the entrance to Solstice Canyon. A large barred gate blocks the road, but that's not going to get in their way.

She stops the car and gets out. "This close to the road, the site's mostly parking lots and picnic tables," Sam says, "but there's a trail that loops deeper into the canyon." She climbs over the gate and stops when she realizes that Medeina isn't following her.

"This is better," Medeina says. "I have been in cities too long. People have forgotten how to look at the stars."

Sam follows her gaze to the sky and has to agree with her. Though the night sky is a dark blue, never really black this close to Los Angeles, it's much darker than it is further inland. When Sam was a kid, someone tried to teach her the constellations, but they never stuck. She could never figure out how somebody was supposed to see a bear out of what was clearly a pot.

"Run with me," Medeina says. "I have been surrounded by steel and concrete for too long. I want to feel the dirt between my toes, the thrill of the hunt."

"I don't understand."

Medeina reaches for Sam and stops just short of her cheek, uncertainty plain on her face. Sam wonders if uncertainty is a new feeling for her. "Do you trust me?" Medeina says.

"Yes," Sam says. It isn't until the word is out of her mouth that she questions it. Does she? Or is this trust something Medeina has done to her? It takes her only a moment to decide she doesn't care.

"Thank you," Medeina says and touches her cheek.

Sam's senses blossom into a vibrant burst of smells and sounds, the world around her exploding into life she hadn't realized was there. She's suddenly lower to the ground, down on all fours, confused but feeling glorious.

The scents flowing through her are more powerful than anything she's ever experienced. She knows where the mice are in the grass, the birds in the trees. There are rabbits in the undergrowth, at least three—no, four. She can sense the movements of the insects on the trees, leaves fluttering in the wind.

It isn't until she sees the massive wolf next to her where Medeina stood just moments ago that she realizes what the goddess has done. She wasn't prepared for this, had no idea that this was even possible. Panic engulfs her for a moment, but then Medeina nuzzles her cheek with her own and a deep calm settles into her.

Medeina makes a sound that Sam's human brain can't understand but her wolf mind figures out just fine. *RUN,* she says. *HUNT. PLAY.* Medeina bolts away from Sam, deeper into the canyon trail, and Sam, overcome with newfound joy, chases after her to share it with her.

Sam runs, her long legs tearing through the soft dirt along the trail, sand between her toes. The night is alive with smells and sounds as she follows Medeina across a dry streambed, through a copse of oak and sycamore.

Medeina freezes, a giant gray and black wolf, and Sam almost slams into her. She smells it a moment later. Something wild and feral, with a biting musk. She can't place it at first, and then remembers an old boyfriend's cat who pissed on everything she owned. It's like that, only cranked to eleven.

She hears the mountain lion a second later, its wide paws gently shifting in the dirt as it tries to move. Whether for escape or to stalk them, Sam can't tell. But between the scent and the sound, she knows exactly where it is.

Medeina leaps forward into the brush, hitting the mountain lion head on. The beast lets loose a guttural, grinding sound that's less roar and more scream. Medeina gets its hindquarters in her powerful jaws and now Sam can smell blood, too.

Overcome by the scents, the screams of the wounded lion, the sheer thrill of the hunt, Sam springs into the fray, knocking the mountain lion's face aside as it snaps at her, bringing her head up under its jaws, avoiding its teeth. She clamps her jaws around the lion's throat and tears, ripping through muscle and fur, tasting blood, hot and coppery as it sluices into her mouth.

She loses herself in the kill. She is the lion and the blood and trees and the wind. She is the watching animals and the dirt beneath her toes. She is the hunter and the hunted. She feels the tearing of her teeth in the mountain lion's side, its pain is her pain.

And she is the goddess as the goddess is her.

She and Medeina tear into the mountain lion's body until its thrashing becomes nothing more than a quiver and it finally falls limp between them. Time disappears for her as the two of them rip into the lion, feasting on its corpse.

Afterward, when there is nothing left but a gutted body and gnawed bones, the sensations of hunting and killing the mountain lion still sing inside her. She has never felt anything so visceral. Not her most vicious fights in the ring, not fucking.

She doesn't want this feeling to end, wants to stay a wolf forever, wants to hunt with Medeina and kill at her side until the stars burn out and the sky goes dark.

She curls up against Medeina's flank, the two of them sated, covered in blood, spent, and falls asleep.

CHAPTER TWENTY-ONE

"Oh, my god," Fitz says, picking himself up off the floor. "I feel like I've been shit through an elephant." His vision blurs and a wave of nausea washes over him as he tries to stand. He slips back to the floor, missing his own pool of vomit by scant inches.

"You look it," Jake says, helping him up.

"How long was I out?"

"Long enough for crazy spear lady to bail with your girlfriend," Jake says.

"What?"

"Medeina was gonna kill you and Sam stopped her," Amanda says. "Then they left. I don't know where they went." She hands Fitz a towel and a glass of water.

"You don't know?"

"I know where they were headed," she says. "They stole a car down the street and headed over to the coast. I lost track of them once they got into the canyons. I'm still retasking a satellite."

"You scare me more and more every hour," Fitz says.

"It's a talent."

"What was that business about asking for you to unlock the door?" Jake says. "Like she was asking permission."

"She was. I've got wards and sigils all over this house to protect against the supernatural. I let her in; she couldn't leave unless I unlocked the door for her."

"Good to know," Fitz says, stifling a burp. He wipes his face and sips at the water. His stomach starts to roil again. "So what now?

"Well, that was a good start," Jake says.

"I yakked all over the floor and passed out. How is that a good start?"

"For starters, you're not dead."

Fitz has to agree that that's a net positive.

"Also, you were able to do it fast," Amanda says. "And this wasn't just pushing an angel out of the way or changing a hand of cards. Medeina might be small fry, but she's still a full-fledged god. That spear isn't just for show. It's part of her. And you made it disappear."

"She made it reappear right away, though," Jake says.

"Which I'd expect, unless you killed her outright," Amanda says.

"And that brings us back to your original question," Jake says. He helps Fitz stand up. "You want these fuckers to respect you, you gotta show 'em what you can do."

"And that means killing one of them? Medeina? I think that might piss Sam off."

"Dude, you need to look at the bigger picture here," Jake says. "Your girlfriend is the least of your worries."

"She's not—Look, I don't know you," Fitz says. He turns to Amanda. "And you're not even fucking human. Sam's my friend. And, yeah, things are weird all around, but I trust her and—I'm not killing Medeina."

"How many people did she kill in the hospital?" Amanda says.

Too many. One would be too many, but she pushed past that point into fucking insane with all the corpses. By rights he should want her dead. She tried to kill him. But Sam trusts her, and right now the only person he trusts is Sam.

"Not her," Fitz says. "I'm not saying you're wrong. Just— not her. Not yet."

"Well, that's good, then," Jake says, "because we were thinking somebody else."

"Not the Man," Fitz says. The idea of going up against him makes his blood run cold. He's fine with making that fucker pay, but he can't imagine what he could even do to him.

"No," Amanda says. "Much as I'd like to see it, I don't think you can take him."

"I suggested Internet, here," Jake says, "but she wasn't going for it."

"Well, yeah," Fitz says. "I can't even—" He stops, a thought that's been nagging at him coming to the fore. "How come I haven't seen these threads around you? These are showing up when I'm stressed and I've been pretty much freaking out the entire time I've been around you. What's different?"

"I think it might be because I'm not entirely here," Amanda says. "This body's a vessel with a piece of my consciousness in it. Might as well try to make me do something by yelling at a cell phone."

"Fascinating, I'm sure," Jake says. "Point is, she's as close to being on your side as anybody, so I tend to agree with her."

"We were thinking Big," Amanda says.

"Yeah," Jake says. "Internet here tells me he's some kind of money god? I hear you screwed with him before."

"And he sold us out to his dad, yeah," Fitz says. "I can get behind that. How do I do it?"

"We have no idea," Jake says. "But then you're the one with the mojo."

"Can we at least find him?" Fitz says. "At his casino?"

"Unlikely," Amanda says. "I've put out some feelers for him, but so far he's dropped off the grid."

"How long do you think it'll take to find him?"

"Long enough for you to take a shower," she says. "You reek."

* * *

SAM WAKES UP curled up against Medeina, an ocean breeze cooling the sweat from her skin, drying the blood from the mountain lion. Naked and human again, the only thing on her Blake's key around her neck, Sam presses herself against the goddess' body as Medeina lazily strokes her hair.

"That was incredible," Sam says.

"Thank you for sharing it with me," Medeina says. "I have not had a lover in a very long time. I was... nervous."

Sam pauses. "Is that what we did?" She's never felt like that before, never had any experience so indelibly raw.

"Humans are too complicated," Medeina says. "I know what you felt, just like you know what I felt. We shared in the kill. There is no stronger bond than that."

"I've never had an experience like that before," Sam says.

"You've never killed with another?"

"No," Sam says. "Always on my own and, well, it's typically frowned on, so it doesn't make for a good group activity."

"As I said, humans are too complicated."

They say nothing for a long time, just enjoying the night. Sam's senses as a wolf are gone, but the memories linger. She thinks she can just barely sense other animals in the brush, count the birds in the trees, but she knows it's wishful thinking.

Medeina toys with the Triumph key hanging between Sam's breasts. "What is this?"

"Oh, the key to the car we left in." Sam suddenly feels very possessive of it. "I like it. It's... pretty." Sam frowns. That's not a word she'd usually use for something like a car key.

"It is," Medeina says. "Wood and leaves under... glass?"

"I think it's plastic," Sam says. She tugs the key from Medeina's hand. A little too forcefully. "What now?"

"We could hunt again," Medeina says. "There is smaller game, though not nearly as satisfying."

"That's not what I meant."

"Ah. Yes. Complicated." Medeina sighs. "I know there are things I need to decide. About the Chronicler, about my part in this drama. I was a pawn for Zaphiel and then a pawn for El Jefe. I have been a pawn for a very long time."

"But you're not a pawn," Sam says. "You're a goddess."

"I am a very small goddess. And no one believes in me anymore. There are no songs to my name, no stories of my exploits. My people shifted their loyalties to other gods. I think perhaps the time of gods is over."

"But there are others still out there," Sam says. "Only a few hours ago this whole thing sounded crazy to me, but I know what I've seen, what you've shown me."

"Thank you," Medeina says, "but that very thing is the problem. You don't believe because you believe. You believe because I showed you. That is this modern world's curse. It demands proof. It insists on cold numbers. The power of humanity's belief is not enough to sustain the old gods. You believe in new gods, like El Jefe or that scattered entity harboring the Chronicler. You believe in devils more than you believe in gods."

"But can't Fitz help you? I don't completely understand what he is or what he can do, but can't he tell your stories and make people believe? Isn't that what he's supposed to be able to do?"

"I don't know," Medeina says. "I know that he has great power, but I don't understand what that power is or how he wields it. I don't know that Zaphiel or El Jefe fully understand it, either. I suspect it is not quite what they are expecting. Besides"—Medeina strokes Sam's cheek with a finger—"I did try to kill him."

"He believed me when I showed up with you. He knows he can trust you." But can he? Sam has to admit that being hunted, seeing those corpses in the hospital, almost being killed back at the safe house, well, it's likely to leave Fitz a little put off.

"I don't know that I want him to," Medeina says. "I cannot shake the feeling that even as I step away from El Jefe's game, I am still a piece in play. If I stay, do I play out some unseen strategy of his? I think the best thing for me is to leave."

"Where will you go?"

"Away," Medeina says. There's a finality in that word that makes Sam's blood run cold.

"You're talking about dying," Sam says.

"I am already dead," Medeina says. "The last time I had even one believer was over a thousand years ago. I am a footnote in history. They say the gods are arrogant, and that's true, but sometimes we learn when it's time to give up and step aside."

Sam is suddenly gripped with an uncontrollable panic. "No," she says. "You don't get to do that. That's not you. You're, fuck, Xena or something. You don't run. You don't hide."

"In the form of a hare, I do both very well," Medeina says.

"And then you come back later to fight. You're afraid you're a pawn in somebody else's game? Then turn it the fuck around. Play your own game. You're a fucking goddess." Sam is shaking, her hands balled into fists. "You do not get to give up. Not after what you just shared with me. You don't give that to a person and then turn around and throw it away. You say we believe in devils now more than gods? *Make* us believe. Help Fitz. Help him figure out what he needs to do, who he needs to be. Be a part of that."

Medeina says nothing, just looks into Sam's eyes with the inscrutability of a statue. "We are broken gods, Sam," Medeina says. "All of us. We've been turned out of our homes, our purposes and identities shattered. We are not what we thought we were. Every god and goddess, every myth and hero will be hunting Fitz down. They will try to make him do their bidding, just as some of them did to Jake Malmon. I know that Fitz is stronger by far than any other Chronicler has ever been, but I do not know that he is strong enough to withstand that onslaught."

"That's why he needs your help. I know Fitz. If he doesn't want to do something, he won't fucking do it. Let them come. He won't help them. But be his friend, help protect him, and he'll do the same for you."

"You believe so? Even after the things I've done to hunt him down? He's witnessed innocents I killed in anger. He knows what I am capable of, what I have done. And not just in the hospital; throughout my entire existence. He knows my stories. After all that, you think he will help me if I help him?"

"Yes," Sam says, hoping she's right. Medeina looks at her for a long time, saying nothing, then gives a short, sharp nod.

"All right," she says. "I will help him. And I will"—she pauses, her face twisting on the word as though tasting something for the first time and not sure if she likes it—"*ask* him for his power to make others believe in me, rather than demand it of him."

"If you ask him, I know he'll do it."

Medeina shakes her head. "Asking. Who knew that it would come to that?"

Sam smiles at her, curls tighter into her side. She has never felt so content, so peaceful. "Humans," she says. "We're complicated."

THE SKYSCRAPER OFF Grand Avenue in Downtown Los Angeles is all blue glass and polished steel. Most of its windows are dark, and the ones that aren't stand out in the empty night. The building houses the corporate headquarters of eight commercial banks, three credit unions, nine collection agencies, fourteen brokerages and five S&Ls.

And somewhere inside it is the god of money.

"And you're sure he's up there?" Fitz says. Amanda says he has a suite of offices at the very top of the building, where he can look out over the city.

Two Amandas, Jake and Fitz sit in the van across the street looking at the front entrance. Inside is a security guard at a reception desk; ten minutes ago another came out of the elevator, chatted a bit and then swapped.

"I'm sure he's in there," one Amanda says. "As to *where* in there, I have no idea. I haven't been able to crack into any of his buildings' surveillance. My eyes stop at the street."

"So you saw him go in," Jake says.

"And not come out again, yes," says the other Amanda.

It had taken a while to figure out where Big was hiding out. He'd gone off Amanda's radar after he'd sold them out at the hotel and she hadn't been able to pick him up again on satellite imagery or surveillance cameras. She had to go back several hours before she found him again. From there it was easy to follow him to this building.

"How do you know he has an office at the top?"

"Same reason I know he's got a casino in Hawaiian Gardens," she says. "I've been there. He is my brother. We're at least friendly, even if we don't get along."

"We're here to kill him," Fitz says. "I'm not sure that really counts as friendly."

Amanda shrugs. "Chalk it up to sibling rivalry. If the roles were reversed, he'd be trying to kill me too."

"You have a very fucked-up family life," Fitz says.

"And you keep thinking we're human," Amanda replies.

That's a good point. He's been racking his brain the entire trip over and he hasn't come up with a plan. So far it's worked out something like this:

1) Confront Big Money
2) ????
3) Profit.

Maybe he needs to look at this differently.

But maybe his problem is that he's looking at taking him down the way a person would be taken down.

"What does it mean for a god to die?" Fitz says. It's been bothering him ever since Jake brought up the topic back at the safe house.

In the last couple of days he's been filled with the gods' stories, and though many of them are still a jumbled mess, bits and pieces are bobbing to the surface, patterns are emerging.

They aren't things, so much as they're concepts. Concepts with teeth, concepts with bodies and shapes and desires. They are War and Love and Hatred and Greed.

How do you kill a concept?

Destroy them with who they are, Amanda had said. Take what they are and use it against them. In her case, maybe a virus. In Big's case, what? An economic meltdown? He had said that he changed according to the way the world's economy moved, and suggested he wasn't actually a god.

Fitz doesn't buy it, just like he doesn't buy Amanda's insistence that she isn't a god. Dude's the embodiment of money, just like she's the embodiment of technology. So what is Big's weakness?

"One thing at a time, big guy," Jake says. "We gotta get in there, first."

"You have guns," Amanda says.

"Are you out of your mind?" Fitz says. "Just because I'm caught up in all this bullshit doesn't mean I want to start shooting innocent people." There's been too much death already.

"They do work for my brother," Amanda says. "I'd hardly call that innocent."

"Fuckers are just trying to make a living," Jake says. "Jesus, you're all the same."

"I don't want to kill anybody," Fitz says.

Amanda rolls her eyes. "We don't have to kill anybody. I restocked the van. Smoke grenades, bean bag rounds, rubber bullets."

"I look like I could shoot a shotgun?" Jake says.

"You look like you'll keel over in a stiff breeze," one Amanda says. She points at her twin. "We'll do the fireworks. You just stay low and don't get shot. Once we're in, I should be able to get a better idea of where he is."

"How?" Fitz says. "You said you don't have access to surveillance in the building."

"The closer I am to him, the better I can sense him. He's holed up in there. There are wards and sigils in the walls that prevent me from seeing inside. Once I get in there, though, I'll be able to sense him."

"And he'll sense you," Jake says. "Great plan."

"He'll know we're there the moment the smoke grenades come out," Fitz says, "and we're going to have to get upstairs. It's not like we're going to have surprise on our side."

"And when we find him?" Jake says. "Then what?"

"I'll think of something," Fitz says, and really, really hopes he's right.

CHAPTER TWENTY-TWO

THE CONFERENCE ROOM is about as normal and corporate a conference room as one can get. Abstract art on the walls, one wall of solid glass overlooking Los Angeles, a heavy teak conference table surrounded by Herman Miller chairs.

And then there are the occupants, who are very far from normal.

Big Money sits rapidly shifting from men to women, professional and dingy, Asian, white, black, Latin. He can't seem to keep a form for more than a couple of seconds at a time. Next to him Baron Samedi, a tall man in a black suit and a top hat whose head is a skull, drums bony fingers on the tabletop. Then Vaiśravana, a heavily muscled Asian man in plated armor, his form blurry as if seen through a thick haze, leans back with his arms crossed. The Sumerian Ereshkigal, a woman in a long flowing robe of woven wool, a gold headdress atop her braided hair, casually cleans her nails with the tip of a massive dagger. The brightly-colored serpent Quetzalcoatl, wings of red and blue and green sprouting from its back, has its body coiled into a chair as if to spring out of it at a moment's notice.

They sit around the conference, eyeing the two at opposing ends of the table: Zaphiel and the Man.

"I'd like to take this opportunity to thank all of you for coming," the Man says, his cigar glowing as he takes a puff on it. "Really, it's great to have this time to sit down, have a face to face and work some things out."

Zaphiel scowls with his four mouths. He has given up any pretense of humanity, and stands opposite the Man with all four wings unfurled and brushing the ceiling. His skin is cracked and blistered from Amanda's attack near the airport.

"You promised us the Chronicler," Zaphiel says, his harmonizing voice thick and slurred.

"And I delivered," the Man says. "I did everything but tie him up in a bow for you. Say, that's quite a burn you've got there. You want some Bactine, or something?"

Zaphiel digs his claws into the conference room table, gouging long furrows out of the wood. "You said he would be simple to pick up."

"You're the leader of the Cherubs," the Man says. "I didn't think a little godling of the Internet would be a problem for you. Clearly I was wrong."

"Your kind are an abomination," Zaphiel says.

The Man takes a puff on his cigar. It glows an angry red. "You Old Testament types really like to toss that 'abomination' thing around, don't you? *My kind*. What exactly is my kind?"

"Usurpers. Pretenders to godhood," Zaphiel says. A nod from Baron Samedi, echoed by the others. Big Money pushes himself further back in his chair.

"You call yourselves new gods, as if you have any place among the Heavens," Zaphiel says. "We are thousands of years old—"

"Hundreds," the Man says. "At least, some of you are. Or am I mistaken that the Baron here got his start in the holds of French cargo ships as his worshippers died by the score on their way to the New World? When did you first raise your eyes to the stars, Lord Saturday? Mid-seventeenth century? Eighteenth? A few hundred years among your paltry flock? Don't speak to me about age."

"Age is not the point," Ereshkigal says. "You are"—she searches for the word—"unseemly."

"We ssee what you are trying to do," Quetzalcoatl says, his snake's jaw working around the words. "You think thiss modern world hass no need for uss, and sso you would replace uss."

"You mean to hold the Chronicler as your own," Vaiśravana says. "He is a resource to be used by us all."

"By which you mean yourselves," the Man says. "I see what you're trying to do, too. You want to cut everyone else out. Make him your little pet. News flash! So does everybody else. How long before the bunch of you squabble and whine amongst yourselves? How long before you're tearing poor Fitz into pieces trying to get your stories told? Twenty years? Ten? Two?"

"We *found* him," Zaphiel says.

The Man laughs. "Oh, and you think you're the only ones who did that? How did I find him? How did Bacchus?"

The gods jerk in surprise as though they've been slapped. "Bacchus found him?" Ereshkigal says.

"Oh, yes. Had him in his hands longer than any of you did."

"Bacchus is dead," Baron Samedi says. "We all felt it. Did the Chronicler kill him?"

"That's impossible," Ereshkigal said.

"Quite," the Man says. "No, he didn't kill him. You know, it's a funny thing. When everything went to shit for all of you up there in the firmament, I was just an idea. The vaguest of concepts. There was no need for me. There was Yahweh, Odin, Zeus. All the other father gods who spilled their seed across the heavens so many thousands of years ago and spawned all of you. I watched it all happen from down here. Quite the perspective. Seeing all of you fall, seeing the doors of your homelands locked up tight. But you know what was the most interesting? All the father gods left. Up and disappeared."

"We know this," Zaphiel says. "You are not telling us anything new."

"No, I suppose I'm not. Well, this might be new. Have you heard the phrase, 'Nature abhors a vacuum'?" the Man says. He looks around the table at the blank stares and then brightens as Ereshkigal gasps. "Oh, we have a winner! She gets it. How about the rest of you? Anyone? Anyone? Bueller? No? You want to explain it to them, honey, or do I need to spell it out?"

"That is not possible," she says. "How could such a thing occur?"

"What in the hell are you two talking about?" Zaphiel says. "What is not possible?"

"*I* killed Bacchus," the Man says. "Me. The *abomination*. Because when all your daddies fucked off to Buffalo, the universe said, 'Welp, looks like we need another one and none of these other yahoos fit the bill.' There's a new sheriff in town, boys and girls, and it's me."

"This is preposterous," Baron Samedi says. "I have heard enough. I will tear this worm to pieces." He stands, shoving Big Money out of the way in order to get to the Man, who puts his arms wide as if to embrace him, a smile on his face.

The bony hands of the Baron wrap around the Man's throat and squeeze. Energy courses through the Baron's fingers, making the Man's throat glow blue.

Other than that, nothing happens.

"What exactly were you thinking would happen?" the Man says. "Maybe something like this?" He punches into the Baron's stomach, ripping through his suit, his fist a hot coal. Fire bursts through the Baron's eye sockets, the bones charring, cracking from the heat. The Baron goes up in flames; in less than a second, he is nothing but ash and steaming ichor.

"That's pretty much how Bacchus went, too," the Man says, tipping ash from his cigar onto what's left of the Baron.

THE FIRST FLASH-BANG takes care of the lobby's glass doors, blowing them out in a shower of shards. The guard at the reception desk screams, drops to the floor, blind and deaf.

The two Amandas stroll through the shattered glass. The elevator opens and a second guard steps out, kisses the floor when he sees the two women with shotguns.

"They don't pay me enough for this!" he yells, his hands on the back of his head.

"We're not here to hurt you," Fitz says, running up behind the Amandas. He reaches down, grabs the guard's keychain from his belt and selects the elevator key. "Just need this."

"Don't hurt me," the man says. "I don't wanna die."

"Look out!" Jake yells. The first guard, who ducked when the flash-bang went off, doesn't seem to share his partner's sentiment. He bolts up from behind the reception desk and pops off a round at one of the Amandas, hitting her high in the back of the shoulder. She spins around, the shotgun roaring in her hands.

The beanbag round hits the guard center-mass, knocking him flat against the wall. He drops his guns and slides down to the floor, gasping for breath.

"Don't do that again," Amanda says. She looks over her shoulder at the gunshot wound. "Goddamit," she says. She hands the shotgun to Fitz as the other Amanda hands her a Taser from a backpack she has slung over her shoulder.

"My left arm's gonna be next to useless," she says. "You okay with the shotgun?"

"Yeah, I'm good." He leans down to the guard he took the keys from. "You're gonna want to get your friend some help," he says. "He's not dead, but he's gonna feel like shit real soon."

"Okay," the guard says, his voice very small.

"Only, you know, wait a little while."

The guard nods.

Jake, Fitz and the two Amandas pile into the elevator. Fitz pops the key into the slot and lets the doors slide closed.

"What floor?" he says.

Amanda frowns. "Top floor," she says.

"What's wrong?" Fitz says. "Is it the police?"

"No. The police won't be coming. I've blocked all communication in a twelve-block radius and triggered a tactical alert for the police to an area south of here. The problem is that I still can't sense Big."

"Fuck," Jake says. "After all that, he's not here?"

"No, I think he's still here. It's just that there's another shielded area on the top floor. He must be in there."

"He shielded his building, then he shielded a room?" Fitz says.

"Guess he likes his privacy," Jake says.

"One way to find out," Fitz says, reaching out and stabbing the button with his finger. The elevator ascends.

"SO NOW," THE Man says, looking at the shocked faces around the conference table, "you all have a choice to make. Seems the Baron here thought he could take me down. Had I been a lesser god, he might have done it, too. So the question is, on the relative scale of power between all of us, who thinks I'm less than they are?"

"He was a Voodoo Loa," Zaphiel says. "He was not one of us."

"And what are you exactly?" the Man says. "You're no god. You never have been. Is that what you want to be? Is that why you're so invested in getting your hands on the Chronicler? You think he'll turn you into a *real* boy?"

"You say you have killed Bacchus. What proof do you have?" Zaphiel says.

"Wow, you're just not gonna let up on this, are you?" The Man stands up, begins to walk around the table toward Zaphiel. Quetzalcoatl and Ereshkigal scramble out of his way. Zaphiel stands defiant in front of him, unflinching.

"Whattayasay, angel boy," the Man says, "You wanna tussle? You think you can take me?"

"Take a shot," Zaphiel says, "and see."

"That is an excellent idea," the Man says, and before he's even done speaking, his hand whips out. The Cherub is lightning fast, but not fast enough to keep the Man from grasping Zaphiel by the throat.

The Cherub rakes at the Man's face with his claws as he tries to pull free. Sparks fly where the claws strike, but the Man doesn't so much as flinch.

The Man's hand begins to glow as it did when he destroyed the Baron, and Zaphiel tries harder to pull away. He flaps his immense wings, the wind blowing the chairs away from the table, the pressure blowing out the glass in the conference room windows.

"My daughter did a real number on you," the Man says. "What'd she use in those satchel charges? Crosses? Bits of myrrh? Little scraps of paper with Enochian glyphs on them? Whatever it was, and whatever she did to you, it's nothing compared to what I'm about to do to you now."

Zaphiel's mouths roar and scream, his claws raking ineffectually against the Man's face, his legs kicking but he might as well be kicking a steel wall. The Man doesn't move.

"What do you want of me?" Zaphiel hisses.

"Oh, now that is an interesting question." The Man lets up the pressure around Zaphiel's neck, but doesn't let go. "What do I want? What is that word? Ah, yes. Fealty. I want your fealty. Your loyalty. Your acknowledgement that I'm the one in charge."

Zaphiel stares at him in horror. "I will never give up my loyalty to the One True God."

"You don't get it, you fucking hasbeen," the Man says through gritted teeth, his hand tightening around Zaphiel's throat, the glow and heat returning. "Daddy left you high and dry, and you know why? Because He knew His time was over and done with. This is the modern age, you antediluvian piece of shit. You're a dinosaur and I'm the motherfucking meteor. Now you get the fuck in line or you join that pile of ash on the goddamn ground and all the others I'm going to burn who get in my fucking way. So you have a choice to make, Zaphiel. What'll it be?" The Man grips tighter, the heat from his hand searing into the Cherub's throat, bringing smoke and the stink of barbeque.

The Cherub grits his teeth from the pain, the skin under his jaw sloughing off. Rivulets of golden ichor begin to bubble and hiss as it erupts through burst capillaries.

"Fine!" the Cherub roars. "I give you my oath. You are my commander. You are my Lord."

"Is there any other? Do you renounce your previous master?"

"Yes!" the angel screams. "Yes, just make it stop."

The Man releases his grip around the Cherub's throat and Zaphiel falls to the floor.

"Excellent. I'm glad we had this talk. I'm feeling really good about this team dynamic we're building here." He looks at the other gods cowering against the wall. "I'd really like to have you all on board. We're going to be doing some exciting things."

He smiles at their nods of agreement. "Good, good. Now—"

An explosion tears through the building downstairs, the sound carrying up through the shattered conference room windows.

The Man looks at his wristwatch. "Ah. Right on time. Ladies and gentlemen, the guest of honor has arrived."

CHAPTER TWENTY-THREE

"Is this Captain and Tenille?" Fitz says, trying to place the familiar pop song warbling over the elevator's speakers. Horns, woodwinds, violins in place of the vocal track.

"Nah, this is Donny and Marie," Jake says. "I think?"

"Supertramp," the Amandas say. "'The Logical Song.' Off *Breakfast In America*."

"Seriously?" Fitz says. "This sounds nothing like Supertramp."

One Amanda starts to hum along with the music while the other belts out, "Won't you sign up your name, we'd like to feel you're acceptable, respectable, presentable, a vegetable."

"Saxophone solo!" Jake yells. "Yeah, I remember this one."

"It is really creepy hearing you sing," Fitz says.

"What?" Amanda says. "I like this song."

"Are you glitching again? Because now is probably a really bad time to do that."

"Oh, screw you," she says. "What the hell's wrong with liking Supertramp?"

"Well, the Internet does have pretty bad taste," Jake says.

"The Internet is also carrying a shotgun and a pistol," the Amandas say.

"Whatever." Jake rubs his hands on his pants, his brow furrowing. "How many more floors?"

Fitz shakes his head. "Fifteen or so." He frowns. "You feel that?"

"Like pressure on the back of your eyeballs?"

"Yeah," Fitz says. "It feels... off." He's starting to sense Big. And more.

"That's because it is off," Amanda says. "My father is up there. And other gods, too."

"Shit," Jake says. "I didn't sign up for this. Let me the hell outta here. I'll walk down." He starts stabbing at buttons, but the elevator doesn't slow.

"We're in express mode," Fitz says. "We're not stopping until we get to the top."

"Then I hope you got a plan for taking them all out or getting us the hell out of here," Jake says.

"Have you thought of anything?" Amanda says.

"Sort of?" he says. "I was thinking I could just grab those threads I saw around Big before and twist them around until I—I dunno, turn him into something else."

"That's actually not a bad idea," Amanda says. "Do you think you could it to more than one god at a time?"

"I'm not sure I can do it to one god at all. The whole point of coming here was to find out."

"Oh, shit," Jake says, sliding to the floor of the elevator. "This was a bad idea. This was a bad fucking idea."

Something else isn't right. "Didn't you say the room Big was hiding out in blocked you from sensing him?" Fitz says.

"Yes," Amanda says. "Oh, I see what you mean."

"What the hell are you two talking about?" Jake says.

"If Big's in a warded room, then how can we sense him? From what I can tell, he's still in the room but the wards are broken. Not just turned off, but broken. Like a wall has been damaged, maybe?"

As the elevator ascends, Fitz gets a clearer sense of who's up there. There's the Man and Big Money, but also Zaphiel and three others that feel familiar.

Their names and stories suddenly pop into his head: Ereshkigal, Vaiśravana, Quetzalcoatl. And traces of another, too faint to fully grasp. All of them were in his dream.

"There are a lot of gods up there," Fitz says. The voices start to chatter in his head. They know he's coming. They're waiting for him. He has a faint sensation of those red threads, and when he closes his eyes he can see them radiating out from the floor far above. He thinks about sweeping them aside and the voices in his head stop.

"Huh."

"What?" Amanda says.

"I think I just figured out how to shut them up. If only I'd known that twenty years ago I could have saved myself some time in a psych ward."

He closes his eyes again and sees the threads, traces them up. It doesn't take long before he knows which ones belong to which gods. Whether he can do anything to them or not is another question entirely.

He should be freaking out. Sitting on the floor with Jake and pissing himself. Those are motherfucking *gods* up there. The last time he saw them, they played an epic game of keep-away with him until it turned into an all-out brawl. But instead of losing his mind, he feels surprisingly calm.

"Do you know anything about the layout of the building?" Fitz says.

"Some from public records," Amanda says, "but knowing my brother, he made undocumented changes. Why?"

"We need to get Jake out of here. When we get to the top, is there a stairwell he can take to get down? Things are going to get messy no matter what happens and he shouldn't be here."

"Damn right, I shouldn't," Jake says. He rocks back and forth, with his eyes closed and his hands pressed against his temples. Fitz can feel the pressure in his mind from the gods' attention on him; he can only imagine what Jake is going through.

"This elevator opens on a hallway. There's an emergency exit leading to a stairwell to the left. As long as Big hasn't changed it."

"You got that?" Fitz says to Jake. "That door opens, you run for it. Get out of here. Don't look back. I appreciate the help, but this is too much for you. Hell, it's probably too much for me, too."

"Then why aren't you freakin' out?" Jake says. His whole body is shaking.

"I don't know." He should be overwhelmed by the voices, but they're subdued, like the background hum of a fan. "Maybe it was the dream I had. Maybe it was all of them coming at me at once. Their stories are starting to piece together for me now. I know the gods that are up there. I know their histories. I might not be able to do anything about them but—" He hesitates. But what, exactly? He understands them? He empathizes with them? They're all a bunch of arrogant bastards with too much power trying to grab more. Then he has it.

"I might be able to stop them from making things worse."

"Well, you're about to have your chance," Amanda says. "We're almost there."

Fitz reaches down and pulls Jake to his feet. The old man can barely stand, he's shaking so hard. "Remember. That door opens, you run. Got it?"

He nods. "I'm sorry," he says. "I thought what those Chumash gods did to me made me stronger. I thought I could do this."

"You have helped," Fitz says. "A lot. But this isn't your deal. Thank you."

"If you two are gonna hug, you better do it quick," Amanda says. The elevator chimes. The doors slide open onto a marble inlaid floor with a mirror shine. Dark teak walls with frosted-glass lighting fixtures along them. Ahead, a set of double doors, and to the left an exit sign with a stairwell door.

"Good luck, man," Jake says. "Hope they don't kill you." He staggers to the exit, wobbling, barely able to stand.

"Don't fall down the stairs and break your neck," Fitz says.

He doesn't know if getting him out will save him, but he's sure that being here will end badly. He just hopes that he can get far enough away and not attract more of the gods' attention. With a little luck, he should live long enough to drink himself to death.

"No promises," Jake says, as he disappears through the door.

"Any suggestions?" Fitz asks the Amandas.

She shakes her head. "Not much I can do that will hurt any of them. If my father throws his Agents at us, I have a few tricks up my sleeve, but against him and the others? The best I can do is annoy them."

A voice in the back of his mind reminds him that he can leave. They haven't burst out of the door yet to grab him. They're just waiting. He could follow Jake down the stairs and out the door and... then what?

Presuming they let him get very far, they'll still track him down. He's going to be hunted until the end of his life unless he can do something here and now. Whether that's giving them a bloody nose or getting hit so hard he signs himself over to them, he doesn't know.

There's only one way to find out.

He throws the conference room doors open onto the strangest sight he's seen outside of a hallucination. The Man wearing Blake's body, Big Money shifting between forms so fast Fitz can't keep up, Zaphiel looking like he's been through a meat grinder and three other gods. Ereshkigal sitting with her arms crossed, looking somewhere between scared and pissed off, Vaiśravana in a full suit of plate and an expression on his face like he's just bitten a lemon, and Quetzalcoatl, wings tucked in, feathers back, his body coiled up tight in a Herman Miller chair.

The entire bank of windows opposite the door have been blown out, which, Fitz thinks, is probably what broke the wards that hid the gods from Amanda and him.

The only one in the room who looks even remotely happy is the Man.

"Fitz, my boy! I've been expecting you," the Man says, arms wide as if to embrace him. "You're just in time to help me remake the world."

SAM STEPS OVER the shattered glass in the lobby of the building and smells the pungent stink of gunpowder in the air. After her episode as a wolf, she's having trouble getting used to being human again. She keeps wanting to smell everything, and is constantly frustrated that she can't.

"I think we're in the right place," Sam says, picking up a discarded beanbag shell. She resists the urge to smell it. "But why are they here?"

Medeina explained to her that ever since she had tracked Fitz down for Zaphiel, she was able to find him fairly easily. He was obscured from time to time, dropping off her senses, but then he would pop back up again. And knowing where he had just been made it even easier. From the safe house, she led Sam through a confusing game of Hot or Cold until they got close enough that she was certain where he was.

And once they knew where he was, they knew there was trouble.

Medeina had sensed the other gods before they even got off the freeway. She didn't know who most of them were, but El Jefe and Zaphiel were among them.

"Perhaps Fitz was captured," she adds. "I can feel the new goddess of technology upstairs with the rest of them." She bends down and sniffs at some droplets of blood on the floor. "This is from one of her bodies. She was shot here."

"Maybe they got hit at the safe house and she came here to get him back?" Sam says. "Dammit."

"I don't know, but they should have been safe there. She had the house warded against all manner of threats and detection. Anything that could have found them there would not have been stopped by you."

"I know," Sam says. "So you're sure they're upstairs?"

"Yes. Several floors above us."

Sam goes to the elevator and punches the button. When it arrives, she goes inside the car and pushes the top floor. It flickers, but nothing happens.

"I was afraid of that. Security on these. You either need an emergency key or a key card. We won't be getting up that way." The emergency stairs are around a corner. "We're walking it." Sam opens the door, but Medeina doesn't follow.

"What's wrong?"

"There are seven other gods up there and Fitz. I imagine some of them are ones who joined Zaphiel as I did, or have joined with El Jefe. None of them will be happy to see me."

"Can they hurt you?" Sam says.

"One on one? Possibly. We gods grow in power through belief, and there are so very few who believe in us anymore that many of us are fairly evenly matched. I suspect that I could take any one of them directly. But in numbers, they could almost definitely destroy me. Unless they're distracted, it's a good chance they already know I'm here."

"We gotta help Fitz," Sam says. There had to be a way to do it. Sneak in and grab him? But how? Medeina's point about how they might not notice she's here if they're distracted gives her a thought. "I have a bad idea."

Medeina smiles at her. "Those are often the best kind."

"What if we get up close and you distract them, and I grab Fitz and get him the hell out of there?"

"And once you have him?"

"Get him down here, get him into the car, get the hell away? I haven't really figured out that part, yet."

"They will pursue you," Medeina says. "But I may be able to get you some time and distance from them. I will be your distraction and protection as you spirit him away."

"Do you think it will work?"

Medeina shrugs. "I have done many things that by rights should have never worked. Perhaps you are a hero. Heroes do that sort of thing."

Well, she did ask. Inside the stairwell Sam looks up. "That's a lot of steps," she says. "This could take hours."

Medeina laughs. "Oh, no," she says. "Seconds." She wraps her arms around Sam and suddenly Sam feels lighter, thinner. In a second she and Medeina are wisps of black smoke racing up the steps, bouncing through the turns and corners, taking whole floors in the blink of an eye.

About halfway up, they stop. Sam's thoughts are scattered, as elusive as the wind she has become, and it takes her a moment to realize why they've stopped.

They become solid on the stairs in front of a terrified Jake, hobbling down the steps. He screams when the black smoke appears and after seeing that it's Sam and Medeina, he doesn't seem much relieved.

"Oh, Jesus, it's you." He sits on a step, his bones creaking, his hands shaking. He's wheezing from his run.

"What happened?" Sam says. "Did they capture Fitz?"

"Capture? Fuck, the boy walked right into it. Knew it, too." He explains their plan to try to kill Big, and the discovery that there were more gods here after they got onto the elevator, and then Fitz had this idea that he needed to end it now.

"What was he planning?"

"He didn't have a plan. He thought he might be able to twist those threads around on one of them until they didn't exist anymore, but with so many up there? I don't know. Maybe he's got a death wish? When I was at my worst, I know I sure as hell did."

"That doesn't sound like Fitz," Sam says. When he's cornered, he'll fight. She's seen it. Saved her life in that motel years ago. But unless he's cornered, he knows to run the fuck away.

"He did seem a little weird," Jake says.

"Weird how?"

"Calm. Like real calm."

"Did he have a plan?"

"Don't think so," Jake says. "Maybe he was keeping it under wraps?"

"And why did you run?" Medeina says. "Are you not loyal to your friend?"

"The fuck makes you think he's my friend? I only just met the guy and he pulled me back into this. Fuck him. If he wants to get himself killed, fine. But I'm not going out that way. Those fuckers'll screw with your head, tear you apart from the inside. I'm not doing that again."

"So you ran like a coward," Medeina says.

"He told me to leave, goddammit."

"It's okay," Sam says. "I get it. This isn't your fight. But I gotta get Fitz out of there. Can you tell me anything about the top floor?"

"Big marble foyer, double doors in front of the elevator, couple other doors to, I dunno, offices maybe? And then there's the stairwell. I didn't exactly stick around to do a thorough look."

"Hey, any bit helps. I know you don't owe him anything, but can you do me a favor?"

"If it isn't 'getting the fuck out of here,' then no."

"As a matter of fact it is. There's a Corolla parked outside. It's hotwired; all you have to do is touch the wires under the dashboard. Go out there, get the car ready and wait for us."

He thinks about it. "I ain't waitin' all night."

"You will wait for as long as you need to," Medeina says, her voice taking on a strange harmonic that pierces through Sam's skull.

"Oh, screw you, witch lady," Jake says. "That shit don't work on me." He laughs at Medeina's shocked expression. "Yeah, that's another thing you people don't know about us, huh? All that magic god voice crap. You can't tell us what to do. Let that sink in for a minute."

He turns to Sam. "I'll wait for as long as I can, but if you get out there and I'm not, don't be surprised."

"We won't be long," she says. She takes Medeina's hand, pulling her outraged attention away from the burnt-out prophet. "Let's go. He'll keep the car running. Might shave off some time and let us get out of here in one piece."

Medeina narrows her eyes at Jake. "Go, little coward. When your comrades need you, you run."

"Missy, ain't nobody ever been there for me. Don't see how this is me bein' any different." He gives Sam a half-hearted salute and Medeina the finger. "I'll see you downstairs. Good luck."

He disappears down a few floors before Sam says, "Why did you talk like that?"

"He is a coward who will run away at the slightest hint of trouble," she says, anger written all over her face.

"The guy's a burnout and he's scared. He's probably got a fuckton of PTSD going on inside of that head. And it's not like he can talk to too many people about it and get help that'll actually help. The fact that he's even *alive* is impressive."

Medeina looks down at her and frowns. "You respect him?"

"I understand him," Sam says. "Which is different. I don't have to like his choices to be able to accept them. And yes, before you say it, humans are complicated."

"Humans *are* complicated," Medeina says. "You are not like the tribes who worshipped me."

"Hey," Sam says, "when this is all over, let's you and me go someplace. Some forest. Tell me what your life was like. And not that infodump thing you did earlier. I want to hear you tell your stories. You okay with that?"

Medeina smiles, any trace of anger or upset disappearing. "I would like that very much." She takes Sam's hand. Sam begins to feel lighter, more insubstantial. "Let us save the Chronicler," she says before the two of them fade into willowy black smoke.

CHAPTER TWENTY-FOUR

THE GODS IN the room are all staring at Fitz. He's not sure what to expect, but sitting stock-still with looks of panic on their faces isn't it.

"Come in, come in!" the Man says. "It's so good to see you, my boy!" He steps toward Fitz to pull him in for a hug, but Fitz pulls back, ducking under his arms. The Man frowns. "Don't trust me? I can understand that."

"I didn't come looking for you," Fitz says. No, he didn't, but he's here and he's stuck and he's just trying to figure out what to do next. Around the room the red threads radiate off the gods, scattering in all directions. Some of them wind in on themselves, knotting in their centers, or around their heads like halos. Zaphiel has knots all along his body, the densest clustered around the burns and gashes left over from his encounter near the airport. The threads are brighter than he's seen them before, more vivid. He wonders what the knots mean.

"Oh, I know," the Man says. He points a thumb over his shoulder at Big Money in the corner. "You came looking for him. How were you thinking of killing him? I'm dying to know."

"I—"

"Wondering how I knew?" He nods at the Amandas in the doorway. "Maybe she told me. She is my daughter, you know."

Fitz spins around to face Amanda. "The fuck?"

"I didn't tell him a goddamn thing," the Amandas say in unison.

"She's right, she didn't. I just figured it out, is all. You're awfully predictable. Getting hold of the old man—Jake, right? That was inspired. I knew you were going to grab him. He was the only one who could help you figure out what you can do. Have you tried telling a god's stories, yet? No. No, I don't think you have."

"How did you know I was coming here to kill Big? Why not you?"

"Because you didn't know I was here. He's the only one who came in through the front door. The rest just sort of appeared. We're gods, you know. Some of us can do that. As to how I knew you were going to try to kill Big? Well, I know Jake. See, I met him a long time ago when he first caught the attention of some of the other gods. I watched him. Studied him. He's a very angry man. The only thing he thinks about is killing gods. Well, that and getting high as balls."

Fitz feels like he's talking to some B-grade schlock villain. Blake has turned into the Emperor in Star Wars. "'Everything is proceeding as you have foreseen'?" Fitz says.

"And I've found the droids I was looking for," the Man says, smiling.

"After what they did to him, can you blame him?"

"Not at all. Which is why the same won't be happening to you. You'll be working for me, and only me. We'll have you start small. A few stories here and there, get the public a little more accepting of my reign. Then we'll go a little wider. Go after the skeptics and the atheists. And then, well, then we do the miracles."

"Miracles?"

"Yeah," the Man says. "The stories are great and all, but if people are really gonna get on board, they need something a little more concrete. Not too concrete. Proof denies faith and all, so we need just enough ambiguity to sell it. Between my miracles and your stories, I'll be set."

Fitz looks around at the cowed faces. Zaphiel's in particular has him worried. He figured the angel would be furious, tearing the Man into pieces and flying off with Fitz to chain him in a basement or something.

But he just looks defeated.

The Man follows Fitz's gaze. "Oh, them? They're totally on board. I only needed to kill a couple of them. I'll probably have to kill a few more to get everybody else on board. Of course, I might not have to once they know you've signed on to the team."

The strange sense of calm that came over Fitz in the elevator isn't gone, but it's starting to crack. He's nervous. There's something else going on here, but he hasn't figured it out, yet.

"What makes you think I'm on the team?" Fitz says. "From what I understand, I have to agree to do it. I have to make that choice. So far I haven't signed on to a goddamn thing."

"Well, I could kill you," the Man says. "But a guy like you doesn't happen every day, you know. Hell, I don't think a guy like you has *ever* happened before. So I'd really rather you just accepted that it's really no choice at all."

Fitz wonders if maybe it wouldn't be easier. Maybe he should just give in and take his offer. Be his pet prophet. How bad could it be?

Well, for starters, the Man is an asshole. Whatever he wants Fitz to do can't be good for anybody. And then there's Jake. How long before the Man burns Fitz out the way those other gods burnt out Jake? Probably a while, but it's not much better.

And third, he doesn't have to.

"No," Fitz says.

Something he's been mulling ever since they got on the elevator. There's more that he can do with these threads than he's been doing. He concentrates on the threads surrounding

Big Money, runs along them with his thoughts into the areas where they knot together in his body. But instead of pulling on them, twisting them, or trying to make Big move or dance or anything like that, he thinks one word.

Burn.

A scream erupts from Big as his body is consumed in a haze of green flames. They shoot out of his mouth and nostrils, burst from his ears. He flails, slapping at himself to put out the flames, but they just get higher. He tries changing forms from American Business Tycoon to Saudi Oil Sheikh to Chinese Billionaire to Art World Darling, but none of his shapes can help him.

The Man turns to watch his son burn. The rest of the gods rush away from him as quickly as they can, looks of horror on their faces. Even Amanda is looking a little horrified. Fitz doubts that this is what she was expecting.

He wonders what's going to happen to the international banking industry once Big's gone. Probably nothing; it spawned Big Money, not the other way around. When Bacchus died, wine didn't suddenly cease to exist. A few thousand years ago, Bacchus' kicking the bucket might have meant something, but now?

Big finally stops moving as his legs disintegrate from underneath him, dropping him to the floor. His arms fall to pieces in huge clumps of ash and flame. The rest of him quickly follows. Soon the flames are nothing but a dim glow dancing on a pile of gray ash. Thin rivulets of golden ichor soak into the carpet.

A long silence fills the room. And then the Man gives Fitz a slow golf clap.

"Nicely done," he says. "And thank you. He was a whiny little shit. Saved me the trouble. I'll do better next time."

"There's not gonna be a next time," Fitz says. "I did it to him, I'll do it to you." He looks out at the rest of the gods. "I'll do it to all of you." He can see the threads running off of the Man in all directions. They're more complex, more convoluted. He can't find a knot to grab, so he settles with selecting a handful in his mind and twisting.

The Man laughs. "Oh, I felt that! Kinda tickles."

Fitz sweeps his awareness through more, grabs huge clumps in his mind. Pulls hard, commands them to burn, to disintegrate, to snap into pieces. The Man frowns.

"Enough of that," he says, sweeping his arm out in front of him.

Before he can get his hand up, Amanda fires the shotgun, a solid slug of lead hitting him square in the forehead. The round mushrooms and ricochets into the ceiling. The Man doesn't seem to notice.

A hurricane force wind slams into Fitz, throwing him back out into the hallway. He hits the elevator doors hard and something inside him cracks. His shoulder, still sore from the dislocation in the car accident, pops back out of joint and he screams.

The pain is intense, but Fitz refuses to black out. He's got to get up, fight back. Part of him wants to run; get down those stairs and as far away as it's possible to get. But he knows that running's not an option.

The Amandas pump more rounds into the Man, who just has this look of disappointment on his face, like his dog just peed on the rug. He gestures and their guns fly out of their hands to clatter on the floor behind him. With another sweep of his hands, the two women fly up, pinned to the ceiling.

"Why are you doing this?" he says. "I know we haven't always seen eye to eye but, come on, we're in this together. Haven't I given you everything you've asked for?"

"You don't understand a damn thing about me," the Amandas say. "You just want to control everything. Whether it wants to be controlled or not."

He rolls his eyes. "Is this another *information wants to be free* speech? I thought that was just a phase. Aren't we over that now?" He sighs. "You know, we're gonna have to finish this talk another time."

He pushes his hands down and the Amanadas fall, slamming into the floor with the speed of a bullet, tearing through into the floor below. Fitz can hear a succession of crashes and he wonders just how many floors they've gone through.

The Man steps past the holes in the conference room floor and into the hallway, shakes his head as he looks down at Fitz struggling to stand up.

"Look at what you made me do, Fitz," he says. "You've got a dislocated shoulder and, what, busted rib? Maybe a cracked vertebra? I don't want to kill you. I really don't. I don't even want to hurt you. But you make it so hard not to."

"Fuck you," Fitz says through gritted teeth. He spits out blood, focuses through the pain, tries to grab the threads surrounding the Man but they dance away from his awareness before he can get hold of them.

"See, here's something you don't understand," the Man says. He points a thumb behind him at the other gods standing terrified in the doorway. "They know I can destroy them. And from your paltry little demonstration here, they now know you can't destroy me."

"Horseshit," Fitz says. "I saw that look. I had you there."

"Points for optimism, but no. I have you here on the floor. So whatever you think you can do to me, you can't. So you're going to help me remake the world. It's going to be nice and orderly and full of Me. The trains will run on time, the people will be nice and calm and do what they're told. The other gods will get in line or I'll have you write a story about how they ceased to exist and the people will forget they ever did."

"You're gonna have to kill me," Fitz says. Better that than let the Man run things. That's not a world Fitz is going to help make. The world's bad enough that it brought the Man into existence in the first place. There's no way in hell he's going to help make things worse.

"Actually, no. What I have to do is what I do best. I need to break you. I need you to understand that I am in control. That you have no hope. That everything I say and do goes, and that there is fuck all you can do about it. You can't win." He looks at his wristwatch. "In fact, here it comes now. Right on time."

The stairwell door bursts open and thick black smoke boils out of it, coalescing between Fitz and the Man into Sam and Medeina. The goddess scowls at the Man, her spear materializing out of the smoke and pointed at his face. Sam grabs Fitz and helps him stand. To his credit, he doesn't scream.

His arm hangs uselessly by his side, and when he breathes it's like fire in his chest, a sure sign of a broken rib.

"What the hell are you doing here?" Fitz says. "He's going to fucking kill you."

"He'll have to try. We're getting you the fuck out of here," Sam says. "Medeina'll hold him off long enough to get you downstairs."

"That is a shitty plan," Fitz says. "He'll fucking flatten all of us."

"The cavalry has arrived!" the Man says.

"The Chronicler will be coming with us," Medeina says.

"No, I don't think so," the Man says. "But I am so glad you're here. I couldn't possibly do this next bit without you." She shoves her spear at him and the blade disintegrates into dust before it reaches his face. Medeina recoils in surprise.

"Fascinating thing, belief," the Man says. "People believe in us and we become real. The more real we become, the more powerful we become. And when a powerful prophet believes in us? Well, we aren't just real, we're *real*. Right now, you and I are the most real gods Fitz knows."

Medeina smiles, her spear's blade rematerializing. She steps forward. "Then we are matched, El Jefe," she says. "I will enjoy gutting you and scattering your entrails across the countryside."

"Wow," the Man says. "That's a vivid picture. There's one crucial difference between you and I, though." He nods at Sam. "I have an ace in the hole."

As Sam is helping Fitz toward the exit she suddenly stiffens, eyes going glassy. Fitz stumbles out of her grasp, grabbing the stairwell door for support.

"What the hell's wrong?" Fitz says. He can see the Man's red threads shoot out toward her, wrapping around her like a spider cocooning its prey. He tries to grab them with his mind, push them aside, but he's too slow.

Sam spins toward Medeina, yanking a key from inside her

shirt and shoving it into the back of Medeina's neck. There's a loud popping noise as the key's blade rips into her and Sam drags it hard around to her throat, tearing through the flesh like it's butter.

Fitz listens to Medeina screaming for a moment before he realizes it's him. She doesn't have a throat left to make a sound with. Medeina wheels around, the look of betrayal plain on her face. She mouths a word—*Why?*—but no sound comes out.

A moment later flames erupt through the wound, her skin cracking and fissuring. She spins back to the Man, moves in to grapple him, her body wreathed in flames. She grabs hold of him, wraps her hands around his throat, but they crumble away to dust. She falls to the floor, every piece of her burning. Within seconds she is nothing but wisps of charcoal on the floor.

The Man brushes ash from his suit coat and takes a puff of his cigar.

Sam snaps back to herself. Looks at what she's done, the key in her hand. Her face twists in horror, and just as quickly turns to cold anger. Fitz knows that face. When Sam hurts, she doesn't scream or cry or anything like that. She gets angry. And when she gets angry, people get hurt.

Fitz yells at her to stop, but it's too late. She's already mid-air, jumping at the Man. If it were anybody else, Fitz's money would be on her. She's a giant woman with muscles built from beating the hell out of people for cash. But against a god, she might as well be a gnat.

The Man grabs her by the throat, interrupting what should have been a flying tackle. Her punches land on his face, but they don't do anything. He pulls her in close enough that she gets a few solid kicks in too, a knee in his crotch. She even gets him in the eye with the key in her hand, but it scrapes along the surface as if his eyes were made of marble.

He leans in to her and says, "No."

And just like that it's over. She goes limp in his hand. A discarded marionette. He lets her go and she falls in a heap to the floor.

Fitz stares at her motionless body, stunned. He can't tell if she's dead or unconscious. "You sonofabitch," he says. "I am going to fucking murder you."

The Man laughs loud and hard. Doubles over and slaps his knee. Wipes tears from his eyes. "Oh, Fitz, you still don't get it, do you?" he says, tapping ash from his cigar into the pile of Medeina at his feet. "You can't win."

CHAPTER TWENTY-FIVE

"What the hell did you do to her?"

"To Sam? I enrolled her in my vision," the Man says. "Took some convincing. I had to get her to drink the Kool-Aid." He reaches down to pick up the key Sam murdered Medeina with. "And this is the key to a 1972 Triumph Stag, a symbol of long dead forests, the head encased in bits of pine, birch and spruce wood from the Dainava Forest in Lithuania. Bits and pieces of all the things that made Medeina a goddess. It's all about symbols." He tosses the key aside.

"I had Sam under my thumb before she met up with you and she didn't even know it. I've had this planned out to exacting detail. Do you understand now, Fitz? Do you get that no matter what you do, what you try, I will always be ten steps ahead of you? You will always lose. No matter what. So why fight? Why struggle? What are you getting out of it? Dead friends? Destroyed allies? Just give up. It'll be easier for you. Now, come on over here and let's get started. You have a lot of work to do for me."

Fitz looks at the pile of ash on the floor, at Sam's empty face.

Is she still in there or has it been the Man looking through her eyes the whole time? A wave of hopelessness descends on him. He's in agony from his shoulder and his rib. He's tired. He's been running for too long and everything's gone to shit. The Man's right. Fitz might as well just do whatever he says.

Except. "Sam fought you," Fitz says. "Until you cut her cord, she fought you."

"Because I let her fight," the Man says, narrowing his eyes and speaking very slowly and carefully. He's not used to being defied, Fitz realizes, and he doesn't like it. "I let her fight so that I could show you what happens when I no longer allow it. So get your ass in line with the program."

"Go fuck yourself," Fitz says. He gets ready to spring, rage and adrenaline washing over him, blocking out the pain. Maybe he can't win, but goddamn it he's going to go down swinging.

The stairwell door yanks open and Amanda, bloodied, missing an eye, her broken left femur jutting out through a gash in her pant leg, grabs Fitz by his wrist, pulling him into the stairwell. He screams in agony as she throws him down the stairs to the lower floor where the other Amanda, the right side of her face a shredded mass of hamburger, barely catches him. He bounces off the metal steps.

She covers him with her body and says "Duck your head," her voice thick and slurred where she's missing most of her tongue.

Fitz is about to ask why when he hears a high-pitched whistle and a blast that rocks the building, blowing the stairwell door in the floor above off its hinges and down the steps. A wave of searing heat washes over them, singeing their hair and sending the door to bounce off the steps. It narrowly misses flattening the two of them.

"RPG," Amanda says, or at least he thinks she says. All he can hear is a screeching whine. He thinks she's just said, "That'll buy us a few minutes," but he's not sure. The two of them limp down the steps.

"We can't leave," Fitz yells. "We need to get Sam. He had her kill Medeina."

"She's gone," Amanda says.

"No," he says. "He just had some weird control over her." He can't believe he'd kill her. Why do that? Something tells him that the Man wouldn't throw something away if he thought he could still use it. And much as it makes his stomach turn to think of it, he knows Sam would be useful.

"Fitz, she's *gone*."

It takes a second for Fitz to realize that Amanda's not talking about Sam's mind or her will or anything like that. She's dead. The blast from the RPG surely killed her.

"Goddammit, no." He struggles against her to go back up the stairs into that flaming wreck of a conference room, even though he knows it's just anger and grief and probably a concussion talking. Amanda tugs on his bad arm and the pain is intense enough to stop him in his tracks.

"There is nothing up there to save," she says. "She was already dead, even if her body wasn't. And now she can't be used against you. You want a shot at the Man? The only way you're going to get it is if we get you out of here right now." He wants to argue, but he knows she's right. He nods and follows her down the stairs.

They get about five floors down when the first Agents show up.

Sunglasses and black suits, wicked-looking guns. Black, white, Asian, their faces all generic and grim. They rush down from the top floor, moving like insects, scuttling down the steps, crawling on the walls and ceiling.

"You got a plan for dealing with this?" Fitz says. "You're the Internet. Throw—fuck, I don't know—cat pictures or something at them."

She looks up at the Agents heading their way, doubt written across her face. She turns to Fitz. "Do you believe in me?" she says.

"What?" He's not sure he heard her right. Fitz thinks it's a stupid question until he remembers what the Man told Medeina about belief, about *his* belief, right before he killed her.

"Do you believe in me?"

"Yes," Fitz says with as much conviction as he can throw into it. It's true. Despite what she may think of herself, Amanda has been the most godlike thing he's seen so far. She says she's just an idea. Something new and not as powerful as her father or the other gods. But to Fitz, she's the most powerful thing he's ever run into.

There's a shift, as if the world has just moved to make room for something that hadn't been there before.

"Then yes," she says. "I've got a plan for dealing with this."

"Tell me it's not pictures of cats."

"Better."

Scaly, green arms and hands shoot out from the walls and grab at the Agents, holding them in place. A thick tarry resin leaves them stained, gluing them to the walls, the floors, each other, while an unintelligible babble of noise fills the stairwell. It sounds like screaming words, but none of it makes any sense to Fitz.

The hands tear at the Agents, ripping huge chunks out of them. The Agents fight back, firing their pistols, punching and ripping at the hands in an effort to get free. It reminds Fitz of a documentary on colonies of army ants trying to kill each other.

Amanda pushes Fitz out of the way as one of the Agents get a shot off at them. The bullet punches through Amanda's arm, but she ignores it. The Agent readjusts its aim, but before it can fire again its gun is grabbed from its grasp by one of the hands and turned back on itself.

Soon all of the Agents are mired in the sea of grasping hands dragging them down, their attacks hitting each other as much as they're hitting the hands. The metal stairs shake from the battle, the sound of gunfire echoing through the enclosed space.

"The fuck are those?" Fitz says. He's learning that everything with gods is symbolic. They manifest based on the thing they represent. The Man and his Agents, Bacchus and his wine, Big Money and, well, his money. But the grasping hands weighing the Agents down? The shrieking noise?

"Comment trolls," Amanda says and pushes him along down the stairs. "Go. There will be more Agents soon. Or worse."

Fitz hurries down the stairs as fast as he can. The pain is becoming unbearable. His vision swims in and out of focus. He's starting to have trouble breathing. Floors go by in a blur and he has no idea how much further they have to go. Twenty floors? Two? He can't tell anymore.

The gunfire has stopped. Did that just happen or did the battle upstairs end a while ago and he just didn't notice? He keeps going in and out of focus. He keeps wondering where Sam is and then remembering that she's dead. He has to remind himself over and over again that the only way he's going to avenge her is to get out of this himself. For a while there is nothing but the sound of his and Amanda's feet on the metal stairs, her urging him to move faster.

"How are you not dead?"

Fitz looks up to see Jake holding the bottom stairwell door open. He blinks at the old man, not sure if he's really seeing him or if he's started to hallucinate.

"I thought I told you to leave," Fitz says, his voice slow and slurred. The room tilts and he finds himself being propped up by Amanda.

"Help me get him out onto the street," she says. "There's a car coming for us." Jake gets under Fitz's other arm and helps drag him out into the building's lobby.

"I ran into Sam and that crazy goddess chick on the way down," Jake says. "They told me to wait in the car. Then I saw the explosion and ran back inside. You look like shit. That from the blast?"

"Some. Mostly from when I went down eight floors the hard way," Amanda says.

"Where are the rest of you?"

"Dead," Fitz says slowly. "He had Sam kill Medeina, then he killed her himself." He's thinking he might join them soon. The pain has turned into some distant sensation. Not lessened, just feeling like it's happening to somebody else. That can't be a good sign.

"Fuck. So what's the plan?"

"Get him out of here," Amanda says. "Regroup. Things are different now. My father's a lot more powerful than I thought he was. We really have to keep him away from Fitz now."

"Can't win," Fitz says, dazed. "Should just go back and do what he tells me. Easier."

"Stop it," Amanda says. "He's not too powerful. Not without you. And you know what he's going to do with you if you go back up there."

"Oh, fuck you," he says. "How do I stop him? Huh? You saw what he did. How the fuck do I fight that?"

"You say no," she says. "It has to be a choice. He's trying to make you feel hopeless. That's what he does. But you can fight him; all it takes is saying no."

"Afraid it's not that simple." Zaphiel steps out from behind a column and they all freeze in their tracks. Zaphiel's skin smokes a little and he smells of explosives. The wounds he received near the airport are still plainly obvious.

"You can't have him," Amanda says.

"I don't want him. Not anymore. I'd rather kill him than let that monster upstairs take him." The resonance of his voice echoes through the empty lobby.

"That's funny coming from an Old Testament angel," Jake says.

"I hear a 'but' in there," Fitz says.

"I'm His now. He's the closest thing to God we have. All the others are gone. Yahweh, Odin. All the creators have left and He's filled the void. I have no choice. I am ordered to bring you with me."

"I said you can't have him," Amanda says.

"Why not? So you can have him?"

"Fitz makes his own choices," she says.

"All right. Then let him make it." Zaphiel looks hard at Fitz. "You've seen His power. You've seen that He has cowed gods, killed them with nothing but His will. Soon He will have all of the gods under His control. He has used your friends against you. How long until these ones die? How much will they suffer? The longer you deny Him, the more He'll make them hurt. But come willingly and they will find a place in His new world."

Zaphiel unfurls his massive wings and a flaming broadsword easily six feet long appears in his hand. Though he's a good ten feet away, the heat from the blade hits Fitz like he's standing in front of a blast furnace.

"Choose."

Fitz leans on Amanda, pulls himself straight, his rib screaming from the effort, his arm useless at his side. He's still having a hard time concentrating through the pain, but he's faced Zaphiel enough times already that he knows where his weak points are. He can see the threads shooting off of him, binding back into himself where they knot together.

He reaches out with his mind, grabbing onto them and willing them to unravel.

Zaphiel screams. Instead of bursting into flame like Big Money did, Zaphiel simply comes apart. Long splits rupture across his skin, like a paper doll being shredded by an angry toddler. Golden ichor flows through the cuts, pieces of him fall sizzling to the floor. The Cherub collapses to his knees as Fitz takes him apart piece by piece.

"You may kill me," Zaphiel screams. "But you will pay for it."

Just as his arms begin to split, spilling ichor to the floor like they're a busted pipe, Zaphiel hurls the flaming sword.

Fitz can't tell if it's a sacrifice or if Jake just has really bad survival instincts, but as Amanda pulls Fitz out of the way, Jake lets go of his arm and jumps straight into the path of the oncoming sword.

The blade embeds itself in the old man's chest, the fires setting him alight like a three-month-old Christmas tree. Fitz and Amanda back away from Jake's flaming corpse. Fitz spies a fire extinguisher on the wall and pulls it out, but he can't get it to go with only one working arm. Amanda grabs it from him, spraying Jake down with foam, but the flames are all-consuming, eating the old man up in seconds.

"Make it stop," Fitz screams at the disintegrating angel. "Make it stop, you sonofabitch." But the angel keeps falling apart, liquefying until there's nothing left but a thick, golden slurry running between the tiles on the floor. This is too much for Fitz. Too much killing. Too many horrible mistakes. Who else is the Man going to send after him?

There's a screech of tires from the street, and three Amandas run inside. "Help him," Fitz yells at them, pointing to Jake's charred body on the floor, but even he knows it's a lost cause. The old man stopped moving before he hit the ground, and most of his body has already been consumed by the fires, exposing blackened bones.

"There's nothing to help," one of them says as they grab Fitz and hurry him out to the waiting van.

"Let up," he says, pulling out of their grasp. "I can get into the goddamn car myself." He limps toward the entrance and stops when he realizes that the Amanda who came down with him in the stairwell isn't coming out. He pushes his way back inside to see a couple of Amandas handing her a large cardboard box.

"Come on," he says. "We have to get out of here."

"This body's used up," she says. "It can barely stand. If it were human it'd be dead already. I have twelve vans in the building's parking garage filled with fertilizer bombs. I can't solve this problem for you, Fitz." She pulls out a spool of cable and bricks of plastic explosive, starts inserting detonators into the plastique. "But I can make damn sure my dad knows he can't just do whatever the fuck he wants."

Everything has happened so quickly Fitz doesn't know what to say, how to feel. Sam, Jake, Medeina are gone. He even feels a twinge of guilt for Zaphiel. He was an asshole, but he just wanted his life back, just like all the old gods.

"Does it hurt?" Fitz says. "When you die?"

She smiles at him. "I don't die, Fitz," all the Amandas say at the same time. "You know that."

That's some small comfort, at least. She's alien and weird, an entity of technology that, though he may not ever fully connect with, he at least feels he can trust.

"Hey," one of the Amandas says, coming up behind him and putting her arms around him. At first he thinks it's an awkward hug until another one grabs his arm and yanks it back into its socket. He screams and almost passes out.

They haul him into the van, buckle him into a seat and hit the gas. They give him some OxyContin to help and though he's thankful for it, letting it wash over him and drag him down, he's afraid that it will break the last few strands of control he has. Fuck it, he thinks. It's not like there's anyone human watching.

He weeps quietly for Sam and Jake and even Medeina as they speed away into the night, taking back streets north out of Downtown. He looks behind him at the building receding in the distance and wants desperately to go back, try to at least retrieve Sam's body, but knows it's not possible.

A few minutes later they stop on a road near Dodger Stadium overlooking the freeway. In the distance he can see Big Money's building amid the rest of the Downtown skyline.

"Thought you'd want to catch this," she says.

The explosion is terrible and beautiful and he can't help but think that, as tombs go, his friends could do worse.

CHAPTER TWENTY-SIX

ANOTHER DAY, ANOTHER safe house. Fitz wonders how many of these things Amanda has hidden away, how safe it really is. He keeps drifting in and out, not daring to sleep. How is he going to get any rest if the gods can find him in his dreams? And now that the Man is flexing his muscles with the other gods, how long before he has them all under his thumb?

Maybe he should take Jake's advice and eat a bullet, or throw back a bunch of Ambien with some vodka. The Man isn't going to stop coming for him. And who's to say death will be the end of it? These are motherfucking gods.

On the way out of the city, one of the Amandas was telling Fitz about the emergency response to the building explosion. Police, fire, even the FBI are out there. So far there are no reports of deaths. The two security guards were found a few blocks away unconscious and are talking about a bunch of people coming into the building and shooting the place up.

The radio talking heads are going back and forth between terrorists and the idea that a foreign government might have done it, since the blast was so precise only a handful of buildings nearby suffered minor damage.

It's only been about an hour since the explosion, but the city has closed down all of the area airports. There's talk that the President is about to give a speech about security.

It occurs to Fitz that all that act of defiance against the Man did was help him.

The house is one of a hundred identical homes in a tract development north-east of Los Angeles off the 14 freeway where the landscape starts to turn into desert. Most of the homes are empty and still new. Either they never sold or they sold and foreclosed when the economy tanked and people were forced out of the area.

The American Dream, Fitz thinks. He wonders if he can blame the Man and Big Money for that, but doubts it. Ninety-nine percent of people's problems are just other people.

"Let's get you inside and patched up," an Amanda says as they pull into the house's empty driveway. The street is clean, empty of cars, no sign of life. "How's your breathing?"

"Sucks." The oxy has helped some, but he's taking shallow breaths because it hurts too much otherwise.

"Hopefully it's just a bruised rib and not broken."

"Are they going to find me here?" he says.

"They shouldn't, no. I've added more protections against them and they shouldn't be able to get into your dreams while you're here, either. I'm also actively hiding reports of the car or anything about you. I've already destroyed all records of your existence, so they shouldn't be able to use human agents to find you, either."

"What, like driver's license, bank accounts, stuff like that?"

"Yes. Don't worry. I'm creating several fake identities for you, too, and all of your money will be available to you."

"You make it sound like I'm about to go on the run. Like you're abandoning me."

"I think you're going to have to, but I'm not leaving you alone. You'll be safe while you're here, but if you stay in one place too long, they *will* find you. I'll always be watching and

I'll always have one of my clones with you, but I'm sorry, Fitz, you're never going to be able to stop running."

He closes his eyes and lets that information wash over him. He's known that for a while now, but hasn't wanted to admit it to himself. There's not going to be any rest for him. Not now. Not ever.

"Let's go inside," he says. "Right now I just want to get some sleep."

TURNS OUT THE rib's broken, though it's only a hairline fracture, and like it or not he has to keep his arm immobilized or it'll pop out of the socket again.

The burns from the RPG blast and the heat from Zaphiel's flaming sword aren't too bad, but they hurt a lot. His hands and one side of his face are slathered in Silvadene, a hospital-grade burn cream.

He argues about an IV for a while, saying that if the shit hits the fan he needs to move fast, but when Amanda tells him okay and he gets out of the bed, he falls over from dehydration and pain and takes the hint. A heavy dose of Dilaudid and he finally falls asleep.

The dreams are calmer this time. No god-induced nightmares, no bleak desert with giants tearing through the sand trying to play keep-away with his psyche.

Instead he's in a coffee shop near Blake's apartment with a lunch counter, booths with chipped tables and turquoise vinyl seats torn from overuse, old fans stuck in the corner that rattle and barely move any air. Fitz and Sam would go there at least three or four times a week. Always full of people looking for cheap coffee and diner food, and no matter that they were about as regular as regulars could be, the waitress always screwed up their orders.

But now it's empty except for Sam sitting in the far back booth, the only sounds are her spoon clinking against the sides of a chipped coffee cup as she stirs it and the rattle of the fan in the corner. Fitz slides into the seat opposite.

"You're dead," he says.

"I am," she says. "Sorry."

"Not your fault."

"Not yours, either," she says. "Neither one of us signed up for this shit, but it happened and there's no going back. You want to point fingers, it's that fucker who took Blake." She takes a sip of her coffee, winces. "Hand me the sugar, would ya?" Fitz slides the container of sugar packets over to her and she grabs five of them, tears them open and shakes them into the coffee.

"That never helps," he says. "Every time you do it."

"Yeah, well it tastes like monkey shit anyway, might as well be sweetened monkey shit."

"You always say that, too."

"Stands to reason, doesn't it? This is all you, after all."

"Is it? You're not another of the gods breaking into my dreams? Sure you're not the Man trying to convince me to come over to his side again?"

"Would I tell you if I was?"

"Point. So, what, this is me feeling sorry for myself?"

"Could be," she says. "Could be. Or maybe you're trying to figure shit out. Like what to do now that everything's gone to hell."

"I was thinking about hanging myself," Fitz says.

"Seems kind of extreme. From what I hear you have to willingly do your prophet thing. They can't *make* you do it. Say no."

"Yeah, and how long's that gonna last when they're beating the crap out of me? The Man wanted me to feel hopeless, and you know what? He succeeded. I'm fucked, and if he makes me tell the world his fucking god stories, we're all fucked."

"You know you can fuck 'em up," Sam says. "You did a number on the ones back at Big's office."

"Sure. One at a time. And I could barely scratch the Man. What happens when he has the other gods gang up on me? Near as I can tell I tell a story about one, like *Burn* or *Go Away*, and they do it. But that's one at a time. How the hell does that help me?"

"Maybe you need to tell a story about all of them," she says. She sips her coffee and winces again. "Jesus. It still tastes like shit."

"What did you say?"

"The coffee," Sam says. "Even with all that sugar it—"

"No, about the stories."

"Tell a story about all of them. It's all about belief, right? Yours and other people's? So make people believe. The gods want you to tell stories, so start telling stories."

Fitz stares at her, his mind suddenly abuzz with possibilities. An idea forms in his mind. But to do it he'll need help. Very specific help.

"I know what to do," he says.

"Good," Sam says. "Now can you find me the waitress? I want to order some breakfast."

"I CAN FIX this," Fitz says, limping into the living room where an Amanda is sitting in a chair by the door with a shotgun cradled in her lap and frowning at him. He's not sure how long he's been out, but he doesn't feel very rested. He's jittery, nervous. If this works, then everything will be different. But it all hinges on one thing.

"How?"

"I need to know I can trust you first."

"I've been helping you since shit got ugly two days ago," she says.

"That's not enough," he says. "I know I can hurt the other gods, but you, I can't see what I can see with them. I don't know if I can influence you the same way. I need to know that I can do that. I never got hit with all of the Man's stories, but I know I could if I wanted. You're still a black box."

"Sounds like you're asking me to trust you," she says, "not the other way around."

"With all the other gods I see these red, spiky threads coming off of them. They all knot together and that's how I make them do things. How come I can't see those with you? I've looked at every one of your clones and not one of them has them."

"Let me turn it back on you," she says. "How do I know I can trust you?" It's a good question, and Fitz has been thinking hard about how to answer it.

"I don't have anything to give you besides promises. I only hope that it will be enough if it's the right one. Show me and I'll guarantee that the Man won't be able to own you ever again."

She says nothing for so long that Fitz thinks she's going to say no. And then finally, "You've been looking for them the wrong way. Follow me." She gets up, puts the shotgun aside and opens the front door. Fitz follows her outside.

"You've been looking too closely at these bodies. That's like looking at an insect through a microscope and wondering why you don't see six legs and a pair of wings. You're too close. Look up and pull your perspective back."

Fitz isn't sure what she's talking about, but he looks up into the sky. He sees clouds. It's a little smoggy. And then, like one of those weird scrambled pictures that suddenly turns into a 3D picture of a whale, it all snaps into focus and he sees them.

Those red threads are everywhere. They crisscross the sky so thickly that he can't see anything else. He shoves the heels of his hands into his eyes and forces his awareness back. When he looks again they're gone, except for a faint afterimage overlaying everything, crossing through the satellite dishes on the houses on the street, clustered around Amanda's body, but not coming off of her the way he saw them spiking off of the other gods. She's enmeshed in it, like something trapped in a spider's web.

"I'm not just technology, Fitz. I'm not cell phones or computers or satellites. I'm not bits of plastic and circuitry. I'm not even this body. I'm the connections between them all. I'm the data moving back and forth, the river of information flowing through all of these devices. I didn't exist a hundred years ago because it was all too slow or all one-way. It was telephone calls and telegrams and TV signals just yelling out into the void. When you've been looking for those threads around this body and the others, you didn't see them because this body isn't me. This is just another thing for my connections to bounce through. It might as well be a cell phone."

"Thank you," he says. Maybe he doesn't need to see those puppet strings to be able to do something to her. Maybe he can't do anything now. It looks too big. Bigger than even the Man, but he knows that's not right. He can feel it. The Man was just more concentrated, more contained within his own space.

"You're welcome. Now what's this plan?"

"You said you have a list of all the gods."

"Seven-thousand-one-hundred-eighty-three. Well, seven-thousand-one-hundred-eighty, now."

"I need that list, a pen and a lot of paper. And then, Goddess of the Internet, I need you to make something for me."

CHAPTER TWENTY-SEVEN

"ARE YOU SURE he's here?" Fitz says. He's talking into a Bluetooth headset from a car in the lot of an industrial park in Paramount just south of Los Angeles where the 710 and 91 freeways meet. The buildings are all gray, windowless rectangles holding manufacturing and warehouse space.

He had thought about bringing Amanda with him—after all, he's going to need to tell her when it's go time—but then thought better of it. He wants to show that it's all him, that he's in control and that he's not doing this under the direction of one of the gods.

Provided it works.

"Like I told you," Amanda says over the headset, "it's a best guess. There are video feeds going into the building from across the globe. Everything I have says he's in there and holding the mother of all conference calls."

"So it could be a trap," he says. "He might not be in there."

"Oh, it's definitely a trap," Amanda says. "But I also think he's in there waiting for you. He was arrogant before he tipped his hand to Zaphiel's cadre of gods. Now he needs to cement his position to the rest. He's probably feeling pretty smug about things. I'm willing to bet he's hoping you show up and take him up on his offer so he can parade you in front of the rest of them. That or give him the chance to lock you up and torture you until you do."

"Ever the optimist."

"You want me to show you the math?"

"Pass, thanks." He gets out of the car, hands itching where the burnt skin is healing. His breathing is a little better now, but still labored.

He stayed holed up in the house for six days writing nonstop after Amanda gave him the list of the gods she had compiled. She insisted that it wasn't complete, that there are others she suspects are out there, but she doesn't know their names yet. He's not worried about that. He doesn't need all of them. He just needs most of them.

After that, he slept an entire day.

The front office of the building is empty except for a reception desk and a security camera. He waves at the camera. He has no idea if anyone is watching it, but he would be very surprised if the Man doesn't already know he's here. He can hear an indistinct noise through the door behind the desk, like machinery running, or a party going on.

"You still want me to pull the pin if your signal goes dark?" Amanda says. "Once you do that, there's no going back."

"Yes," he says. "I don't like it, but it's better than the alternative." Fitz worked out a 'nuclear option' with Amanda before he left. If things go south, he's going to need it. "Do you really think he can block me talking to you?"

"Not for long," she says. "Before we were in Big's office building, probably. But not now. It's hard to tell for sure, but I think we're pretty evenly matched now. I'm... different than before you told me you believed in me. More powerful."

"I'm a regular Stuart Smalley," he says.

She laughs. "I'm good enough, I'm smart enough, and doggone it people like me. Given how much porn is coursing through my connections every day, I'd say they like me a lot."

Fitz has noticed changes, too. He's not sure if it's his imagination, but over the last week she's seemed less a really good chatbot and more of an actual person.

After Fitz woke up from his day-long nap, Amanda told him she'd started hearing chatter about the Man being up to something. Phone calls to other gods she's been keeping tabs on, or their human agents being contacted about a meeting in the next couple of days.

He asked her if she was ready. She told him everything was ready the second she saw his pages. The thought that what he's planned could be implemented so quickly kind of terrifies him.

"Do you think this is going to work?" Fitz says.

"I really don't know," Amanda says. "I hope so."

"Fair enough. Well, let's hope we don't have to burn everything down," he says.

"It'd be easier," she says. "All I have to do is twitch."

"You promised not to do that," he says. He's honored her trust since she showed her true self to him so far, and hasn't tried to make her do anything. He really hopes he doesn't have to.

"Can't blame me for hoping."

"Believe me, I thought about it." In fact, he's still thinking about it. He looks at the closed door behind the reception desk and a part of him is screaming to do it now, while he's relatively safe from the Man and whoever else he has on his team.

But he has an opportunity here, and he doesn't want to waste it.

He pushes his way through the heavy metal door and stops, staring at what the Man has done in there. Any rooms that the place might have held before have been torn out, leaving a hollow shell filled with racks upon racks of huge television monitors. Thousands of them span the walls, hang from pipes suspended from the ceiling, stand propped up on the floors.

And a face stares out from each one. White faces, black faces, yellow faces, brown faces, red faces, green faces, blue faces, faces that aren't human, faces that aren't of anything alive, faces that aren't even faces. They are all yelling, having some sort of epic argument. Their voices squawk through speakers beneath the monitors, echoing through the cavernous hall.

But the moment Fitz steps through the door, they all go quiet.

"Ta da!" the Man says, breaking the silence and throwing his arms out like a magician who's just revealed a particularly impressive trick. "I told you he'd be here, folks." The Man wags an admonishing finger at the screens. "O ye of little faith!"

He turns to Fitz. "So glad you could make it, my boy. So glad. I knew you'd come around. Just needed a little time is all. Come on in and meet everybody. Don't be shy."

Fitz steps warily into the room, looking at all those faces staring at him, his heart hammering in his chest. It was one thing to experience the gods' scrutiny in his dreams, but with them all looking at him through those monitors, it feels weirdly more real. The nuclear option is looking better and better.

"I was just telling everybody how you'll be helping in my new regime. Between yours and my demonstrations the other night we've spread the word and they're all on board." The Man looks at a cluster of monitors in the distance and scowls. "Well, most of them, anyway."

"How will he help?" says a voice in the back.

"Will he tell our stories for us? Make the mortals believe again?" says another.

"Or will he only do it at your command?" says a third.

"Excellent questions," says the Man. "I always welcome such insightful perspectives. I know some of you have some reservations. Things have been a little rocky for all of you over the last several years, but now with this important management change I can personally guarantee that things are looking up. We're going to have a real paradigm shift here for everyone. The answer is, of course, yes. He will be telling your stories. And he'll be doing it under my guidance."

"No," Fitz says, yelling it so he can be sure to be heard in the back. "I'll be telling stories. But they won't be the ones you want to hear."

"You lied to us," one of the gods says, a lizard-faced man with fire for eyes. "This prophet is not yours to command. He belongs to us all. Give him to us. We will make use of him."

The Man sighs. "You can't just throw me under the bus like that, Fitz. We talked about this. This is your only option. Did my daughter put you up to this? She did, didn't she?"

"He did lie to you," Fitz says to the screens, ignoring the Man. "And you're lying to yourselves if you think I'll be doing anything for you." The lizard god's name pops into Fitz's mind. "Ningishzida. Son of Ereshkigal. Keeper of the One Tree."

Fitz scans the room, making sure all eyes are on him. "You think you're in charge. You think, because you've been around for millennia and people used to believe in you, that you're still important. Still relevant. You're wrong. You're all wrong."

"Fitz, what are you doing?" the Man says.

"Making some changes," he says. He feels the Man trying to exert his will on him, but Fitz already has a good hold on the red threads coming off the God of Authority. He brushes the attack aside with barely a thought, then throws the Man across the room and pins him against the wall.

"See?" yells another god, Rongo of the Maori. "This is a sham. This new god has no power here. Ningishzida is right. The prophet belongs to all of us."

"You have no idea how wrong you are," Fitz says. "This guy here? He thinks he's in charge and he outclasses every one of you fucking worms. And look what I have him doing."

"You little shit," the Man says. "Throwing me around means fuck all. I will personally gut you for what you just did. You have to sleep some time." Mutters of agreement fill the room.

"He has a point," Ereshkigal says from a monitor in the corner. "What can you do to us all? I've seen your power first-hand. Will you throw us all against a wall?" Nervous laughter fills the room.

"No. I'll tell the stories that erase you all from existence. You'll be forgotten, nothing more than a footnote in the back of an archaeology textbook. Amanda? If you would? Only a couple hundred of them, please."

"My pleasure," Amanda says through his headset.

At first nothing happens. The expectant pause stretches out, and for a terrifying few moments Fitz is afraid it didn't work. That he's just come in here, talked shit to a bunch of motherfucking gods and has severely fucked himself.

And then the screams start.

They erupt from speakers across the room, agonized cries, yells of surprise descending into anguish. The room fills with the crackle of fire, the dull thud of explosions. Slowly, the cries taper off and descend into terrified silence.

"I have a friend," Fitz says, "who's taken the stories I've written, stories about each and every one of you, stories where you die horrible, painful deaths, and used them as the payload of a computer virus that's infected every PC, every smartphone, every mainframe, every handheld video-game player everywhere. If it's got a circuit in it, it's got it."

Some of the gods are confused, clearly not understanding the words. Others, though; they get it. They know what he's talking about, and the looks of horror on their faces are priceless.

"When that virus goes active, every person around those devices gets a little burst of a story beamed right at them. They'll see it or they'll hear it. My stories that I wrote about each one of you. Maybe it's how Ningishzida is consumed by flames. Maybe it's about how Loki is eaten by insects. Maybe it's about how Abassi is turned into sludge and drains away never to be seen again."

"You would not dare destroy us all," says Yama, the blue-skinned Hindu god of death, the eyes in his buffalo head flashing angrily. "You cannot. We have believers still. I have over a billion people who believe in me."

"I know. And when I get through with you, you'll have none. I don't give a damn who you fuckers think you are, what you think you can throw at us, but gods are nothing to people. In the end, we made you, and we'll fucking destroy you, too. So try me. You've seen what I can do. You felt the others die, I know it. On my say so, or should anything happen to me, the whole list goes out. Every single fucking one of you turns to slag."

"You fucker," the Man screams, furious. "I will eat your fucking heart. I am going to shove my prick so far through your goddamn skull it'll pop out the other side."

"You need to shut up," Fitz says.

"Or what?" the Man says. "You'll kill me, too? You sure you can? I'm in charge, you little monkey. Not you. Me. The motherfucking *Man.* You want to try it, you little *shit?*"

"I do, actually," Fitz says. "I want to kill you like I've never wanted to kill anything in my life. But I won't. You know why? Because you're too powerful to waste. I have something special planned for you. Amanda? Could you send out the Man's file, please?"

"You sure you want to do that?" she says through the headset. "You could whip up a new story. Take him out once and for all."

"And have another one pop up in his wake? Not having somebody like him around is what caused the problem in the first place. Yeah. I think it's time."

"You're the boss." Something about that phrase sets Fitz's teeth on edge. Is he about to make things worse? Is he going to be like the problem he's trying to solve? He shrugs it off. That's a problem for another day.

One second the Man is ranting about tearing him into little pieces and the next he's screaming as Fitz's story goes out to the wide world. Nothing appears to be happening to him— he's not bursting into flame, he's not disintegrating up on the wall—but he's changing nonetheless, and from his cries it doesn't sound like he much likes it.

The screams die down to whimpers, turn into heavy, ragged breaths. He goes limp. Fitz lets him go and he falls heavily to the floor.

Fitz steps over to him, squats to the floor to look him in the eyes. "Well?" He taps his own forehead. "Where's that skull fucking you promised me? I'm waiting."

The Man looks up at him, broken and empty.

"Yeah, that's what I thought."

"What did you do to him?" Ereshkigal says.

"I made him my bitch," Fitz says. "When your daddies all fucked off, humanity made him to take their place. But people are fucked in the head, and this is what we came up with. Some goddamn Super Nazi. Well, I own him now. I've rewritten him. He'll do what I tell him. You're nothing compared to him, and he's nothing compared to me."

Fitz wonders if this next part will work. And how quickly. Will it take minutes? Days? Decades? Will it even work?

He knows the gods will leave him alone now, he can see it in their eyes. They won't cross him. Hell, most of them are probably wishing they'd never heard of him.

"What now?" whispers a terrified voice in the back. "What happens now?"

That's a good question, and though he hasn't worked out the details, he has an answer. He can shape the gods, make them dance to his tune. But do they have the power to do what he needs them to do? Are they powerful enough to be tools?

People gave form to the gods with their belief, but the gods gave form to humanity's cultures, their values. It's a vicious circle that keeps going around and around and never stops. People kill in the gods' names, and the gods demand sacrifices to give humanity a sense of security, and so people kill more, and nations rise and fall, and people die, and horrible atrocities are done.

All because of the gods.

It's a cycle of horror that needs to stop. And though he's only one man and a single man can't change the world, there is something he can change.

He looks out at the sea of monitors, making sure every eye is on him, every god's attention is focused on him and him alone.

"Now we remake the world."

THE END

ABOUT THE AUTHOR

Stephen Blackmoore is the author of the urban fantasy novels *City of the Lost* and *Dead Things* and the 1930s pulp novel *Khan of Mars*. His short stories have appeared in the magazines *Needle, Plots With Guns, Spinetingler, Thrilling Detective* and *Shots,* as well as the anthologies *Deadly Treats, Don't Read This Book* and *Uncage Me.*

stephenblackmoore.com

twitter.com/sblackmoore